The Rising

The Andovia Chronicles Book 2

Tiffany Shand

DEDICATION

For my mum, Karen.

ACKNOWLEDGMENTS

Editing and proofreading by Olivia Seaton and Dark Raven Edits

Cover Design by Kristina Romanovic

MAP OF THE LOWER
R E A L M

EREDEN

Spirit
Grove

Crystal
Palace

ALARIS

VARIUM
old city

GLENTEL

ANDOVIA

N

NW NE

W E

SW SE

S

RING OF
SORROW

REALM OF THE
UNDERSEA

JORIAM

SLAVE
ISLANDS

DRAGON ISLANDS

URSAIA

DORINGA

CHAPTER 1

Nyx Ashwood perched on a tree branch and listened to the sounds of the forest around her. Her long pink hair fell in loose strands from her braid and her enormous purple wings hung loose behind her, fluttering like leaves in the breeze.

"Concentrate and listen with your mind," Ambrose told her. "Listen to the sounds around you. And sense any potential threats." The druid perched on a tree stump, his long red beard flapped in the breeze, and his dark eyes were fixed on her. He clutched his staff and tapped it on the ground, impatient.

Nyx fidgeted, uncomfortable from being stuck in one position for so long.

Noises buzzed around her. The sound of the wind rustling through the trees. The twittering of birds and the faint jingle of laughter from sprites overhead. She had no idea what Ambrose expected her to feel. She had grown better at using her mind whisper abilities over the several months since she had come to live in Andovia, but she didn't feel like she had full control over them yet.

"I am," she grumbled. Her backside had already gone numb.

"Good, now concentrate on listening with your mind."

She wondered what she was supposed to be listening for. Her senses didn't warn of any potential threats.

Why couldn't Ambrose just tell her? The old druid always liked to be cryptic. After several months of training with him, that still annoyed her. All he told her was she should 'use her inner senses to detect potential threats'. That way she could hone her mind whisper abilities, just as she had mastered a mental shield. The sounds of people's thoughts didn't overwhelm her anymore. It helped a lot, but Ambrose still insisted she had a lot to learn.

Nyx scanned the forest.

Ambrose's mind remained closed off to her since he had a mental shield, too. It made him much harder to read. Part of her was happy at not being subjected to his thoughts, but at the same time it would have been easier if she could listen to them once in a while.

The faint whisper of thoughts echoed around her from sprites, dryads, and other fae that inhabited the forests of Eldara, the eastern territory of the realm of Andovia.

Nyx was sure he planned to get someone to sneak up on her. Maybe Darius, Ranelle, or Lucien. Or perhaps his friend, Alaric.

Her brow creased. *Come on.* If there was someone here, she should be able to pick up on their presence. Something prickled at the edge of her mind as someone crept towards her.

Nyx flung out her arm and hit whoever it was with a blast of magic. She could also move things with her mind and channel the power through her hands.

Someone cried out, then she heard a crash. She opened her eyes.

Bright sunlight streaked through the heavy canopy of trees. Darius Valeran, druid, and the man she worked for, lay on the ground. She worked as his servant—at least in her official capacity. Most of the time she worked with Darius. Her duties included working around the forest in the Forest Guard and working in the resistance.

"Ow!" Darius groaned. "Why did you knock me down?"

"Because I enjoy it." She smiled. "And Ambrose told me to sense potential threats."

"I didn't mean you had to send him flying." Ambrose shook his head. "You were just supposed to *sense* a potential attack."

"My mind told me he was a threat. A threat means I react and make sure my enemy can't hurt me." Nyx flapped her wings and flew over to Darius, hovering above him.

Darius scrambled up. "Am I your enemy now?" With his long blond hair, chiselled face, and blue eyes, he looked as handsome as ever, even though his black tunic and trousers were dusty.

Nyx pondered the question. Once, she had considered him her enemy when he saved her from execution. After she had been falsely accused of murder, he had taken her into custody. As a former slave, she had no right to a trial. Instead of handing her over to his elder brother, Prince Gideon, he had convinced his father, the Archdruid, to let her be his servant. The Archdruid was a spiritual leader and the highest authority over all Magickind. No monarch or official was equal in rank to him.

"You're my friend," Nyx said finally. She never thought she'd admit that. Or that she would call anyone, let alone a Valeran, a friend. In some ways, he was more than that after they had been through so much together.

As well as being highest in rank, the Archdruid was infamous for waging war all over the world of Erthea and enslaving countless races. Realms could rise and fall at the Archdruid's whim. Nyx had thought Darius was the same when she first met him. But she had been wrong. Instead, he despised everything his father stood for.

Darius gave her a smile and brushed off his clothes.

"Good, Nyx, but you shouldn't always react with violence," Ambrose warned.

"You said search for threats which I did." She flew back over and landed on the branch she had been perched on.

"Did you sense me?" Darius furrowed his brow. "I'm immune to your power so you shouldn't have felt my presence."

That was true. Darius wasn't completely immune to her mental abilities, but his touch seemed to neutralise them. No one had come up with an explanation as to why, though.

"I knew you were there, even though you are cloaking yourself. I can pick up your presence a lot more easily than I used to." She tossed her long braid over her shoulder.

Ambrose stilled in his seat, his eyes glazing over. Nyx knew he was receiving a message from someone.

"We will practise again later," he said after a moment. "It appears we are being summoned to the palace." Ambrose leaned on his staff and rose to his feet.

Darius groaned. "I wonder what my father wants now."

Nyx's stomach lurched. She hated the palace. And even more so being around the Archdruid and the prince. As the second-born son, Darius was allowed much more leniency and chose to live separate from court life.

"Can I stay here?" Nyx asked. "And practise?"

Ambrose arched an eyebrow. "Your place is with Darius, as his servant. We have to keep up appearances."

Nyx scoffed at that. No one would notice if she were missing. Even when she did follow Darius around at the palace, people acted like she wasn't even there.

Darius waved his hand in dismissal. "Stay and practise. I will call you if I need you."

"Are you sure you can find your way home?" Ambrose asked her. "It's easy to get lost in this forest."

"I'll be fine."

She spent almost every day in the forest or flying around it with the druid. It never frightened her. It felt welcoming. She always felt more at home here than at the palace.

Nyx breathed a sigh of relief when both men trailed off. She closed her eyes and scanned the forest with her senses. The three territories that made up the island of Andovia always felt like they were made of magic itself. There was so much life and energy here. She lowered her mental shield a little further. Inside her, her power pulsed, like a dam waiting to burst. The darker side of her gift was her influence. She could compel others and force them to obey her.

Ambrose had warned her not to use that unless she had to. Her influence was much harder to control than her other powers. And it ran the risk of enslaving someone. Nyx had been lucky no one had been enslaved by her power before now. Most people only fell victim to it for a short time.

Ambrose had also told her that her influence was always active. Over the years, she must have learnt to hold it in, or she would have enslaved the human tribe she had once lived with. Nyx couldn't remember any part of her life before she ended up with the tribe. People here insisted she looked like a true Andovian with wings and colourful features. The original fae of Andovia had become enslaved to the race of Silvans. They were also fae but considered themselves the first race of all Magickind.

She let her senses take in every part of the forest again. Something prickled at the edge of her mind, warning of danger. Nyx opened her eyes and remained perched on the long tree branch. What had she sensed?

The forest looked the same. She unfurled her wings. Could she sense the exact location of the threat? She knew it was close, but not where.

Nyx lowered her head and pretended to meditate again.

A dark figure sprang towards her. Nyx caught the flash of a blade. Her assailant's face and body were covered from head to toe in black leather.

Nyx raised her hand. Waves of invisible energy rippled against the attacker, who flinched. But her power hadn't flung them away from her. Damn, why hadn't it worked?

She couldn't believe someone had come to kill her again. Nyx looked around for any kind of potential weapon and called on her magic again. A tree branch broke off and flew towards her attacker.

Her attacker leapt up onto another branch before her branch had a chance to hit them. How did they move that fast? They didn't move like Lucien, so Nyx doubted they were a Lykae.

Nyx had had enough of people trying to kill her. She hadn't used her touch on anyone in a while. Maybe it was time to compel them and find out who had sent them. Touching someone made compulsion easier, but she could release her power from a distance if she had to.

The assailant came at her again. Another flash of silver caught her eye as they threw a knife at her.

She waved her hand and sent the blade hurtling away from her. "Why are you trying to kill me?" Nyx demanded. "Who sent you?" She scanned her assailant with her senses. Maybe then she could at least figure out what they were. Nothing came to her.

What did that mean? Nyx had spent weeks practising and identifying different Magickind all over Andovia. Usually, her senses told her something. But not this time. Nothing. No thoughts came to her, nor did she sense anything else other than a strange tingling feeling.

Her assailant pulled out another blade.

Nyx knew if she couldn't hear the person's thoughts, she might not be able to use her influence either. She flapped her massive purple wings and took to the air. She rose high above the dense canopy of trees. Below, her assailant leapt from branch to branch. Moving with unnatural speed.

"Good luck catching me now." Nyx grinned. She glided over the sweeping, massive forest. Trees stretched out before her. She would fly off into Avenia and find the druid. Once she was clear of the assassin, she would open a portal to get there quicker. Flying all the way there would take a couple of hours. Time she didn't have. Maybe he could help her figure out why someone wanted to kill her. Again.

Was it because of that damned prophecy again?

Something silver flew through the air. Straight towards her.

"Holy spirits!" Nyx swore and dove out of the way.

One by one more flashes of silver came at her.

How could that assassin have managed to track her? How could they even see her? The canopy should have hidden her from view.

Nyx flapped her wings harder. The knives turned and spun back towards her after she dodged them.

She drew magic and concentrated on pulling a glamour around herself to hide her from view.

More knives whizzed around her. Obviously, her glamour spell had done no good. She realised the blades must be enchanted somehow or they would have fallen to the ground by now. How did they do that? She turned and flew in the opposite direction. Nyx knew she couldn't risk flying back home or the assassin would follow her. She had to make sure she lost them first.

Nyx dove through the thick canopy of trees and glanced behind her again. The blades were still following her. Leaves and branches smacked against her. Nyx turned left then right as she dodged different trees. She ducked around a large tree and scrambled onto a branch. The knives came straight at her. Nyx raised her hands and green light sparked between her palms. The blades hovered there. Something pushed back against her magic. The assassin had to be somewhere nearby to use their power.

Her mind raced. Why couldn't Ambrose have taught her some defensive magic? He'd been so focused on her getting her powers under control. She needed to know how to protect herself when her powers proved useless against someone.

Come on. She pushed back, using the full strength of her powers. *Go back!*

More force repelled against her. Nyx used her free hand to trace runes in the air. Light exploded around the hovering blades. They fell away and dropped into the tree line.

A blast of magic shot up through the air. Nyx dove out of the way and straight through the canopy. Branches whacked against her, hard. She didn't care if she ended up with a few bruises and shot past the trees. A quick glance over her shoulder revealed a ball of light following her.

Would she ever get free of the assassin?

Nyx swerved around the trees. How could she get the assassin off her trail? She considered calling Darius, but she didn't want to bother him. Too bad she hadn't been able to use her influence on the assassin earlier.

Nyx gasped as she collided with a branch. The air left her lungs in a whoosh as it struck her chest. The magic was about to strike, and she knew it.

Gasping for air, she turned and traced one rune after another. The runes shimmered with light, and energy exploded around her. Nyx bit back a scream as it knocked her through the air. Leaves smacked against her as she fell. She flapped her wings but fell too fast to gain any momentum.

Static sizzled against her skin as she hit a field of energy.

What was that?

Nyx slumped to the ground. She took a deep breath. The ball of light was gone. But was the assassin?

She scrambled up and scanned the area with her mind.

"Help me…" a voice rasped.

Nyx froze and spotted an old man with long white hair a few feet away. He lay slumped against an oak tree. Dark stains covered his long blue robes. His long grey hair fell in a tangled mess past his shoulders, and his dark eyes pleaded with her.

She put her hand over her mouth to stifle her alarm and rushed over. "Spirits, who did this to you?"

"Listen to me. You cannot let her rise again. If she comes back, she will destroy us all…" he rasped.

"Who? What are you talking about?" Nyx hated feeling useless.

No one had taught her anything about healing magic. She tore off part of her tunic and pressed it against his wound. "Who did this? Don't worry, I will call for some help."

Druid? Nyx called out to Darius with her mind. *Druid, I need your help.*

No answer came.

"Please, promise me…" The old man gripped her hand. "I kept your secret all these years. If she rises again…" He let out one final shuddering breath and his body went limp.

"No! Come back," Nyx begged. "Damn it, druid, why won't you

answer me?"

CHAPTER 2

Darius followed his mentor, Ambrose, back into the great hall at the Crystal Palace. The great domed building stood like a massive jewel glittering in the sunlight. How he hated this place.

To his displeasure, the hall was full of people. He had hoped it might just be a meeting with his parents. No such luck.

Darius groaned. Why had he been summoned before the entire court? He despised the court, and his mother knew that. Nor could he fathom why he had been summoned either. He never came here unless he had to.

"Why do you think we have to be here?" he whispered to his mentor.

Ambrose shrugged and used his staff to push his way through the crowd.

Darius repressed a sigh. Why couldn't they stay at the back of the crowd? He hated being on display at the front. If his mother saw him, she would tell him to join her on the dais. Then he'd be centre stage in front of everyone. Ambrose stopped when they reached the front. Darius stood behind him and hoped he hadn't been seen. If he kept his head down maybe he wouldn't be.

On the raised dais at the head of the hall stood the intricately carved throne of the Archdruid. Tree branches twisted and wound around it, along with crystals. On it sat the Archdruid, Fergus Valeran, himself. His father had short blonde hair and icy blue eyes. He wore his usual white fur trimmed tunic and white hose. A white gold circlet adorned his head. The Archdruid was the highest authority on the sphere. A voice of the gods—that was what some people called him. He ranked higher than any Magickind, monarch, or authority on Erthea. Power rolled off him like waves crashing against rock.

On a smaller, much plainer throne perched his mother, Lady Mercury. She was more striking than beautiful, with long black hair swept back and her dark eyes scanning the crowd. Her red velvet gown looked almost modest compared to Fergus's gaudiness.

Darius had no doubt his mother had been loving every moment since Fergus' other wife had been imprisoned.

Around him were the many Silvans who made up the high fae. All of them looked more human than fae, with their dark hair and dark eyes. But an aura of light shimmered around their skin with a silver hue. They all wore fancy clothing and jewels, and blended in with the opulence of the great hall. Diamond chandeliers hung overhead. Gold filigree bordered the walls along with bejewelled suits of armour holding dazzling weapons.

The whole place struck Darius as a complete waste. Thousands of starving and mistreated slaves scattered the lower realm. Yet his parents preferred to gain more wealth and power rather than help others. Every Archdruid always turned bad. The power came from Erthea itself. With it, they could cast spells and bend someone to their will. And Archdruid's possessed strength beyond anything other mere Magickind could fathom.

Some said the Archdruid could wield the power of the gods. Darius knew his father was strong, but he was no god. Even if he did portray himself to be one. He would bring his father down. Both his parents, if he had to.

Darius felt out of place among all the grandeur in his simple Forest Guard uniform with a black tunic, a jerkin, and dark trousers. People chatted around him. All wondered what the Archdruid was about to say. He wished they would get on with it. He raised his mental shield and some of the noise around him went away. He went to pull a glamour spell too, when Mercury called out for him.

He groaned. Why hadn't he pulled the glamour earlier?

His half-brother, Gideon, stalked out and took up position nearby. Gideon had long, dark blond hair, dark eyes, and dressed almost as richly as their father.

Darius caught Gideon's glower and Mercury beckoned to him. He reluctantly made his way over to his mother.

Mercury rose from her throne and gave him a stiff embrace. "Your father has an announcement," she grumbled. "May the gods help us all."

Fergus rose and raised his hand. At once the entire hall fell into silence.

"What is he announcing?" Darius leaned in close so he could whisper to his mother.

"We'll find out soon enough." Mercury moved back to take her place at the Archdruid's side.

Darius headed over to his brother.

Gideon scowled when he saw him. The two had never been close. He was only a few months older than Darius.

"Do you know what this is about?" Darius asked him.

Gideon shook his head and said nothing.

"I have an announcement," Fergus' voice boomed through the room. "A few months ago, Queen Isabella, my former wife, was stripped of her title for causing the deaths of several fae and endangering my realm."

Gideon stiffened beside him. Gideon had been furious at his mother's efforts to break the veil between the worlds and ignored things when Isabella opened rifts to the underworld. All in her attempt to find the former Andovian Queen who had ruled until a century ago. Isabella had never revealed why she wanted to find the Andovian Queen's spirit.

Darius was only glad Isabella was being punished for the deaths she had caused and hoped they wouldn't have to deal with darklings again. Darklings were shadow creatures from the underworld that she had used to do her bidding. They had killed several people, including Nyx's foster father.

This was it. His father would finally condemn Isabella to death. Innocent blood had been shed at her hand and she would pay for her crimes. His father would do the right thing for once.

"But..." Fergus went on.

Oh, holy bloody spirits. Darius clenched his fists. Had Isabella found a way out of her prison? Or had she somehow found a way to avoid punishment for her crimes?

The double doors to the great hall opened and Isabella herself walked in. The crowd murmured in confusion.

Mercury's eyes flashed, but she didn't lose her composure.

Gideon looked stunned.

Odd, Darius expected him to have known.

Isabella looked nothing like her usual frivolous self. Her long rose gold hair fell loose around her shoulders. She wore a pale white loose robe and appeared to be a shadow of her former self.

Darius had never seen her look so demure. His mouth fell open.

"She is a priestess in the Order of the Blessed and she will instead serve penance for her crimes. She will no longer bear the rank or title of queen. Instead, she will be allowed to spend her days serving the gods," Fergus told everyone. "But she will no longer be recognised as my wife either."

A flash of triumph passed over Mercury's face before she regained her composure again.

Darius couldn't believe it. How could they have let Isabella come back after everything she had done?

No, penance wouldn't justify the people she had killed.

He turned to Gideon. "Did you know about this?"

Gideon glowered at him. "Of course not. I thought they would execute her." His fists clenched. "She can do what she likes. I want nothing more to do with her. She almost destroyed my realm!"

"You're not just going to let her come back into the palace, are you?" Darius demanded. "Even if she's not queen anymore, she's still a danger to everyone here. Maybe even to you. She almost destroyed Andovia. Are you willing to let that happen again?"

Gideon's eyes narrowed. "Why would you care about what happens to me, brother? You and I have no love for each other."

"True, but I care about what happens to this realm. Are you willing to take the risk of her destroying everything again? You have to do something."

Gideon gave a harsh laugh. "What do you expect me to do, brother? The Archdruid has the true power in this realm. You should know that."

Darius blew out a breath. How could Gideon stand back and just let his mother worm her way back in? Spirits, his brother had no spine. He dreaded to think what kind of Archdruid Gideon would make some day. Although sometimes he wondered if Gideon would ever take the throne. Fergus would never relinquish his power. Not after everything he'd done to take power in the first place over a century ago.

Fergus rambled on and Isabella greeted everyone from the court as if she had only been away on a trip. Not locked up in a prison cell.

Once the announcement was over and the Archdruid left, Darius hurried over to his mother. "I need a word with you," he hissed.

To his surprise, Mercury obliged him. They headed outside into a small private garden reserved only for the Archdruid. But Fergus never used it, so Mercury did.

"How could he let that woman out of prison?" Darius fumed. "How could you let him bring her back here?"

"I did not let your father do anything. The council of elders decreed it so." Mercury scowled. "You know there are greater powers in this world than us, boy."

"Father wanted her gone, didn't he?" Darius demanded. "Why didn't you do something to make sure she stayed gone?" He knew about the high council of elders. Made up of the most powerful of Magickind with the Archdruid among them.

Darius had only seen them a couple of times when he had been dragged before them. Or to meetings. Mercury liked sitting in on the meetings too, but she had no authority among the council. The council of elders went above the Andovian council, too. Isabella had some sway over them as a high priestess and the former fae queen.

Mercury snorted. "Isabella convinced them she was working for the good of Andovia. The former Andovian Queen's power was legendary. If Isabella found and controlled her spirit, she would have the ability to control everyone." She cackled. "She's making a move against your father and he's too blind to see it."

"Overthrow Father?" To Darius, that seemed almost impossible. Fergus hadn't reigned as Archdruid for almost a century and become the most feared Archdruid of them all for nothing.

No Archdruid who came before him had brought so many realms to their knees.

"Of course. If she overthrows your father, she can place her son on his throne. She can be the Archdruid in all but name."

"I'm not so sure. Gideon was furious with her. He claims to want nothing more to do with her." Darius ran a hand through his hair.

Mercury laughed. "Oh, and you believe him? You are a fool, boy. Gideon will always be loyal to his mother. Nothing will ever change that. But do not worry. I'll be keeping a close eye on that fae whore. I

14

helped your father get his throne. I will not allow anything to take it away from him."

Darius sighed. "And what if she starts killing again? Will Father just let her go again?"

Mercury waved a hand in dismissal. "We've all had to take a few lives here and there. She didn't kill anyone of importance. That's why she was able to escape execution." Her lips curved into a smile. "I hear your brother is leaving, too. So we won't have to worry about him either."

He wasn't surprised by her disregard for others. Innocent lives meant nothing to his parents. Such were the games they played to hold on to their power.

He would find a way to keep an eye on Isabella and stop her. He'd convince his parents she was a true threat. Maybe he could take comfort in the fact that Mercury would have her eyes and ears watching her. His mother would let no one near Fergus' throne. He could be sure of that.

"Where's Gideon going?" It was unlike his brother to leave the realm.

"How should I know? I heard he's travelling or some other nonsense. I'll just be glad to be rid of him."

"Where will Isabella be living now? At the palace?"

"No, your father refused that. She will reside in the great temple."

Darius didn't know whether to be relieved or worried by that.

"I want to take you before the council of elders again," Mercury changed the subject.

He gaped at her. "What? Why?"

"Because it's been years since they examined you. You are of age now. It's time they tested your powers."

He scowled. "What you mean is you want them to test me to see if I have the potential to be the Archdruid." He shook his head. "No, Mother. I want nothing to do with them. I'm no Archdruid and I never will be."

"You could have extra training. You could become a great druid. Instead, you waste your talents by running around the forests of Eldara." She rolled her eyes. "I had such high hopes for you, boy."

Darius scoffed. "I'm happy working in the Forest Guard. I'm sorry to ignore your plans for me to become a druid sorcerer, but that's not who I am."

"Where's your fae shadow?" She glanced behind him, as if she expected to see someone there.

He furrowed his brow. "My what?"

"That ridiculous-looking fae girl with pink hair and those ugly wings."

"Nyx is busy, and she's not ugly." Darius knew he should have kept his mouth shut.

Mercury's dark eyes widened. "Really? You seem very fond of that slave."

"She's not a slave. She is a servant. And no, I'm not." Darius knew he could never let his mother know how much he cared about Nyx. She was a good friend, but nothing more. If Mercury suspected he cared for her, she would use that to her advantage.

Light flashed as Nyx herself suddenly stumbled towards him. "Druid, why didn't you answer my calls?" Nyx was covered in leaves and dirt. Part of her tunic had been torn off.

"Show my son some respect, girl." Mercury glowered at her. "Do not address him in such an informal way."

Nyx paled and bowed her head. "Apologies… Lady Mercury…" She sounded out of breath.

"That's not much of an apology. You should show respect to both me and my—"

"Fine, apologies, Lord Darius." Nyx brushed some leaves out of her hair.

"Prince Darius," Mercury corrected.

Darius scowled. "Mother, she can call me whatever she likes. I'm not a prince."

"Yes, you are. Honestly, boy, I sometimes wonder why you went to so much trouble to get a title and your own lands when you don't—"

"It's been a pleasure, Mother." Darius gave her a formal bow and grabbed Nyx's arm. "Don't say anything else," he hissed in her ear.

Once they were clear of the gardens, Darius let go of her. "What happened to you?"

Nyx scowled at him. "Someone tried to kill me, and I found a man dying." She put her hands on her hips. "Why didn't you answer my calls?"

Darius was taken aback. "I didn't hear you call for me."

"I did. More than once. Were you blocking me?"

He shook his head. "Of course not. But we have another problem. Isabella is back."

Nyx's eyes widened. "You need to come and help me figure out who killed the man in the forest. Tell me about Isabella on the way."

Darius sighed, but she was right. One of his duties was to keep the forest in order. "Where is the body?"

"In Varden Forest."

He groaned.

"But that's not all. The man who died gave me a strange warning," Nyx went on. "He told me I can't let her rise again."

Darius had no idea what that meant and had a feeling he didn't want to find out either.

CHAPTER 3

Nyx still wasn't sure how she got from the forest to Darius so fast. She'd been desperate to see him and tell him what happened. Then she had somehow found herself with him.

"How did you transport yourself here? I didn't see a circle on the ground." Darius wanted to know after they reappeared in the forest. He had created a circle so he could transport them there.

"I don't know," she admitted. "I needed you. And I was angry because you weren't there. I had to watch that man die. Why didn't you answer me? You could have helped!"

The trees became less dense as they passed through and in the distance stood a yellow stone guard tower.

Darius groaned. "Nyx, how did you end up here? We're miles away from where I left you."

"I told you, an assassin attacked me and chased me. I couldn't read the assassin either." She scowled. "But I didn't feel a shield. It's like their mind was impenetrable. How is that possible?"

"Perhaps they were immune, or you didn't detect the shield," Darius said. "At least I know why I didn't hear your call now."

She furrowed her brow. "Why not?"

"Because we're close to the old city. Observe." Darius picked up a rock and threw it towards the tower. Light flashed, and the rock bounced off.

"What old city?" Nyx had never heard of it before. But then she hadn't spent much time in the territory of Avenia either.

"The old city of Varden. It used to be the capital of Andovia

18

before my father took the throne. Legend says it fell out of the sky, but I doubt that's true. My father planned to claim it for himself a hundred years ago, but he was forced out."

Andovia was made up of three different territories. Avenia, Eldara, and Migara. It had once been one domain that had been divided up into separate territories after the Archdruid had conquered the realm.

"Fascinating. Can you concentrate on the dead man now?" Nyx gestured to the body at their feet.

"You don't understand. The city is warded so magic can't pass through it. Did you hit the shield or go near it?"

Nyx nodded. "I flew into it earlier when the assassin chased me. Then I found him."

Darius knelt beside the body. "What did he tell you?"

"Not much. Just that he kept a secret and that we couldn't let her rise again. He never told me who he was." Nyx wished she had thought to ask. She had been so focused on saving him it hadn't even crossed her mind.

"He is high fae. I recognise him from court."

"So, he's a lord?"

Darius nodded. "A low ranking one, but yes. He didn't have much more than the title." He examined the wounds. "These wounds look shallow. It would have taken him a while to die. And he wasn't killed here."

"How do you know that?" Nyx frowned.

It always fascinated her how he seemed to know so much. She craved that knowledge. Although she had found a calling, she still didn't feel like she had a true place.

Darius and his friends all had their places. Where did she belong?

"We'll take him to the guard station—I need to report this," Darius said. "Since I am a Forest Guard my general should let me investigate."

"Good. Now why is Isabella back?"

"She's a priestess. She still has some power."

"I'd say it would be a big coincidence if she wasn't the one responsible." Nyx crossed her arms.

"Nyx, you know we shouldn't jump to conclusions. We don't know how or why he died yet."

Darius called his general with his mind, and two more forest guards came out to see the body and scour the area. They didn't find any sign of where the man might have come from.

Nyx stood there and stared at the guard tower of the old city. She couldn't make out much beyond that, as everything was covered by trees. Something struck her as familiar about the place. Like a memory from a dream that lay just out of reach.

"Nyx, come on. We need to go," Darius called out. "There's nothing else to find here."

She didn't budge. Just continued to stare.

"Nyx?" Darius came over and put a hand on her shoulder. "Are you alright?"

She shook her head. "Why can't people go in there?"

"I told you it's impossible. The shield covers the entire area. Anyone who tries to get through will either be repelled or destroyed."

"But why? Who put the shield there? Who lived there?"

"The Andovians. Which were made up of fae and druids."

"Your grandfather did that?"

Darius shook his head. "My grandfather was old and mad. My father killed him, claimed his throne, and cemented his place in history when he conquered this realm and waged war for the next few decades. Legend says the Andovian Queen cursed the city to keep it from him."

"How do we know that man didn't come from there?" Nyx frowned. "He had to come from somewhere. And he's right outside the city."

"There's—"

Nyx unfurled her wings and took to the air. She scouted the area. Every time she flew close to the city, she got hit by the shield. Then she flew down back to Darius and followed him back to the guardhouse.

When they arrived at the guard station, Alaric, the chief of the overseers, was there, along with Ambrose. Overseers served as guardians and keepers of knowledge. Alaric often worked with Ambrose, so it wasn't unusual to have him around.

Darius' general frowned at the body. "What were you doing near the old city?" he demanded of Nyx. "No one goes near there. It's the Varden's territory. They watch over the old city." He was a tall, muscular man with long dark hair and wore a similar uniform to

20

Darius.

"I took her there," Ambrose spoke up. "To another part of the forest. Nyx must have got lost when she was flying back."

Nyx opened her mouth to mention the assassin.

Don't say anything, Darius warned her in thought.

She closed her mouth again. Why couldn't she mention the assassin? It was the truth. But she had learnt Ambrose and Darius kept their secrets and didn't trust many people. Maybe they didn't want word of the assassin spreading. But that made no sense to her. The assassin could have killed that poor man, too. They didn't seem convinced, though, since the assassin had been busy chasing her.

"Right, I got lost," Nyx agreed. It was true enough.

"Valeran, go and question the Varden. Find out what they know. I doubt they will want to investigate. Their only mission is to check the old city and watch over their forest."

"Someone died there. Wouldn't they want to know about that?" Nyx asked.

"The Varden only care about their own kind." General Killian shook his head. "Watch yourself, Valeran. We're not on good terms with them after what that damn Dragon Guard did."

"I'll take the body and see what I can discover about the cause of death," Alaric said. "To me, it looks like he may have been tortured."

"I still say he came from the old city." Nyx crossed her arms. "I didn't sense any magic being used around me, like if someone transported themselves from somewhere. He didn't look like he had the strength to use magic either."

The general frowned. "Did you see him walk out of the old city?"

"No, but… He was on the ground when I discovered him."

"Walking in and out of the city is impossible. The place has been sealed off for over a century," General Killian stated. "Besides, there's nothing there but ruins."

Nyx knew that was wrong. She had seen glimpses of buildings that looked intact when she had flown over it. Although it had been hard to see everything because of the shield and dense tree foliage.

Ambrose used his staff to transport them, and the body, to Alaric's house.

Nyx always found the overseer's house fascinating. Tubes bubbled and fizzled as they zigzagged around the room. Strange machines whirled and books and other objects covered every available surface.

"Nyx, tell me everything that happened after I left you in the forest," Ambrose instructed.

So she did. How the assassin chased her. How she couldn't read them. And how she ended up finding the dying man.

"He told me he kept my secret all these years. And something about if she rises again—and that was all he said before he passed." Her mind raced. "What could he have meant? I've never seen him before." Had the man somehow known her? If so, how?

Perhaps he knew her when she was a child? She couldn't remember anything before she had ended up with Harland.

"He was probably delirious from being tortured," Ambrose remarked. "He may not have meant you."

"Did you hear anything in his thoughts?" Darius asked. "Was he telling the truth?"

Nyx bit her lip. Why hadn't she used her powers? She could have got all the answers she needed from him. "No, he… I tried to help him. I didn't think…" Tears pricked her eyes.

"He was beyond saving." Darius squeezed her shoulder.

Alaric took the body to another room.

"I will go out and talk to the Varden," Darius went on. "Nyx, are you up to coming?"

She sniffed. "Do you need me to?" She wanted some time alone. To think and maybe do some research in the Hall of Knowledge.

"I'd rather you came with me. The Varden might respond better to a fae."

"What's the Varden? Isn't that what you called the old city?" Nyx furrowed her brow. She had heard them mentioned before but didn't know what they were.

"They're guardians of the forest and they named themselves after their city. They protect all of it and the fae who live there. And they guard the old city."

"Why? What's in the old city to protect?"

Darius shrugged. "I have no idea. The Varden are very secretive."

"Nyx?" Alaric called out. "Can you come in here?"

Nyx headed over to the other room. She winced when she caught sight of the man's face again. His eyes were now closed, at least.

"Nyx, can you see if you can pick anything up from him?" Alaric motioned towards the body.

"We need someone to watch Isabella," Darius said as he and Ambrose came in. "Do we have someone in the resistance who could help?"

Ambrose nodded. "I know someone. Perhaps you and Nyx should go and stay at the palace. You might be able to keep a closer eye on things there."

Darius and Nyx both gaped at him. "I'm not living at the palace. You know how much I hate it." His hands clenched into fists.

"How can I live there? The whole reason I came to live with you and became the druid's servant was to hide my powers." Nyx couldn't believe Ambrose would even suggest such a thing.

"There's an assassin after you. You might both be safer there," Ambrose stated.

"Have you gone mad?" Darius demanded. "Neither of us are going to the palace unless we have to."

"Nyx, I want to see if you can read anything from the body. Use your powers and see if you can read him," Alaric suggested.

"Read him?" Nyx stared at the overseer in confusion. "But he's gone. My powers don't work on the dead."

"He's not been dead for long. There could still be residual energy you might be able to pick up on." Alaric motioned her over.

Nyx hesitated. She didn't want to look at the man, let alone read him, to see if there was something left.

Ambrose shook his head. "No, you should run along. Find out what the Varden know. There won't be anything left for her to find."

She took a deep breath. "No, I will see if I can read him." She reached out and put a hand on the man's shoulder.

Nyx closed her eyes and let her senses flow free as she scanned the body. She didn't know what she expected to see. After all, she had never used her powers on someone dead before.

At first, nothing came to her. For a moment, she wondered if there was anything left for her to sense. If the man's spirit had moved on, wouldn't his energy have gone with him? She didn't know how dead bodies and magic worked.

Come on, show me something. Who were you? Who killed you?

After a few moments, she found herself in a dark hallway. This didn't surprise her. She often saw this when she entered someone's mind.

This hallway looked different than others she'd seen before

23

though. Only two doors appeared to be visible. Odd, most people's minds were full of endless doors that unlocked their memories and past experiences.

Nyx headed over to the first door. It flashed in and out of existence. She guessed that was because this man's body was now an empty vessel. It had no soul and not much energy lingering behind.

She reached out, and the door opened at her touch. Light and colours whirled around her. Darkness surrounded her like a heavy shroud. Black and unyielding.

Her heart pounded in her ears as fear slid over her, icy and unrelenting.

Where was she? Was this where the man had been during his final moments before she found him?

"You need to tell me where they are, Thyren," a woman's voice came from the shadows, but Nyx couldn't make out a discernible figure.

Was that Isabella? She strained to hear and see more, but nothing became clear.

After a moment, a shaft of light illuminated a figure. The man, Thyren, was tied up and bound to a table. "I already told you everything I know. Why don't you just let me go?" He struggled against his restraints and Nyx could see he was too weak to put up much of a fight. "You'll never find them. They are hidden and long gone from this world. Why would you want to bring them back? If they came back, they would rain terror down on us all."

"Because I need them!" Something silver flashed in the limelight as the woman plunged a blade towards him.

Nyx drew back and gasped as the memory faded from her mind. Her heart still pounded as the man's lingering fear ran through her.

"Are you alright?" Darius reached out a hand to her as he came over. "What did you see?"

Ambrose furrowed his brow. "Did you see something? Unbelievable. There shouldn't be anything left for you to read. Not after a soul has already passed on."

She shook her head as if to shake away the awful things she had seen and felt. "His name was Thyren. I saw him being tortured by a woman."

Ambrose gaped at her. "Where was he? Who was torturing him? Did you see who it was?"

"No, I couldn't see her clearly. I didn't recognise her voice either. But she kept asking him where to find *them*. Not where to find her." She ran a hand through her loose strands of hair. "Odd, I thought he might have been talking about the Andovian Queen. Perhaps I was wrong."

"We'll see what we can find when we go back to Varden Forest." Darius took hold of her hand and led her towards the door. "Ambrose, call us if you or Alaric find anything else."

Nyx wondered what kind of nightmare she'd walked into now. Between the man's murder and the assassin that had been sent to kill her, she couldn't fathom how the two things might fit together. One way or another, she would have to figure it all out.

CHAPTER 4

Darius decided to get his dragon, Sirin, and fly back to the forest. He knew taking the dragon with him was a risk, but it was easier than using a circle to get to the forest. The shield around the old city made transporting anywhere in the forest unpredictable, and they might end up in the wrong place.

Sirin stood several feet taller than him, with large spikes and iridescent white scales.

"Why do you want me to come with you?" Nyx asked as she clung to his back as they glided over Varden Forest. "You said they might talk to you if you had a fae with you. What does that mean?"

"The Varden aren't fond of my father. They're distrustful of outsiders and they especially hate the Dragon Guard," he explained. "The Dragon Guard burnt down part of the forest a few years ago on my father's orders. It was one of their numerous attempts over the years to break through into the old city."

Darius knew he wouldn't receive a warm welcome from the Varden. Most of the Forest Guard couldn't get near them either, and avoided them whenever they could. Ambrose had a good relationship with them, which was the only reason they let him come and go freely.

"So the Varden are fae too?" Nyx asked.

He nodded. "They are winged fae—one of few races who are still free. Varden aren't a race of fae. They named themselves after the city after their queen was killed, they are true Andovians. My father has tried to wipe them out before but they're strong."

"Why does your father want to destroy every race?" Nyx growled. "Is it because they're fae? If he wipes everyone out, there will be no other races left in Erthea."

Darius winced. "No, some fae races are aligned with my father. Look at the high fae and the elves. All of them are on his side." Sirin glided out of the treeline. "Anyone who goes against him and the elders is an enemy. As is anyone they can't control."

"Why do they want to control everyone? Who are the elders?"

"The high fae. They consider themselves the first race. All other races are inferior to them." He scowled. "That's one of the reasons I work with the resistance. To fight for a better future."

"What are elders?"

"A group of Magickind. Old and powerful. They portray themselves as gods. They control most of Erthea. Some elders work for the Order of the Blessed, serving as priests and priestesses. They serve the gods that the Silvans worship."

Nyx frowned. "So that's who Isabella works for?"

Darius nodded. "That's how she escaped execution." Darius turned his head to look at her. "But Ambrose is getting one of our allies to watch her."

"I still think she's trying to kill me. Why can't she accept I'm not part of the prophecy?"

"We don't know if you are or not." Darius guided Sirin lower, and they descended through the trees.

"I'm not," Nyx insisted. "Just because I'm a mind whisperer doesn't make me part of that prophecy."

An ancient prophecy foretold two beings who would either bring about an age of peace or an age of great darkness. Many Magickind believed it would bring about the dark times again and plunge Erthea into chaos. One of the beings in the prophecy was said to be a fae who could wield great power with their mind, which made people suspect it might be Nyx since she was the first mind whisperer to appear in over a century.

Sirin circled around the trees and Darius told her to land.

"Maybe we should continue on foot. If the Varden think I'm one of the Dragon Guard, they may attack us." He climbed off his dragon. "Sirin, go. Stay close by." He activated the runes that he had inked on her skin so she would remain hidden. Sirin roared and then soared into the air. "Don't use your powers on the Varden. They are very powerful and if they sense what you're doing, they may consider it an attack."

"An attack? Sometimes I can't stop myself from hearing people's thoughts. You know that."

"That's why Ambrose has you working so hard to control your gifts." Darius cast his senses out and scanned the area with his mind.

The forest vibrated with energy, but he knew the Varden were well shielded. They were kin to the dryads and knew how to hide themselves from strangers. Most of them could fly too, so he wouldn't be surprised to see scouts positioned nearby. Others rode on horseback.

Darius didn't know what they would do if the Varden saw them as a threat and attacked. Sirin's mind merged with his, and he used her keen eyesight to focus on the forest below. The heavy green and brown canopy swirled with a riot of colour. No trace of any of the Varden came to him, though. All he sensed were some of the usual fae.

"I want to learn more magic," Nyx blurted out. "More than using mind whisperer abilities."

Darius frowned at her. "I've been teaching you magic."

"Yes, basic magic. I want to know more. I need to do more." She threw her hands up in exasperation. "I had to watch that man die today because I didn't know a damn thing about how to help him."

"Not everyone can perform healing magic. Your magic might not even be able to do healing spells," he pointed out. "It took me years of study and training to learn everything I know. You can't learn everything all at once. Plus, you've been training with Ambrose."

"That is too focused on me gaining control over my mind whisper abilities. I have better control now. My power isn't a danger to anyone. I need to learn more. There is a lot more to my magic than just moving things and hearing thoughts and influencing people." Nyx pushed her hair off her face as a few strands blew over her eyes. "You have the knowledge I crave. I used more strange runes today when I was fighting with the assassin."

Darius furrowed his brow. "Do you know what they meant?"

A few months ago, he had seen her using strange runes that weren't part of any runic system he had seen before. Further research hadn't revealed where they had come from, either.

Nyx shook her head. "I never do. They just come to me, and

instinct takes over." She bit her lip. "Maybe we should do a mind sharing."

His mouth fell open. "What?"

"A mind sharing—Ranelle mentioned it. We could share knowledge. I could gain yours and it might be enough to give you whatever repressed magical knowledge I have."

"Nyx, mind sharing is… It can be dangerous. I know you're desperate for knowledge but there are no shortcuts when it comes to magic." Darius didn't want to consider what the consequences of a mind sharing might be. He'd never performed such magic before and possessed secrets that were better left unsaid.

"I need to know how to defend myself against the assassin. I don't know if my influence will work on them either. And you said I can't carry a sword." She crossed her arms at that. He knew how much she missed having a weapon of her own. She had always carried one when she lived with her human tribe.

"You can't have a visible sword. If someone sees you with it, it will lead to a lot of unwanted questions." Questions that he couldn't answer. She was supposed to be his servant. Servants didn't carry weapons. Especially not fae servants who worked for a Valeran.

"I need more than a sword. I need to know how to defend myself in ways other than with my mind whisperer powers. This assassin was different—my powers were useless on them."

"Different how?"

"The fae Isabella sent after me before were just under fae. Outcasts. This person was trained to kill. They used magic I've never seen before. I think they can move things with their mind like I can. Or somehow control weapons and use magic to find their intended target."

Darius didn't want to think about that. He hoped Ambrose's friend could keep a close watch on Isabella. They had to find a way to bring her down, but it wouldn't be easy. Not with the Order behind her. He couldn't be sure Isabella was connected with the assassin chasing Nyx and the man who had been killed.

First, they had to find out what the Varden knew.

"Shouldn't we at least consider the idea of mind sharing?" she persisted.

He sighed. "We'll look into it. Now we have work to do."

He agreed she needed more magical knowledge but didn't think mind sharing was the right way for her to get it. Mind sharing was too unpredictable. Any number of things could go wrong. Besides, he couldn't be sure it would even work due to his immunity to her mind whisperer abilities.

Darius scanned the area again as they pushed through the trees. Still, he sensed nothing.

"Nyx, can you sense anyone nearby? There are fae all over this forest. Just like our forest. I can't sense the Varden. They're probably shielding themselves from me. What do you sense?"

She furrowed her brow. "There's too much chaos for me to find anything."

"Concentrate. Move past the background noise and see what else you can hear."

Nyx closed her eyes. "The dryads are discussing why we're here. I told you, I can't hear the Varden. There's too much chatter going on—there are over a hundred minds inside this forest."

Darius scanned the elements further. Deep around them, energy hummed through the earth and surrounding wilderness. His senses tingled as he caught a hint of fire.

"This way." He motioned for Nyx to follow. They made their way through the trees.

"I hear the faint buzz of thoughts, but I can't make out what they're thinking," Nyx remarked. "Where do the Varden live? In the trees or on the ground?"

Darius shrugged. "I—"

A blast of light shot towards them. Darius jumped and Nyx shot into the air.

A winged fae with long brown hair came riding out on a white horse. She aimed a staff weapon at them that was crowned with a blue shape, almost like flower petals.

"Darius Valeran, how dare you step into the home of the Varden again." The woman pointed her staff at him. "You know your kind are not welcome here."

"You let him into the forest earlier." Nyx flapped her wings furiously as she hovered beside him.

"In the outskirts of the forest, yes. Yet you dare to find our home now." The fae levelled her weapon at him.

"I have no quarrel with the Varden. A high fae was found dead a couple of hours ago. I need to know if you saw anything. And an assassin also tried to kill my servant here." He motioned towards Nyx.

Nyx scowled at the word "servant".

"And you came to accuse us?" the Varden guard demanded.

"No, I—" Darius shook his head.

The woman shot another staff blast of magic at them. Darius raised his hand, caught the energy between his fingers, and snuffed it out. If this woman wanted a fight, he would defend himself. He pulled out his sword and kept his magic at the ready.

Nyx narrowed her eyes, and the staff flew into her grasp. "Could you please stop trying to kill us? We came to talk to you. So please tell us what you know about the high fae that I found dying."

She gave Darius a quick smirk. *See. Told you I'm getting better control of my powers. I can't hear her thoughts, though.*

The fae stared down at her now empty hands, then back at Nyx. "How did you—?" She gasped. "What are you?"

Nyx put the weapon down at the horse's feet but didn't hand it back to the fae.

Darius didn't know whether to be pleased or horrified by Nyx's actions. He had told her to be careful, but patience wasn't her strong suit.

"Velestra, I'm not your enemy." He motioned for Nyx to take a step back. "Can you tell us what you know?"

Velestra sighed. "The dryads saw him stumble from the old city. But I don't know how that's possible. No one can enter there. The shield won't let anyone through—not even the Varden."

Darius frowned. "Are you sure? No one has set foot there since—"

"Since your father destroyed half the city and made most of the Andovians slaves." Velestra scowled.

"Velestra, is there something hidden in the city?" Nyx asked. "The high fae said he kept a secret. And he couldn't allow her to rise again. Does it have something to do with the Andovian Queen?"

All colour drained from Velestra's face.

"Do you know what he meant?" Darius let go of his sword. *Nyx, do you sense anything from her?*

No. I can't read her. She has a shield around her mind.

"It means nothing. The man was weak from torture. You won't find the killer here. I suggest you look among your own kind."

31

Velestra bent and grabbed her staff. "Your father's queen has been meddling with powers she has no business with." She swung her horse around and rode off into the distance.

CHAPTER 5

Nyx was relieved when she finally got to go to the great library that evening. She always loved visiting the place.

Once she got through the main library, she pressed the orb on the statue of the Andovian goddess Awa. Nyx always found it strange being transported to the Hall of Knowledge. Even more strange was the Silvans keeping a statue of the Andovian's goddess up since they had their own gods and beliefs.

Light flared around her and a few seconds later she reappeared outside a large white marble building with massive pillars and statues guarding the entrance way.

She hurried inside the beam of light which flashed over her as it scanned her. She never would get used to the odd sensation of being scanned by the ancient detection system.

Nyx let out a breath she hadn't known she'd been holding as the beam of light faded and she hurried inside.

She found her friend, Ranelle, already there.

Ranelle looked flustered. "Gods above, is there a priestess looking for me in the library? Was anyone asking for me?" Her fiery red hair hung loose around her shoulders, and she had dark circles under her emerald eyes.

Nyx shook her head. "No, why?"

"Because they told me I'm going to be moved to the temple. They said my apprenticeship should not only be at the great library." Ranelle ran a hand through her flaming red hair. "If I refuse, my apprenticeship will end. I don't have anywhere to go. I won't go back to my father." Her fists clenched. "He will have me married off like a broodmare. Where is Darius?"

"Talking to Ambrose, but he won't be long. I came because I need to do some research." Nyx squeezed her shoulder. "Why don't you want to stay at the temple?"

Ranelle sniffed. "Nyx, this is a nightmare. I liked my old mentor, but some priestess says she's taking over my training." Ranelle scowled. "I don't even worship the Silvan gods. I'm not from Andovia. I swear this is all Isabella's fault. I know she was a nightmare, but funding for the great library and a lot of other places has been cut since she was removed from power."

Nyx gave her a sympathetic look. "Don't worry, you can stay with Ambrose if need be. You won't have to leave."

"Who is leaving?" Lucien trailed in behind them. He was in his usual rumpled shirt and dark trousers. His mane of unruly brown hair fell past his shoulders and his amber eyes roamed over them. "Oh, are we finally going to be rid of you, dragon?"

"Lucien, shut up. Or I'll use my influence on you," Nyx warned.

Lucien flinched and raised his hands in surrender. "What did I do wrong?"

"You intruded where you're not wanted, wolfsbane." Ranelle glowered at him. "Maybe Nyx should use her influence. Nyx, make him think he is a mouse. He has the mentality of one."

Lucien glowered at her. "I came to tell you the high fae was tortured to death. His injuries show signs of healing, so it was prolonged," Lucien said. "And no, I don't need to leave. I'm an overseer, which means I have the right to be in our sacred Hall of Knowledge. The overseers were the ones who created this place. Not the Archdruid—even though the druids claim to be the ones who did so."

Darius came in a few moments later. "I haven't been able to find out anything else about the high fae."

"Who is the priestess who is forcing you to go to the temple?" Nyx asked Ranelle.

"Lyra Duncan. She is a new priestess who works alongside Isabella in the great temple. She was the only priestess there until Isabella moved in."

Darius frowned. "You have to go to the temple? Why?"

"Because Isabella isn't queen anymore. Funding for the great library and apprenticeships has dwindled. Either I move out to the temple and continue my training there or I return home to Lulrien." Ranelle gave Lucien a deadly look. "If you say one word, I'll make Nyx's influence look like a wet cloth."

Nyx bit back a smile. She knew Ranelle and Lucien came from the same realm in Lulrien. Their races, lykaes and wyverns, had been enemies for centuries. Ranelle and Lucien often called each other names and bickered.

Lucien held up his hands in surrender. "I never said anything."

"Good." Ranelle scowled.

"You can come stay with Ambrose. He wouldn't mind," Darius added.

"Or you could come stay with me," Lucien added. "Alaric wouldn't mind either. I'm sure we can learn to live with each other."

"Live with you? Gods above, I'd rather die!" Ranelle laughed.

The four of them sat down at one of the tables and discussed the day's events.

At least that seemed to calm Ranelle down.

"So, Isabella is back and a high fae was tortured and killed in the old city?" Ranelle furrowed her brow.

"I still don't understand how no one can enter the old city. Who put the shield up?" Nyx arched an eyebrow. "Someone must be able to bring it down. Somehow."

Ranelle shook her head. "No one knows. Legends claim the queen did it in her moment of death. I have read accounts saying a great light filled the sky and forced all the Archdruid's forces out."

"I don't see how anyone could get in and out of the old city now, though," Darius remarked. "Even my father couldn't bring that shield down. How could anyone else if they weren't the Archdruid?"

"Maybe the shield was designed to only keep certain people out." Ranelle shrugged. "I can't imagine they wanted your father or any of his forces there after they enslaved the Andovian people."

"Tell me more about the Andovian Queen. Who was she?" Nyx glanced between them. "She's connected to all of this somehow."

"Agreed. But I don't understand why Isabella would want to bring her back." Lucien steepled his fingers. "The Andovian Queen was her enemy and the Archdruid's. Why resurrect someone who was once a threat to them?"

"Because she probably thinks she can control the queen." Darius

35

scowled. "Isabella knows her power at court is waning so she's making a play for the throne."

"The Archdruid's throne?" Ranelle's emerald eyes flashed. "You must be mad. Your father would never let anyone take him down. I doubt your mother would either."

"Why not? If she had enough of the elders and high fae on her side, she could control the throne through Gideon. We need to keep a close eye on her and find out if she had the high fae man killed."

"The most ideal place to keep an eye on Gideon, Isabella, and the rest of the court is to be part of it," Ranelle said, and gave Darius a pointed look. "Which means you need to take your place at court. Nyx could go with you, she is your servant."

Nyx flinched, unsure why Ranelle would even suggest such a thing. She couldn't be at court, and especially not around Gideon. It had taken months to convince him her powers were negligible, and she wasn't part of the prophecy.

"I can't live at court. Look at me." She motioned to her wings and bright pink hair. "I'm too different to fit in with their elegance."

Nyx always stood out in Joriam, where she had spent the last seven years of her life. Once her ears had been pointed, but Harland, her foster father, had cut them off. He cut her wings too, but they had healed themselves. Her hair often changed colour too. She had settled on pink because she always liked the bright colours and she had enjoyed being different from her tribe in some ways. For that alone, the tribe had despised her.

"Other Andovians work at the palace," Darius pointed out. "I can't live there either. I left when I was twelve and I don't want to go back."

"You have an estate if you don't want to live at the palace. Need I remind you of that?" Ranelle tapped his head. "You are a prince, and you have other titles, too."

Darius waved her hand away impatiently. "I don't claim any of those titles. They're what I've inherited and what my mother got for me."

"You and Nyx are the only ones who can go to court," Lucien agreed. "And the dragon—I mean Ranelle, can watch Isabella in the temple."

"Being in court means you can get close to your father as well," Ranelle said. "And find out what Isabella and the elders have

36

planned."

Darius held up a hand. "No one is going to court. Gideon has left. So there's no point in being there. My father doesn't even take Gideon to see the elders. How do you expect me to do it? My father pays no attention to me or the rest of his children."

"What about the assassin?" Ranelle asked. "If someone is chasing Nyx, we need to do something. Are you sure you saw nothing you could identify them with?"

Darius scowled but said nothing else.

Nyx shook her head. "They wore a mask, and I couldn't read them. I couldn't even move them." She sighed. "Who would be immune to my powers? Aside from the druid, I mean."

Ranelle shrugged. "I've been going through old archives of the great library, but I still can't find anything about mind whisperers. I'll see what I can find at the great temple. They have records too. If Isabella wants to find the queen, she must know something about mind whisperers. The queen was one."

"She was? Why didn't anyone mention that?" Nyx frowned. "Is that why Isabella wants me dead?"

Darius shrugged. "We have no way of knowing if you have any connection to the queen. She died over a century ago. My father wiped out her bloodline because he feared someone would rise against him. You can't be related to her."

"How can you be sure of that?"

Hope blossomed in her chest. Maybe there was another mind whisperer out there. Someone like her who could help her figure out where she came from.

"Nyx, my father slaughtered the queen and her family. He told me stories about it when I was a child. After he killed them, he had every mind whisperer in Andovia executed."

"Then how am I here? One must have survived."

"Are you sure you can't remember anything?" Darius prompted. "If you were around ten when you ended up in Joriam you must remember something."

"A mind sharing might be beneficial," Ranelle remarked. "Nyx can get your magical knowledge and maybe it would bring forth her memories. Then you could access whatever magical knowledge she has."

"There are other ways to retrieve lost memories." Darius rose from his seat. "We'll try that first."

Nyx's shoulders slumped. She craved magical knowledge almost as much as she longed for the memories of her long-lost past. She was sick of people coming after her. One way or another, she would prove she wasn't part of the prophecy.

The prophecy spoke of two things. One fae of great power and one born of fire. Together, they would bring about a new age either for great good or great darkness. Nyx knew she couldn't bring about an age of anything, so she couldn't be one of the chosen.

Nyx jumped. "What does that mean? What else can we try to do?"

"Other spells that are far less dangerous." Darius turned and called out for the keeper.

The keeper appeared a few moments later. It was a being created to watch over the hall and gather information from the extensive records when required. It also served as a guardian and protected the hall and all its knowledge.

She repressed a sigh. Nyx wished she could ask him more about what kind of spells they would be trying and when they could try them. Somehow, Nyx felt her missing memories would help with this whole situation. Although she couldn't begin to imagine how.

"Keeper, can you bring us all the information you can find about the old city?" Darius asked. "Bring us records and accounts of the day the shield went up and anything else you can find. Anything that mentions the city could be important."

"And about the Andovian Queen," Nyx added. "Bring us records of her as well."

An alarm rang out. The sound shrill as a bell.

"What does that mean?" Darius shot to his feet.

"It means there's an intruder." The keeper blurred away in a rush of light.

"Intruder? Someone followed us here?" Ranelle's eyes widened.

Arrows shot through the air towards them. Nyx ducked, then she and Darius ran in the direction the arrows had come from.

Ranelle and Lucien ducked underneath the table.

Nyx scanned around but still found no one on either floor above them.

She raised her hand to deflect an arrow, but someone's magic pushed back. As quickly as it started, the attack stopped, and silence filled the room.

The keeper reappeared a few moments later. "The intruder escaped before I could find them."

Nyx wondered what she could do to keep the assassin at bay. If they could follow her into a shielded place like the Hall of Knowledge, what else could they do?

CHAPTER 6

A couple of days passed. Ranelle knew she couldn't put moving to the great temple off any longer. She gathered up what few possessions she had and packed everything into a small sack. She hadn't had much when she had bartered passage to Andovia three years ago. The librarian had needed help and offered her lodging in return. The library had been home. Among the familiar sights and smells of the books, she had been comfortable.

Ranelle hated to leave but knew she didn't have a choice. Her father hadn't given her a penny. Everything she'd achieved since coming to Andovia, she'd earned for herself.

The great temple loomed before her. All white stone and marble. She headed up the steps. This place reminded her of a small palace rather than a temple. The wyverns didn't worship any gods. They had been cursed centuries ago by another Archdruid. Since Ranelle was half fae, the curse didn't fully affect her. She could still use her wings, even if she couldn't transform into a full wyvern.

Ranelle clutched her sack and gulped as she headed through the main part of the temple.

A large mosaic covered the ceiling with a scene depicting the first race. The Silvans. Peaceful, blond, and ethereal. Fae, but more human looking. Tall, graceful. The perfect race—or at least that was the way they saw themselves.

Although beautiful, Ranelle felt uncomfortable looking at it. She knew she was different. She was glad her wings were pulled back inside her body. People in Andovia hated her wings. They claimed she was a demon. Ranelle ignored them for the most part. She wasn't ashamed of what she was.

She wandered by the rows of pews. The walls of the apse were covered in images of different gods and goddesses.

How that priestess thought she could learn anything here, Ranelle had no clue. She didn't even know all their names. She had studied the history of Andovia, of course, but their gods rose and fell. Ranelle wandered up to the high altar, which glittered with the sign of a pentacle. Each point representing the four elements and a place of spirit.

The temple looked like so much space had gone to waste.

What did anyone expect her to do here?

Only the Order of the Blessed lived here. Priestesses who were loyal to the so-called gods. Ranelle scowled up at the scrutinising gaze of the gods.

"What are you doing in here?" A sharp voice made her jump.

Ranelle clutched a sack to her chest as Lyra Duncan came over. Her long black hair fell in wispy tendrils and her blue eyes bored into Ranelle. "You were supposed to report here days ago. What took you so long?"

Ranelle bit her lip. "My mentor allowed me to stay a few days longer at the library." It hadn't taken much convincing. Ranelle had needed that time to do more research in the Hall of Knowledge.

Gods, she would miss the library and being able to go to the hall whenever she needed to. There, she had a wealth of knowledge right at her fingertips. Which often helped when Darius and Lucien needed help.

Lyra's lip curled. "Your mentor was far too lenient with you. Come." The priestess grabbed Ranelle's arm and dragged her through the temple.

Was that necessary? She hadn't done anything wrong.

She didn't want to be here. But she didn't want to impose on Ambrose, either. Plus, she would have unprecedented access to Isabella here in a way no one else would. Or at least she hoped she would. She had learnt everything she could about the Order of the Blessed from the outside.

The Order seemed to keep their secrets close and only told people what they wanted them to know.

Ranelle knew she would have to be on her guard here. She was determined to help find out what Isabella was up to. And perhaps learn more about the elders. The elders were a mysterious race. From everything she had learnt about them, she knew they were bad. They were the true power on Erthea and controlled everything. Perhaps they had been the ones who had wanted to enslave her race too.

Lyra dragged her down a long corridor. Crystals lit up the walkway. Lyra let go of her when they reached a tiny room that looked like a cell.

Good gods, was Lyra going to lock her up? Was it somehow punishment for being associated with Darius, perhaps? Or because she hadn't arrived when the priestess had expected?

"You will sleep here. Put your sack down and follow me. We have much to do."

She dropped her sack on the bed and followed Lyra back into the passageway. "What will I—?" Ranelle asked.

Lyra glowered at her. "Learn to only speak when spoken to."

Nyx had offered to come with her and Ranelle wished she were there to support her. But Ranelle had known bringing Nyx to the temple would be foolish though, especially if Isabella had sent that assassin. Besides, Nyx never knew when to keep her mouth shut. Ranelle did. Her father saw women as subservient. How disappointed he would be if he could see her now. She knew when to hold her tongue.

Lyra led her down another corridor. How many rooms and passages did this place have?

Lyra pushed open a set of large double doors. Ranelle gasped. An entire library stretched out from floor to ceiling. The stone walls were dirty and crumbling with age in places. The fireplace stood empty, and the room smelt musty.

"The library needs organising and cataloguing," Lyra said. "It's impossible to find anything around here."

"But… But this could take years to go through it," Ranelle protested.

"If you want to be a scholar, then I suggest you put your skills to good use," Lyra snapped. "Many priestesses would kill for a chance to live and train here."

"I'm not a priestess and I never will be. Your gods are false and corrupt." Ranelle put a hand over her mouth.

Good gods, why had she said that?

Nyx must be a bad influence on me.

Lyra's eyes widened, yet her lips curved into a smile. "We are not what we seem, Ranelle. You would do well to remember that. Get to work. You will hear the noonday bell for our meal later."

Lyra left her alone, and Ranelle breathed a sigh of relief.

How in the realm would she catalogue all these books? The great library held thousands of tomes, and all of them were kept in meticulous order. How did anyone find anything here?

Ranelle rifled through a few titles. One was a copy of the Silvan's holy book. Another was a ledger of food and supplies. Ranelle pushed them aside in disgust. She hoped she might have access to information here that the library and the hall didn't possess.

Now, from the sound of it, she was going to be forced to live in a virtual prison and work like a slave. She couldn't run away, not yet. Not while she could still spy on the temple and learn what she could about the order.

She picked up a pile of books and started arranging them into different stacks.

A cloud of dust swirled around her.

"Glan," she muttered the druid word for clean.

The dust around her faded as light sparkled around the room.

After she had arranged a few books, Ranelle left the library and wandered around the temple.

There were dozens of rooms and many of them lay empty. That struck her as odd. She cast her senses out, careful in case someone felt her presence.

In the next the room she spotted Isabella.

Ranelle smiled. Maybe things were looking up.

CHAPTER 7

Nyx sat back on her bed and read through the notes Ranelle had given her for a memory retrieval spell. It said she had to sit somewhere quiet and recite the spell. Darius suggested she try it.

Nyx stared at the gnarled, knotted bark walls. Living on top of the tree had scared her at first. Now she couldn't imagine living anywhere else.

She closed her eyes and imagined her protective grove around her. Trees surrounded her on all sides and formed a protective ring. Only faint slivers of light came through the heavy canopy. Nyx had been coming to this place in her mind for as long as she could remember. One of her earliest memories was of someone telling her to go there. Who had told her? She couldn't remember.

Harland had told her she had been found lying under an ash tree as a child. She had known her name was Nyx, but not much else. Or at least that was the only name she could remember. No one had been certain how old she was. Around ten or so they thought. She had spent seven winters with Harland.

She pushed all thoughts of Harland away. He was dead and gone. She defeated his spirit. He couldn't harm her anymore.

Nyx recited the spell. In truth, she had no idea if it would work. She had never cast a spell before. Those strange runes she kept drawing had to come from somewhere. Nyx waited for something to happen. Something to signify the spell had worked. She opened her eyes again. Everything in the room looked as before. Same walls. Same table covered with discarded books. Same blue linens over the four-poster bed.

She got up and paced. Had the spell worked?

She recited it again. Nothing.

Had she done something wrong?

Nyx considered asking Ambrose for help, then remembered he had gone out. The druid would have to do. Nyx headed down the hall towards Darius' room. She knocked and waited. No answer came.

So she opened the door and peered in.

Candles lit the room with a faint glow. His room looked similar to hers. A four-poster bed stood on one side. A table and chair sat in the corner, covered with books and maps. Weapons lined the walls along with rows of books and a pile of clothes lying at the end of the bed. Nyx bit back a smile when she thought of the fuss Ada would make if she saw them.

Darius sat in a circle on the floor, crossed legs and naked from the waist up. His eyes were closed.

Nyx sighed. She knew not to interrupt him when he did this. He could be in the middle of a spell or something. She needed to know why her spell wouldn't work.

Too bad she couldn't visit Ranelle at the temple either. She couldn't risk going there for fear of being seen by Isabella. Maybe Lucien could help? He knew about spells too since he was training to be an overseer.

"Did you want something?" Darius' voice made her jump.

"No. Yes. I don't know." Nyx pushed her hair off her face. "Are you busy?"

"No, I was meditating. It's rare to have quiet moments around here."

Nyx averted her gaze when she caught herself staring at him. Her cheeks flushed.

"The spell Ranelle gave me… it didn't work. Why not? I did everything she said." She moved past the candles and slumped onto the floor beside him. She kept her gaze on the floor to avoid looking at him. Then wondered why it bothered her so much. She had spent every day with him for months. She had seen plenty of half-naked men before. Especially when she used to work in a tavern.

"There can be a lot of reasons why spells don't work." Darius rested his hands on his knees. "Timing, power, emotion. Those can affect magic."

"See, this is why we need to do the mind sharing. I need to know these things." She blew out a breath. "I need to know why I can't remember anything."

"What is your oldest memory?"

She furrowed her brow. "Being taken to live with Harland and Mama Habrid. Before that, everything else is a blur. I don't even remember waking up under a tree like they said."

"Maybe something traumatic happened. The mind can block things out when it doesn't want to remember."

"Like what? If something did happen, wouldn't I have remembered something by now?" She threw her arms up in exasperation. "I don't remember anything. Harland never told me I had any injuries when I got brought to the slave market. Injured slaves aren't very attractive."

"Didn't you say Harland used to buy slaves who had magical abilities?"

She nodded, and a heavy weight settled in her chest. Her foster sisters had magical abilities as well. Different from hers, but it had bonded them together. "I wish I knew where my sisters were. I keep wondering what happened to them." She sighed. "I must've come from somewhere. I want to know where. If there're others out there like me." She tossed her plait over her shoulder. "It would be nice to meet another mind whisperer. To know I'm not the only one."

There had to be other mind whisperers out there somewhere. Magic was usually passed down through a bloodline. So one of her parents had to have been one.

"Maybe it will help you to focus on something specific." He held out his hand. "I can lend you my power. It might make the spell more effective."

Nyx reached out and grasped his hand. His fingers laced through hers. "Are you sure this will work? Your touch neutralises my powers," she pointed out.

"I put a shield around my skin, so my touch won't affect you."

Energy tingled against her fingers. She recited the spell again, and Darius's magic washed over her. She closed her eyes and waited.

"Concentrate on breathing, let your mind take you back." His voice sounded almost faraway even though they were sitting next to each other.

Nyx let her mind drift and found herself standing in a hallway. A door lay at the far end, dark and out of reach.

Nyx made a move towards it but found she couldn't. The closer she moved, the further away the door became.

She let out a low growl. "I can't reach them. Something is stopping me."

Darius frowned. "That's odd. Perhaps your mind isn't ready to remember yet."

Nyx snorted. "I'm more than ready to know what happened to me, druid."

"There's another spell we could try, but it involves high magic."

High magic came from outside nature. It came from the spirit and things around you.

She hesitated. She knew how much he struggled to control high magic. It brought out a darker side of him. "Are you sure you can do this?" She arched an eyebrow at him.

"Of course I can." Darius looked down and Nyx realised their hands were still clasped. "If it helps you, it's worth it."

"Do the spell. I will hit you if you lose control." She bit back a smile.

Darius chuckled. "I hope that's not necessary."

Darius chanted a spell. Light flashed around them. Nyx closed her eyes and waited. She didn't hold out much hope that something would happen this time. Still, she enjoyed being close to the druid. It felt good to be able to touch him without fear of her powers being neutralised for once.

Nyx almost pulled back when she realised what she was thinking. Why would she feel anything for the druid? He might be her friend, but that didn't make him anything else. He could never be anything more than a friend to her. They were from different worlds.

She found herself standing in the dark hallway again. The door was closer now, but not much. At least that took her mind off Darius.

"Do you see anything?" Darius' voice sounded far away.

Nyx didn't reply and made a move towards the door. Once again, something held her in place. "I can't reach the door," she groaned.

The more she pushed, the further away the door became. They were her memories, and she'd be damned if she would let anything stop her from reaching them.

She struggled forward and reached for the door. Pain tore through her head. She doubled over and struggled for breath.

"Nyx, what's wrong?" Darius asked in alarm.

She gasped for breath again. Why couldn't she breathe? Why did it hurt?

Darius muttered some strange words and light flared between his fingers. She closed her eyes and whimpered. "I'll call Ambrose." Darius slipped an arm around her.

"No!" Nyx moaned and held onto him as she took a few deep breaths.

He stroked her hair and held her. "Are you sure you're alright?"

"Why can't I open the door to my memories?"

"I don't know. Maybe you're not—"

"I'm ready," Nyx ground out. "I need to know where I come from."

"We'll find another way."

"The mind sharing?" She rested her head in his lap. She doubted she had ever been this close to a man before.

"I don't think that's a good idea. Especially after what happened."

"At least that would probably work."

"Mind sharing is more than just sharing knowledge. You share each other's memories, too. Things you would never want to reveal to anyone."

Nyx shook her head. "You've already seen my darkness and know my secrets. I'm not afraid to see yours."

Darius sighed. "There are some things I can never share with anyone."

She looked up at him. "Why do you never let anyone close to you?" That was one thing she had noticed during the past months they had spent together. Aside from Ranelle, Lucien, and herself, he didn't let anyone else get close to him. He didn't pay attention to women, even though many often paid attention to him. Aside from them, he kept everyone at a distance.

"Because if people get close, they get hurt."

"That sounds lonely." She reached out and laced her fingers through his again. "Everyone needs someone, druid. Even you."

Darius held her hand and continued to stroke her hair.

The sound of a door closing echoed down the hall.

Nyx bolted upright. "I—I should go."

"You should. It's late."

Nyx turned to move; her face flushed. What had she been thinking? Holding his hand like that? She scrambled towards the door.

Darius caught hold of her and captured her mouth in a kiss.

Her eyes widened. She returned the kiss. She found herself wanting more, but Darius pulled back.

"Night, Nyx."

"Good night, druid."

Nyx headed back to her room and ran her fingers over her lips. Her heart and her mind raced. Why had he kissed her? He looked as surprised as she had been. She enjoyed it. No one had ever kissed her before. No boy had ever even liked her before. All the males back in her human tribe had tormented her. Romance was something she didn't think she would ever have. Not with her mind reading abilities.

Did he feel something more than friendship towards her?

Nyx had no idea what she felt for him either. She liked him well enough. They spent every day together. But what did that mean now?

She shook her head and pushed all thoughts of Darius away.

Ambrose had already warned them to not become involved. He had a point. Darius was the son of the Archdruid, and she was a former slave. How could they ever be together?

Nyx slumped onto her bed heavily. The thing that bothered her most was she couldn't access her memories. Had something bad happened to her?

She fell asleep with questions racing through her mind.

"Do you really think the spirits will help us?" Nyx flinched as tree branches thwacked against her head.

The Spirit Grove always made her a little uneasy. The first time Darius brought her here, she'd been afraid. The trees flashed with different colours. Red, green, pink, blue. Like they were part of this world, yet somehow not.

Voices whispered in the wind. The Spirit Grove was a place where the veil between the worlds was thinnest. Spirits could come and go freely here.

The druids often came here to commune with them. The druids didn't worship gods the way the rest of Magickind did. They respected spirits—both of nature and souls that had passed on.

49

"They usually give messages."

He unclipped his sword belt and removed his longbow from his back, along with his daggers.

No one could carry weapons into the Grove. The druid never told her why, though. Probably some unspoken rule. Nyx couldn't fathom why spirits would be bothered by weapons if they couldn't be hurt by them. At least she didn't *think* they could.

"Are we going to see the Great Guardian again?"

She had met the mystical Guardian once. Nyx still didn't know much about her. Other than the Guardian protected the sacred grove.

Darius shrugged. "She doesn't appear that often." He pushed through the tree line.

Nyx made a move to follow, and a wall of energy blocked her way. "Ow, druid! Why can't I get through?"

Oddly, she'd never had a problem entering the Grove before.

Darius rushed back over and waved his hand in front of the entrance to the Grove. No energy blocked his way. "Do you have any weapons on you?"

"Do I look like I do?" She motioned to her sleeveless tunic and hose.

"What about the bracelet I gave you?"

She glanced down at silver band on her wrist. It didn't look like much, but it turned into a sword.

Darius gave it to her months ago. She had taken to wearing it more often now an assassin kept stalking her.

She sighed and slipped the bracelet off, then dropped it beside his weapons. Still, a wall of energy barred her way.

"You need to apologise to the spirits."

"Why? I forgot about the bracelet."

"Nyx, just apologise. The spirits don't like weapons. Certain metals repel them."

"Fine. Spirits, I'm sorry. I meant no offence." She waited, and half expected a response.

None came.

Darius reached out, grabbed her hand, and pulled her through.

She breathed a sigh of relief.

They carried on walking. The Grove grew darker as the trees became denser. Coloured light flashed around the dark, skeletal outlines of the trees. Voices whispered all around them, but she couldn't make out what they said.

Nyx couldn't hear any thoughts either. Spirits were different from living minds, but Darius said she might hear them since they were made up of energy.

She and Darius didn't say anything. It felt almost wrong to speak here.

He kept hold of her hand and she flushed when she thought back to their kiss last night. Nyx still didn't know how to feel or what to think about that. Were they more than friends then? Did she want them to be more than that?

A chill ran over her senses as they prickled with recognition.

"Stop, someone's here." She gripped Darius's hand.

He furrowed his brow. "Where?"

"It's the assassin. I feel them. They're nearby. Damn, we don't have any weapons." She hoped their magic would be enough to fend the assassin off.

"They can't enter this place. No one with ill intentions can."

"How can you be so sure of that?"

"The spirits blocked you, didn't they?"

"Maybe we should go after the assassin, then. If we could capture them—"

"Nyx, we need to know what we're up against. Besides, the assassin isn't our only concern."

Nyx remained on edge as they reached the centre of the Grove. The light here grew brighter and bathed them in a rainbow-coloured light. After a while, the assassin's presence faded.

"They've gone." She slumped onto the ground beside Darius.

"See, told you they can't enter." Darius let go of her hand, then bowed his head in respect to the spirits. He closed his eyes and told her to listen. To ask the spirits what they wanted to know.

Nyx bowed her head too, but her mind raced. What did she want to know? So many things, but she didn't know where to begin.

Why is the assassin after me? Why do they want me dead? They were the two most pressing questions for her.

Darius would ask about the murder and Isabella, anyway.

She waited. Only the faint murmur of voices greeted her.

Nyx opened her eyes when her senses tingled.

The Great Guardian sat a few feet away from her. Behind her, a glowing white tree flitted in and out of existence. The Guardian stared at her, expectant.

"You." Nyx scrambled up and bowed her head. She knew better than to disrespect this woman.

"Nice to see you and the young Valeran are working together."

The Great Guardian had told them to work together when Nyx had first come here. Nyx scoffed at the idea back then, but she couldn't imagine not being with him now.

"Who sent the assassin to kill me? Was it Isabella?"

The Guardian's beautiful skin beamed like moonlight. Her dark hair fell past her shoulders and her lavender eyes sparkled. Her lilac gown glittered, too. Nyx couldn't be sure if it was magic or a trick of the light. "You will discover that in time."

Nyx groaned. She hated cryptic messages. "I need to know now. I'm tired of people trying to kill me." She brushed dirt off her hose. "I'm not part of the prophecy."

"Can you be certain of that?"

She sighed. "Am I?"

The Guardian smiled. "All in time. You're asking the wrong questions."

"Alright. Who killed that man I found dead outside the old city? Was it the assassin?" She crossed her arms. "Did Isabella order his killing?"

Her power pulsed deep inside her. She knew it would be stupid to use her powers on the Guardian. But she scanned the woman with her senses. Nothing but crashing waves of power greeted her. Old, like time itself.

The Guardian had pointed ears, so Nyx guessed she might be some kind of fae.

"There's more than the assassin at play here."

She glanced over at Darius; he still had his eyes shut. He seemed oblivious to their conversation. "Can you tell me anything useful?"

"Secrets lurk in the shadows, you will have to shed light on them to find the answers you seek."

"That makes no sense." Nyx scowled. "Why can't you give me some real answers?"

"All of your questions are tied together. I will say that. The assassin, the murders, Isabella and her."

"Her?" Nyx furrowed her brow. "You mean the queen?"

"She—" the Guardian gasped, and her eyes blurred to white. Her body trembled.

"Guardian? Are you alright?" Nyx didn't get a reply. "Druid?"

Darius didn't respond either.

She reached out and touched the Guardian's arm. Energy jolted between them. Her eyes snapped shut as a vision dragged her in.

A woman with broken wings hanging from her back screamed as fire consumed her body, tied to a burning stake. Her screams grew in pitch, then light exploded around her so intensely it stung Nyx's eyes. Fire burned through the sky around the old city. The light blurred around a stone crypt, then a strange symbol appeared.

Nyx winced as her vision blurred and darkness crept in around her.

CHAPTER 8

Darius sat listening to the spirits, but everything they said remained jumbled.

"Must not rise."

"She will return."

"City has fallen."

A scream tore him out of his meditative state. Darius opened his eyes and found Nyx on the ground, clutching her head.

"Nyx, what happened?" He spotted the Great Guardian a few feet away, her face ashen. "What's going on?"

"She touched me when I had a vision. She must not have known not to do so."

Darius knelt and put his hand on Nyx's shoulder. "Will she be alright?"

"It will soon pass." She rose and turned to leave.

"Wait. What did you see?" He caught hold of Nyx as she slumped against him.

The Guardian frowned at him. "You know better than to question me, Darius Valeran."

He cursed himself. He did know better. "I'm sorry. Nyx must have rubbed off on me."

Nyx groaned as she opened her eyes. "My head!"

He stroked her hair and murmured something to soothe her.

"What did you see?" Darius asked the Guardian again.

The Guardian hesitated. "Just make sure nothing tears you apart. You must stay together, no matter what."

"Why is that so important?" Darius asked.

"I think you already know the answer to that. Don't let anything part you. Not even people you trust." Her lips twitched. "You will find the answers you seek. Look to the star." She vanished in a bright flash of light.

Darius guessed Nyx might be dizzy, so he laid back on the ground. He pulled her with him. Hopefully, the earth would help ground her.

Nyx rested her head against his shoulder and squeezed her eyes shut.

"What did you see?" he asked her.

The murmur of voices around them faded.

Darius kept his arms around her, enjoying the feeling of having her close. He stroked the back of her wings, surprised by how soft they were. He knew the fae considered someone touching their wings an intimate thing. He'd always wondered what they would feel like.

"A woman… She was burning." She opened her eyes and stared at him. "She was… broken. Her wings were torn—like someone ripped them apart." She shuddered. "Then it changed. It was so fast. I saw someone with a knife, then a block of stone and a strange symbol."

"What kind of symbol?"

She shrugged. "I don't know. It happened so fast. The Guardian saw more than I did. She cut me off—I felt it."

"The Great Guardian has unfathomable power, so that doesn't surprise me. We'll figure out what it means. Can you get up?"

"I don't know."

"We can stay here as long as you need to."

"Did the spirits tell you anything? The Guardian told me everything is intertwined. Isabella, the assassin. Everything."

"She told me to look to the star. I have no idea what it means."

"Why does she have to be so cryptic?" Nyx sighed.

"I guess it's from living for so long."

"Well, if I get to live a long time, I'm going to give people straight answers."

Darius smiled. "I hope I'm around to see that."

"Oh, you will be. You're stuck with me, remember? We'll still be riding around on Sirin, too. Chasing sprites, no doubt."

He laughed. "Spirits, I hope not."

"Alright. Where do you want us to be?" Nyx leaned up on one elbow. "In Andovia or somewhere else?"

He shook his head. "I don't think about the future much. Everything in this world is too uncertain." Thinking about the future never seemed very important to him. He didn't like to plan that far ahead.

"I don't care as long as I'm with you. We both know you'd be lost without me." She gave him a playful shove.

"You won't leave then?" He arched a brow.

"Why would I?"

"You said you'd find a way to get freedom no matter what."

She pursed her lips. "That's... true, but I have freedom here. More than I'd have elsewhere."

"So is that the only reason you'll stay then?" Since Nyx arrived in Andovia, he had been afraid to find her gone one day. Despite their kiss, and everything they'd been through, he wondered if she would still leave given the chance. Deep down, he still feared it.

"I have friends here. This place feels like home. I won't leave unless I have to."

"Promise you won't leave." He reached up and caressed her cheek. "Promise you'll stay no matter what happens."

Nyx looked away and shook her head. "You and I both know we shouldn't make promises we can't keep. One day I might not have a choice about leaving."

Darius sighed and sat up. "You're right. We shouldn't make promises." He took her hand. "Except one. I won't lose you no matter what happens."

"You can't be sure of that."

"I'm sure of how I feel about you."

Nyx hesitated and brushed her lips against his. Darius pulled her in close and deepened the kiss. He couldn't deny how much he wanted to be close to her. After a few moments, they pulled away from each other.

"What are we doing?" Nyx flushed.

"No idea. We should get going."

She nodded. "We should. You have guard duties. And I have a lesson with Ambrose."

They began the trek out of the Grove.

"Will you be alright?" Darius asked for a few moments. "I mean, after the vision? Maybe I should take you—"

"I can find Ambrose by myself." Nyx unfurled her wings.

"But the assassin—they already followed you once today. Maybe it would be safer if we stuck together."

"I can handle them. Don't you have patrol today?"

"Fine, just be careful. That's a promise you have to keep."

"When am I not careful?" Nyx grinned.

"I could list all the occasions, but we would be here a while."

She gave him shove. "You be careful too." She flew off without a backwards glance.

Darius gathered up his weapons once he got out of the Grove.

Sirin sat waiting for him. *I saw that.*

Saw what? He furrowed his brow.

The dragon huffed. *You have feelings for her.*

"Don't be ridiculous." He clipped his sword back around his waist and sheathed his daggers, then swung the bow over his back.

I feel what you feel, remember? The dragon snorted. *I know what you feel for her.*

"You know I can't afford to care for anyone. Not even her."

Anyone he cared about could be used against him. It had happened before.

"Come, we have to patrol."

Later that evening, Darius headed to the Flying Dragon Tavern, where Lucien worked most evenings. He headed straight to the bar.

Long tables with benches covered the centre of the room and smaller tables were dotted around the sides. Huge oak beams hung overhead and covered the tavern's dark walls. The stench of cheap ale hung in the air.

Lucien came over. "Something wrong?"

Darius furrowed his brow. "How do you know?"

"Because you look worried." Lucien pulled him some ale.

"I need to know how to find the assassin. And stop Isabella." He sighed. "I have a bad feeling something will happen to Nyx."

"Be careful. I might start thinking you have feelings for her. Which you pretend you don't have."

Darius scowled. "I... I can't."

"You do. We all see the way you look at her. Frankly, I worried there was something wrong with you, since no man or woman has ever turned your head before."

"Just give me the damned ale." He grabbed the tankard. Its contents sloshed over the bar. "There must be a way to find the assassin."

"Why not go straight to the source?"

"The source?" His frown deepened. "Nyx?"

"No, the person who sent the assassin after her."

"You mean Isabella." He rubbed his chin. "What if it's not her?" He couldn't be sure if his former stepmother had sent the assassin or not. Since others seemed to believe Nyx might be part of the prophecy that foretold the coming of the next dark times, it could be anyone.

"You have magic and a mind whisperer at your disposal. Use them."

"I can't be sure either of those things would work against her."

"You're the Archdruid's son. Start acting like it. Isabella isn't queen anymore, and she doesn't have the same kind of authority that she used to have."

Darius gulped down the bitter ale. "So I confront Isabella." He considered it. Could he even do that without severe repercussions? He never dared to directly go against his stepmother before. That would have been pure suicide. "What about the assassin? They got into the hall and tried to follow us into the Grove."

Lucien raised his eyebrows. "They're determined. That's why I said go straight to the source. See if Isabella is responsible."

"What if all that does is expose me to her? You know how careful I have to be."

"You have to take risks sometimes."

The tavern door creaked open, and a cloaked figure came in.

Darius scanned the person with his senses and caught the familiar tingle of a druid. "Yasmine?"

A dark-haired young woman with blue eyes looked out from beneath the hood. "Valeran." She smiled and gave him a brief hug.

"What are you doing here?" Darius was surprised to see his pirate friend here. He motioned to her to follow him to a quieter part of the tavern where they wouldn't be seen or overheard. "Is something wrong? You haven't lost your ship again, have you?"

"No, I won't let that happen again." Yasmine scowled. "I'm collecting supplies."

Darius sat down at a table with her. "Have you brought any newcomers?" He knew the assassin had to have come from somewhere. Bartering passage on *The Vanity* wouldn't be out of the realm of possibility.

Yasmine shook her head. "No one. We have a few refugees on board but they're headed elsewhere."

"Are you sure no one left the ship?"

"Quite sure. Will and the crew are with them. So I thought I'd stop by to say hello. Where is Nyx?"

He shrugged. "At home, I suppose. Have you found—?"

"No, I haven't found anything about her foster sisters. I will keep looking."

Darius hoped one day he could find them for her. But right now, he had more pressing issues to deal with.

CHAPTER 9

Nyx walked into the tavern. A lot of fae and other Magickind frequented the Flying Dragon. She and Darius often went there to see Lucien or just to relax. Here they could be themselves.

She headed over to the bar. "Do you think you could help me track the assassin?" she asked Lucien quietly.

"If I caught their scent, I could track them."

"Good, will you help me set a trap?"

"Why are you asking me to help you instead of Darius?" He arched a brow at her.

"Because we both know he won't like it." She knew Darius wouldn't be very happy if she used herself as bait to lure the assassin out.

Lucien glanced over at a barmaid. "Olive, can you cover for me?" he asked the doe eyed fae.

She nodded. "Don't be gone long."

Nyx glanced over at the far corner of the room. She knew Darius was there, even if she couldn't see him.

"An old friend came to visit," Lucien added.

"Yasmine. I know."

"How?"

She rolled her eyes. "I can hear thoughts."

Everyone's thoughts were there at the edge of her mind. She didn't fully raise her shield because she feared the assassin might have followed her.

"Alright, let's go."

She and Lucien headed out into a nearby alleyway. Shadows danced all around them from flickering torches and candles from the nearby houses.

Ranelle flew over and perched on a roof. Nyx had called her to come and help them. The more eyes she had around her, the better. They needed to be prepared for anything.

Nyx wandered further into the alley. The buzz of minds around her was distant.

Are you shielded up there? she asked Ranelle. *I don't want the assassin to sense you.*

I'm cloaked, believe me. Where is wolfsbane?

I'm close. Lucien had shifted into wolf form to remain out of sight.

And be ready for anything. She moved further down the alleyway. She kept her senses on alert. *Come on, I know you're lurking around here somewhere.* Nyx had felt the presence of being followed throughout the day.

She doubted the assassin would have given up.

Lucien and Ranelle's thoughts buzzed on the edge of her mind.

Wouldn't this be the perfect place to strike her down?

Lucien, Ranelle, do you see anything?

Nothing, Ranelle replied.

Nor I, Lucien added.

They must be around here somewhere.

Maybe they got tired. You and Darius moved around a lot during the day.

*They followed me to the hall and around the forest. They must be—*Nyx froze as her senses tingled. With what she didn't know. Recognition perhaps.

She didn't call out to the others yet and carried on walking. An arrow whizzed through the air towards her. She waved her hand. It fell to the ground with a thud. *Lucien, Ranelle, they're here!* Nyx shot into the air.

Lucien ran around the corner. *Where are they?*

"Over on that roof." Ranelle sprang off the roof and motioned to one of the opposite houses.

Lucien shifted back into human form, then blurred to keep up with Nyx.

She spotted a dark figure jumping from rooftop to rooftop.

Curse it. How could the assassin move so fast? She flapped her wings harder to keep up.

Ranelle trailed behind, she couldn't fly as fast as Nyx.

Lucien blurred below her. His rushing thoughts echoed at the edge of her mind.

Lucien, try and catch up with them. Cut them off. Nyx glided over the rooftops and had to ascend so she wouldn't collide with them.

On it. Lucien shot down another alley.

Nyx lost sight of the fleeing figure and cursed. Once she found them, she'd use her touch on them and force them to talk.

Someone cried out in alarm, followed by a loud crash.

She shot over the rooftops. Lucien lay on the ground, but there was no sign of the assassin.

She swooped down beside him. "Where did they go? Are you hurt?"

"They stunned me. I'm supposed to be immune to magic."

"You're not immune to mine," she pointed out. "Where did they go?"

"I think they headed in there."

A huge dome shaped building loomed ahead. The great temple.

Nyx had never gone in there.

"They went inside?" Ranelle frowned as she landed beside them.

"Good, let's go in." Nyx checked her wrist to make sure her sword bracelet was in place.

"That's a bad idea. If Isabella—"

Darius appeared in a flash of light. "What are you doing?"

"The assassin is in there." Nyx motioned to the temple. "We need to get in."

"Let's go. I need your help in there."

Her mouth fell open. She had expected him to say no and protest about it being too dangerous.

"You can't—" Ranelle protested.

"Nyx, come on." Darius motioned for her to follow.

Nyx hurried up the steps after him.

"Wait, you can't go in. Do you want Isabella to—" Ranelle ran to keep up with them.

Lucien blurred to catch up.

"Just tell us where Isabella's chambers are," Darius said.

Nyx still couldn't believe he wanted to confront Isabella, but she would be right there with him to help.

What are you going to say to Isabella? She switched to talking in thought so they wouldn't be heard.

This place felt eerie. Shadows danced around the marble walls like wraiths. She didn't like this place at all.

Use my powers and get some answers. I need you there to read her.

"Wait, you're what?" Nyx gasped.

"Luc, Rae, go and search the temple for the assassin." Darius waved his hand.

Ranelle opened her mouth to protest.

"Come on." Lucien grabbed her arm and dragged her away.

"Are you out of your mind?" Nyx put her hands on her hips. "I need to go find the assassin. Seeing Isabella—"

"You can go after the assassin if you want to, but I need some answers." Darius walked off.

Bloody stubborn druid! She sighed. As much as she wanted to find the assassin, she couldn't let him do this alone. If something went wrong, something might happen to him, and she wouldn't allow that. The assassin would just have to wait for another day.

Spirits, help me. She hurried after him.

CHAPTER 10

Darius fought to keep his nerves under control as they headed towards Isabella's chambers.

I still think this is a bad idea. Why not just let me use my powers? Nyx asked.

Because we don't know if your touch will work on her. Darius pushed his nerves away, but his heart still thudded in his ears.

How do you know your magic will work? Nyx arched an eyebrow at him. *You don't know what kind of protection she has.*

She had a point. He couldn't be sure his powers would work.

I'll be using higher magic. It should work.

Higher magic didn't just consist of spells. Sometimes the energy came from outside nature. Like blood or other energy sources. Higher magic was more elaborate and bordered on dark. Some claimed it went against nature itself. His father used higher magic, but Darius struggled with it.

And if it doesn't? Nyx grabbed his arm. *You're putting us both at risk if your plan fails.*

I have to do something. Lives are at stake. Just make sure you read her. He stopped at the end of the hall where Isabella's chambers were.

Wait, you're going to use magic to force her to talk, aren't you? She stared at him in disbelief. *Gods, Darius, you can't do that.*

Do you have a better idea? He frowned at her.

Yes, use my touch on her. It's safer than you—

No, it's not. If you use your touch and it doesn't work, you'll be exposing yourself. It's safer all round if I do this.

You lose control using higher magic.

If you don't want me to do this, don't come in. Go home.

As much as Darius wanted her to be there to read Isabella, he wouldn't force her to do it.

Nyx blew out a breath. *No. I'm not letting you expose yourself either. We stay together. The Great Guardian said that's important.*

Good. Let's go. Darius yanked the door handle open and headed in.

The chamber opened into a small room. A single bed draped with old furs stood on one side. A fireplace and a small table stood on the other. The room looked nothing like what he had expected. Ranelle had to have got the room wrong. Isabella would never stay somewhere this spartan.

But Isabella herself sat in the corner, staring out of the window. Her rose gold hair hung loose about her shoulders, and she wore a plain black dress.

Nyx shut the door behind them.

"Isabella?" Darius approached her, she didn't respond. Her gaze seemed far away.

"Isabella?" Nyx tried instead.

Still, the former queen didn't budge.

"Stepmother." Darius knew she hated being called that. He put a hand on her shoulder.

"Why is she not responding?" Nyx frowned. "What's wrong with her?"

Darius drew magic. This kind of magic didn't require spells. All that mattered was desire and will. This was the way higher magic worked. "Talk to me." His voice came out harsher and colder than he'd intended. Power thrummed through his fingers. This was the very kind of magic his father used to impose his will on others.

Isabella turned. "What are you doing here?"

"We need to talk to you." Nyx crossed her arms. *Is your magic working?*

I think so.

Something doesn't feel right about her. Look at her eyes. They seem… empty.

Darius had noticed that. The will. The power. The authority seemed to have vanished from them. She looked nothing like the nasty, arrogant woman he'd known.

Isabella flicked her gaze to Nyx. Her eyes flashed, but she didn't say anything. That surprised him, too.

Why hadn't she berated them for intruding? She'd be angry at Nyx, no doubt. Isabella didn't allow anyone to defeat her.

"Did you send another assassin after Nyx?" Darius demanded.

"No. Why would I? I'm serving penance for my crimes."

Nyx snorted. *Does she really expect us to believe that? I know she is somehow involved. She has to be. Who else would want me dead?*

Is she lying?

She shook her head. *I don't sense any signs of deception. Unless she can prevent me from reading her.*

I don't think she can. She feels... compliant.

But she feels strange. There's something not right with her.

"Thyren—a high fae was found dead outside the old city. What do you know about that?"

Isabella blinked. "Nothing."

Darius leaned in. "Isabella, I know you were plotting to take my father's throne. You still plan to do that, don't you?"

Isabella shook her head. "I am serving my penance."

Darius repressed a sigh. *This is us getting nowhere.*

Do you think your touch will work on her? He didn't want to risk Nyx becoming exposed, but his magic didn't always yield the results that hers could.

I'm not sure my touch will do much good. Nyx drew back. *I can feel your magic working. It's forcing her to talk.*

What do you sense?

Her mind is... blank. She's not feeling much of anything.

The door burst open. A dark-haired woman with blue eyes stared at them. "What are you two doing in here?"

Darius and Nyx jumped.

He relaxed. "Lyra—we were um... just visiting my stepmother."

Who is that? Nyx asked.

Lyra Duncan. The chief priestess here. She is an ally and friend. She helps the resistance.

"Indeed. It is a little late for visitors." Lyra motioned for them to follow her out. "Good night, Isabella."

"Good night, priestess."

Isabella turned her attention back to the window.

"Get some rest," Lyra told her. "I will see you at morning prayers." She closed the door behind them. "Darius, you're playing a dangerous game coming here."

He rubbed the back of his neck. "I know, but—"

He'd known Lyra almost as long as Ambrose. At least he knew he could trust her.

"But you couldn't help yourself." Lyra sighed. "You're lucky she didn't—"

"She didn't seem… like herself."

"She was odd," Nyx agreed.

"Isabella has lost everything. Such a heavy fall from grace can change a person." Lyra motioned for them to follow her down the hall.

Nyx scoffed. "No one changes that much unless they're forced to."

Lyra stared at her. "You must be the mind whisperer Ambrose tells me so much about."

Why would Ambrose tell her about me? Nyx sounded perplexed.

Because they're… friends. Well, more than that. We can trust her.

"It's late. Why don't you both come and have some tea before you go home?"

"We can't. We have someone else to search for." Nyx tugged on his arm. *We need to find our assassin.*

Rae and Lucien haven't found anything. Let's find out what she knows, too.

Darius hesitated. "Lyra, has anyone new been staying at the temple recently?"

"No, why do you ask?"

"Because the person who's been sent to kill me ran in here earlier." Nyx glared at the priestess.

"That's disturbing. Olaf!" the priestess called out.

A troll stomped round the corner. He towered over them.

"Olaf, be a dear, and search the temple and the living quarters for an intruder."

Olaf grunted and stomped away.

He's the unofficial guard for the temple, Darius explained. *Trolls are hard to kill since they are immune to most magic.*

"Good night, Lyra."

Nyx and Darius headed home. "What's wrong with Isabella?" Nyx asked once they were lying in his room.

Darius rubbed the back of his neck. "I don't know. She seemed… so different."

She scoffed. "I doubt anyone could change her that much. She felt odd when I touched her."

He nodded. "I know."

"Then what's wrong with her? Her mind was blank. Like when I read a man who had lost his mind."

"Do you think Isabella's gone mad?"

"No. Her mind didn't feel broken. At least I don't think so." She sighed. "I don't know. Things were so much simpler when I only had human minds to contend with."

"She felt different to me as well. Her hatred for me seemed diminished." He shook his head. "That didn't seem like Isabella at all. She's always despised me and thinks I will somehow take the throne away from her son."

Darius could never understand why Isabella viewed him as a threat. He wasn't one. He didn't have the power or inclination to take his father's place on the throne. Gideon had been born to be the next Archdruid, not him.

"Maybe she is an impostor. That could happen."

"Why would anyone impersonate her?" Darius half smiled.

"Think about it. Isabella could work from the shadows and have a repentant puppet in her place." Nyx sipped her tea. "She wants the throne."

"No, that was her. I would know her energy anywhere. A glamour spell can't mimic that."

"Maybe she found another way." Nyx leaned back on the bed and yawned.

"Why didn't you like Lyra?" He arched an eyebrow.

She shrugged. "Because something doesn't feel right about her. Besides, I'm not quick to trust anyone. You of all people should know that."

"She's not so bad once you get to know her. She taught me about control. Maybe she could help you."

"I can control… things by myself." Her eyelids flickered. After a few moments, her head lulled against his shoulder.

He considered carrying her to her own bed, but instead pulled her closer. Darius waved his hand, and the candles snuffed out.

CHAPTER 11

Ranelle couldn't believe Darius would be foolish enough to confront Isabella head-on. They headed through the sweeping hallways of the great temple.

Lucien stalked ahead of her and kept sniffing the air.

She glowered at him. He had to be the one who talked Darius into this foolishness. Nyx wouldn't have had time to do that. This sounded just like something wolfsbane would do.

"Have you lost them?" she hissed.

She didn't like talking to him in thought unless she had to. Plus, talking in thought took more energy for her. The only time she didn't struggle with it was if Darius or Nyx reached out to her with their minds. Communication with them was easy because they had both formed mental paths with her. Her path to Lucien wasn't anywhere near as strong.

Not that she minded that. She'd rather avoid him at all costs, anyway. All he did was irritate her.

No, I haven't. Keep your voice down, Lucien replied. *Do you want them to hear us? And stop glaring at me.*

How do you know I am glaring? Ranelle crossed her arms.

Because I can smell your anger and I can feel it.

Who says I'm angry at you? She was, of course, but she didn't have to tell him that.

You're always angry at me for no reason.

She gritted her teeth. *Just focus on finding the assassin.*

Why did Nyx and Darius always have to leave her alone with him? She detested being around him. They knew she and Lucien were enemies. They only tolerated each other because of their friendship with Darius.

Ranelle didn't like wandering around the halls of the temple, either. Shadows lurked everywhere, and she always felt like someone was watching her. Yet no one ever appeared.

Only a handful of priestesses and priests lived there. Lyra was the only one she saw every day. The others never seemed to be around much. Lyra said they were out preaching the word of the gods. Ranelle didn't mind though, she preferred to keep to herself.

Lucien sniffed again. *The assassin's sent is growing fainter. We need to move faster.* Before she could say anything, he turned, picked her up and then blurred away.

She yelped as they moved so fast her head spun.

Do be quiet, girl, Lucien grumbled.

She couldn't believe he had dared to pick her up without even asking. *Put me down right now, or I'll set you on fire!*

Your fire won't work on me, dragon.

I'm not a dragon. I'm a wyvern! Now put—

Her anger only seemed to make him move faster. Ranelle raised her hand to conjure a fireball, but her stomach recoiled. She swallowed hard and put her arms around Lucien's neck to hold on. Hitting him with a fireball would have to wait until later.

I will maim you for this! she growled at him.

He had the audacity to smile at her.

They shot out of the temple and into the middle of a crowded street. The cold night air hit her face.

"They're on the roof," Lucien murmured.

"Where?" She craned her neck to look up. "Let go of me so I can fly after them."

"I move a lot faster than you can."

"I can see more from the air."

"You can't move as fast, can you?"

She sighed. "Move then."

Lucien blurred again and Ranelle bit back a scream.

Moving with lykae speed felt different from flying. So much faster. Colours and sound blurred in shadows and specks of light as Lucien moved through the crowded city.

Where are they going? Ranelle wanted to know.

My guess would be the forest. They probably think they can lose us there.

Hurry up. I thought you could move faster than anyone?

I'm trying to, but they keep jumping.

Do you think they can fly?

Doubtful, but they might be able to levitate.

We need to trap them. Know any good spells?

Aren't spells your forte? He arched an eyebrow.

She scowled. *I'm a keeper of books. That doesn't mean I know every spell in creation. You're an overseer. You can access their knowledge.* She had always envied that about him. All overseers could tap into centuries' worth of knowledge of spells, potions, and other information just by using their minds.

Not all of it. I haven't met the person I'm supposed to protect yet, so my powers haven't fully matured.

Ranelle wasn't so sure about that but said nothing.

Besides, overseers are meant to protect and teach others. We are not trained to be warriors, Lucien added. *I do have a couple of crystals that might form a trap, though.*

Good enough. Now get them.

I can go faster, but you won't like it.

She groaned. *Move it!*

Lucien's eyes flashed gold. This time Ranelle did scream.

Are you trying to announce our presence to the whole realm? Lucien rolled his eyes.

Ranelle closed her eyes. She would vomit if she had to endure this much longer. A few moments later, they came to an abrupt halt.

She opened her eyes again. Trees stood around them like dark, looming giants. She knew she shouldn't be surprised they'd got so far, so fast. She was, though. At least she could get on solid ground now. "Put—"

Lucien gripped her tight and dove out of the way as a blast of light came at them. They hit the ground hard.

She winced. Lucien took the brunt of the fall. *Let me go.*

No, I'm immune. You're not.

You are not immune to everything.

Don't argue with me on this. For once, just trust me. I don't want anything to happen to you.

A blast of light hit against his back.

Can you smell what magic that is? Ranelle buried her face against his chest as his body shook.

I don't know. Strong. Like Nyx. Fae perhaps, but I can't be sure. Hold on. Lucien rolled out of the way but still kept hold of her.

Where are they? She couldn't get a good view because his body blocked her vision.

Up in the trees. To my left. His eyes flashed gold again.

You need to let go of me. I'll distract them while you jump.

No, what if—?

We're supposed to trust each other, remember? So trust me. Keep them focused on me.

Rae—

Odd, he never called her Rae. Under normal circumstances, she wouldn't trust him. But they needed to work together if they were going to stop this assassin.

Lucien groaned. *Be careful.*

She rolled out of his grasp. Ranelle sprang into a crouch and threw two fireballs at the dark shape of the figure obscured by branches.

The figure dodged them. She yelped as magic blasted around her.

Lucien, go. She ducked behind a tree, then threw another fireball.

He yelped as a blast of magic knocked him to the ground. *Curse it, they're blocking every move I make.*

Ranelle couldn't understand that. How could anyone anticipate Lucien's moves, given how fast he moved?

They must be a seer or have some kind of mental ability to predict such a thing.

Rae, I need you to divert their attention away from me.

What do think I'm trying to do? Her wings popped out of her back, and she shot into the air and hurled more fireballs.

The assassin continued to wave them away, so the fire dispersed.

Curse it! Think. She had to do something.

Ranelle raised her hands and threw fireballs at the branches.

The dryads would probably never forgive her for this. But she would make sure the fire didn't spread.

Lucien leapt up onto a branch and grabbed the assassin. The assassin punched him, then spun into a kick. He staggered and made a grab for them.

72

Ranelle flew higher and raised her hands to contain the flames to that tree.

A blast of energy shook the air. Lucien yelled as he plummeted towards the ground. A flash of silver came at Ranelle. She dodged it and lunged towards Lucien. Lykae or not, she knew falling from such a height would hurt him.

She grabbed his arm. The force of his descent almost pulled her to the ground as well. She ascended to gain momentum. Lucien wrapped an arm around her waist to get a better hold.

"The assassin is gone," he groaned. "Why didn't you go after them?"

"Because I was busy saving you." Ranelle flapped harder until they reached a branch.

She and Lucien scrambled onto the branch, and she quelled the flames surrounding them.

"Why didn't you go for them?" Lucien frowned.

"Because you were falling."

"I'm a lykae. A fall like that—"

"It could still hurt you. You're not invincible." She sighed. "Can you track the assassin?"

He shook his head. "They are long gone. I'm not sure I could have gotten that close to them. Their magic was so strong."

"What do you think they are?" Ranelle pushed her hair off her face. "I've never seen anyone anticipate our every move like that."

Lucien shrugged. "Fae perhaps. A skilled and highly trained one, that's for sure. Whoever sent them hired the best. They're not some cheap cut-throat hired in a back alley."

"We need to come up with a better trap. I think we need Nyx and Darius to do that."

"We'll figure something out. Despite their escape, we have learnt a few things tonight. Not many Magickind can anticipate moves and extinguish fire. They fought with their mind and magic. That takes skill."

"They must be fae or even a trained druid. Or sorcerer."

"Sorcerers are gifted with magic. Their mental powers were too strong for that. My guess would be a fae or a druid." Lucien grinned. "We work well together."

"I suppose we do. Maybe you're not so bad. For a lykae, I mean."

CHAPTER 12

Nyx tossed and turned in her sleep. The woman on the pyre stared at her with hollow eyes. "My vengeance will come," the woman said.

Nyx bolted awake. Sweat dripped down her face. Good gods, what had that been? Why had she seen that woman?

Slivers of light crept in through the open window. She gasped for breath. It took a moment to realise she wasn't in her room or her bed.

She realised she must've fallen asleep in Darius' bed. It had to be close to dawn now, so she had been here all night. She turned over and buried her face in the pillow.

Who was that woman? Why did she seem to haunt her?

Darius murmured something in his sleep, and his arm around her tightened. His touch felt comforting, so she leaned back into his embrace. Nyx closed her eyes and waited for sleep to take hold again.

A while later, sleep hadn't returned. She sighed and sat up. She knew she should sneak back to her room before Ambrose or Ada got up. Her heart still raced. Maybe she needed to calm herself, so she glanced over at Darius. She never got a chance to stare at him much. And never this close.

His brow furrowed even in sleep.

Nyx still had no idea what they were now. Friends didn't kiss each other and fall asleep in each other's beds. Were they lovers then? No, lovers did more than kiss. She knew that well enough.

Did he feel something for her? He said he didn't want to lose her. But would he ever want more than friendship with her? Would she? She never thought anyone would want her for being fae, much less a mind whisperer. She never allowed herself to feel attracted to anyone. No one had mattered before him. No one ever took the time to know her well. Except, it seemed, the druid.

After a while, she headed out.

Nyx found Ambrose at the dining room table when she came out for breakfast.

Ambrose glared at her. "Use your powers."

She gaped at him. "What?"

"Use your powers," he repeated. "What is Ada thinking?"

Ada came in carrying a tray of tea. The brownie didn't look the least bit concerned by Ambrose's sudden hostility.

"Why?" Nyx wondered if he wanted to test her again.

"Just do it!" Ambrose slammed his hands down on the table so hard it rattled.

She lowered her mental shield. "She's wondering why Darius isn't up yet. She thinks you're being a loathsome toad to me." He wanted to know what Ada thought, so she told him.

Ada frowned. "Master, I—"

"Never mind." Ambrose waved the brownie away.

Nyx didn't need to read his mind to sense his anger.

"Something wrong?" She slanted her usual chair and plopped down into it.

"Now use your touch on Ada."

Her mouth fell open. "What? No. Why would—?"

"I need to see your powers are still working."

"Why?" She narrowed her eyes.

"Just do it!"

Nyx hesitated as Ada came over to her. She couldn't fathom why Ambrose would want her to do such a thing. She only used her touch when she wanted to compel someone. Or in self-defence.

"I'm sorry," she told Ada and gripped the brownie's arm.

The one she should be using her touch on was Ambrose to find out what his problem was. Energy shook the air like thunder without sound and the table trembled.

"Now command her," Ambrose demanded.

"Ada, stab Ambrose with this." Nyx handed her a fork.

Ada didn't even blink as she took the fork and headed over to Ambrose.

The elder druid shot to his feet. "What are you doing?"

"You wanted proof my powers are working. There you have it." She returned his glare. "Why are you doing this? Why would you want me to use my powers on her? You're the one who lectured me on the importance of not using my touch on the innocent." She turned to the still advancing Ada. "Ada, put the fork down." She then waved her hand to release the brownie from her power.

Ada complied and blinked. She stared down at the fork. "What am I doing?"

"Ask Ambrose." She sat back in her chair and crossed her arms.

"Ada, leave us."

The brownie scurried away without so much as a backwards glance.

"I had to be sure you haven't lost your powers." Ambrose took his seat again. "Do you listen to nothing I tell you?"

"Of course I do!"

"Then why did you spend the night in Darius's bed?"

She gaped at him. "What Darius and I do isn't your business. We're not doing anything wrong."

"I warned you, you can never be together. Deep down you know your powers come at a heavy price."

"What are you talking about?"

"Mind whisperers can't sleep with anyone. If you were with someone in that way, you risk enslaving them with your power."

"I've used my full power on him before. My touch doesn't work on him."

"You can't be sure of that. You are a mind whisperer; he is the son of the Archdruid. If your powers don't separate you, that will." Ambrose reached across the table and took her hand. "I'm just trying to save you future heartache. I see the way he looks at you. The way you look at each other. End this now before you get in any deeper."

She couldn't believe Ambrose was lecturing her about this. She'd known he wouldn't approve, but...

"We are both of age and I have feelings for him, too. I'm not giving up on that."

"In what world could the two of you be together? How do you know his immunity won't neutralise your powers if you were together?"

"Stop meddling in matters that have nothing to do with you," she snapped. "I might be a mind whisperer but—"

"But you are still enemies. That will become apparent in the future. End it now before this causes you more heartache."

Pain stabbed through her chest. Could she do that? Could she end things with Darius after they'd finally grown close?

"No." She didn't want to give up her chance of happiness just because he didn't approve of them being together.

"Do you really want to risk your powers or his soul over this?" Ambrose snapped.

Nyx gripped the edge of the table. "Of course not. My powers and his soul aren't at risk."

"How can you be sure of that?"

"I know. We are connected. I think you know that too."

"Don't say I didn't warn you," Ambrose added.

Nyx felt sick to her stomach and had to force herself to eat.

"Morning." Darius gave them a smile as he came in that soon faded. "Something wrong?"

Ask your mentor. Nyx gulped down the rest of her tea and rose.

"You have training with Lyra at the temple this morning," Ambrose told her. "She may be able to help you more than I can."

Training with Lyra? Why?

"Is this because of our… disagreement?" Nyx narrowed her eyes.

Ambrose shook his head. "I came to tell you that last night, but you weren't in your room."

Fine, she would see what the priestess could teach her. Anything to get away from Ambrose.

Nyx headed outside, jumped off the edge of the tree house and flapped her wings. An invisible wall of energy appeared in the air and blocked her descent. Instead, she stood suspended in mid-air. *Darius.*

"Druid!"

Darius came outside to join her on the platform. "What's wrong?"

She scowled. "I told you, ask your mentor."

"He said I shouldn't be with you. So, I guess he knows you were in my room." He rubbed the back of his neck.

"He made me use my powers on Ada!"

"Why would… Oh, my immunity and your touch." Darius winced.

"I haven't lost my powers and I won't enslave you."

"Look, don't let him bother you." He pulled her in close. "Ambrose can disapprove of us all he likes."

"Why do I have to train with Lyra?" She still wondered if Ambrose was sending her to train with the priestess to punish her.

"She has mental powers."

"Is she like me?"

He shook his head. "She's a druid with fae blood. Just go and see what she has to say. Maybe she can help you more than Ambrose can."

She sighed. "Fine, I'll see you later."

Nyx flew off. She never imagined she'd be visiting the temple again so soon. Her mind raced with thoughts. What gave Ambrose the right to judge her and Darius?

Things wouldn't be easy for them, but she wasn't about to give up. Not when they had barely begun.

She glided over the forest. Normally, the sight of it brought her peace. This place was home. But it did nothing for her today.

When Alaris came into view, she muttered a curse and flew to the ground. Fae weren't permitted to fly over the city. They weren't really permitted to fly at all, but being Darius' servant afforded her some luxuries.

She folded her wings down and made her way through the crowded city. She kept her head down. Most people here didn't like fae, much less fae that stood out the way she did. Nyx still couldn't imagine how the priestess could help her.

Ambrose had taught her what he could, and she had gained more control. But she still needed to learn more. Not just about control, but so many things. Like where she'd come from and what she was meant for. There had to be other mind whisperers out there somewhere.

Nyx hesitated when she reached the temple's massive double doors. Should she go in through the main entrance? Or go through the side door as she had last night?

She was technically a servant. Still, she wanted a good look at the temple. To see what was good about it.

She pushed the door open. It grinded like aged bones. Nyx winced at the sound. Now everyone in the temple would know she was there. She walked in and kept her senses on alert.

The temple stretched out before her, with its domed ceiling and marble walls etched with gold. It looked nothing like the old temple her tribe had used back in Joriam. That had been little more than a stone ruin with no roof and trees growing around it.

A high altar stood at the end of the massive sanctuary. A symbol of a twelve-pointed silver star glistened above it.

Nyx gasped. The same star she'd seen in the Guardian's vision. *Druid?* She reached out to him with her mind. *I found something.*

What? Darius sounded curious.

The star from my vision. It's a symbol here in the temple. What does it mean?

It's a symbol dating back centuries. It's the sign of the gods.

Nyx frowned at it. *It's a symbol of the Twelve.*

Twelve, what? How do you know that?

I just do. She sighed. *I wish I knew where all this knowledge came from. Maybe there's a way we can find out.*

How?

We'll see. I'll be out patrolling all morning. Have fun with Lyra.

I doubt that.

"Pretty, isn't it?" Lyra's voice made her jump.

Nyx ended her connection with Darius and turned around. How had the priestess managed to sneak up on her?

"I guess, but it doesn't give me a good feeling." Nyx wanted to slap herself and put a hand over her mouth.

Should she apologise for talking out of line? She knew she always had to watch herself whenever she went to the palace but didn't know how to act around the priestess. Just because Darius and Ambrose said she was an ally didn't make her one.

"As well, it shouldn't. Now it's just a reminder they are gone from this world."

"What? Gods are real?" Her frown deepened.

"The Twelve are more than gods. They have been here since Erthea began."

"Where are they now?" She had never expected to come here and start talking about gods. Did that mean gods were real? She would ask Darius about it later. From everything she had learnt from the druids, gods weren't real.

"Gone or forced into hiding by the Archdruid."

"He killed them?"

"No, they can't be killed. I don't know what he did to them. He destroys everything."

"Ambrose said you were going to train me. How do you plan on doing so?"

"Indeed. I know you've been struggling with your powers."

"My powers are… more controllable than they used to be."

"You don't have complete control, do you? You're afraid of what you are."

"I never said that." Nyx scowled.

Why did this priestess presume to know anything about her? She didn't know Nyx. Plus, something didn't feel right about her.

Nyx scanned the priestess with her senses. No buzz of thoughts came to her. Nothing else did either. Not even an inkling as to what Magickind she might be.

Lyra's eyes widened. "Do you do that around the Archdruid?"

"Do what?" Her frown deepened and her heart pounded in her ears. Had Lyra somehow sensed her using her powers? If so, how? No one ever sensed when she read them.

"Read someone. You're strong but your technique is sloppy."

Sloppy? How could reading someone be a technique? She just did what she'd always done when she wanted to know something about someone. Used her senses and waited for them to tell her something.

"What are you?" Nyx narrowed her eyes.

"I'm a priestess. I serve the old gods. I served the Andovian Queen herself before he… before he destroyed her." Lyra's fists clenched. "I can help you master your gifts, but you have to be willing to learn."

"If you're not a mind whisperer, I doubt you can help me."

"Come. We need to practise somewhere more open than this oppressive place." Lyra grabbed her arm and light flashed around them.

Nyx gasped when they reappeared in the forest. Trees spread out all around them, a mix of green, gold, and brown.

Lyra nodded. "Much better."

Nyx couldn't work out what the priestess was. Druids used circles and cast spells to transport themselves places. Or opened portals, which required more power. Most fae couldn't transport themselves anywhere. Or at least she didn't think they could. A small circle of standing stones surrounded them.

"Where are we?"

"In Varden Forest."

"Won't the Varden mind us being here?"

Lyra snorted. "The Varden are my friends. They won't mind a bit." She smiled. "Come, sit." She sat down in centre of the circle and put her hands on her knees.

Nyx still wasn't sure why they didn't just stay in the temple.

"If you aren't a mind whisperer, can you really help me?" She slumped to the ground.

"I grew up around them. I was a priestess to the queen herself." Lyra pushed her long, dark hair off her face. "I'm probably one of the few people left alive who remembers them. Other than Ambrose."

"Ambrose? What do you mean?"

"Well, he was mated to one of them, of course. Didn't you know?"

Nyx gaped at the priestess. "No, I didn't."

"Let's begin. Show me your power."

"Alright then." She reached for Lyra's arm.

"No, no, no. I meant let your power flow free. I want to see how well you control it."

Nyx grabbed Lyra's arm and let her power flow free. Energy surged from her into the priestess. It shook the air around them and sent leaves flying.

Lyra flinched and slapped her hand away. "Your touch won't work on me. I have a block made by the queen herself. Your touch won't work on your own kind either."

She sighed. No wonder she couldn't hear anything from the priestess. "Show me your power. Lower your shield and let it flow free."

"Are you mad? I've spent months learning to hide my power. I can't let it free."

"You are in a protective circle. You can't be sensed in here." Lyra furrowed her brow. "You don't trust me. Good, you shouldn't trust anyone but yourself. It will keep you alive. Don't let your feelings for that Valeran cloud your judgement either."

Nyx sighed and let her power flow free. Orbs of light sparkled around her fingers.

Maybe Ambrose had sent Lyra just to lecture her about her relationship with Darius. But the priestess didn't seem that interested in the topic. She wouldn't mention it further.

"You're holding back." Lyra frowned.

"I am not!"

"Yes, you are. I can see it. You're afraid of what you are." Lyra sneered. "Afraid won't help the people around you."

Nyx gritted her teeth. "I am not."

"Yes, you are. You've lost control of your power before. And you'll do it again."

Her hands clenched into fists. What was this woman playing at?

Her power pulsed through her, desperate to be free from the tight rein she kept on it. It wanted to get out. But could she do that? Everything in her screamed to keep her power in.

"Never let anyone see your curse," Harland had always told her.

"Don't let your power free. You must hold it in, or you'll be a danger to everyone," Ambrose said.

"You will lose control. It's inevitable. Perhaps you'll even enslave the Valeran you care so much about."

"No!" Nyx screamed.

Power burst out of her. Thunder shook the air without sound. Leaves whirled around like a tornado. The stones trembled under the force of her power.

Lyra grinned. "That's much better."

Nyx clenched her fists and squeezed her eyes shut. She grappled to get control over her magic again. Ambrose was mad to think this woman could help her. All Lyra did was infuriate her.

"Stop!" Lyra grabbed her wrist. "To control your powers, you need to control your emotions. Panicking and forcing them into submission isn't wise."

"But Ambrose—"

"Ambrose isn't a mind whisperer—despite being bound to one. Concentrate on your breathing and calm yourself."

Nyx took a deep breath and her heart still thudded in her ears. Everything inside her screamed at her to get her power under control again. More leaves whirled around them.

"I sense druid magic inside you. Have you been sleeping with the Valeran?"

"That's not your business." Nyx was breathing hard. After a few moments, the leaves finally settled.

"There. You see. Control will come if you let it."

"I can't afford to be reckless. If anyone finds out how powerful I really am—"

"You are powerful, and you need to embrace it if you want to survive in this world."

She blew out a breath. "Why can't I remember where I come from? I need to know if there are others out there like me."

"That knowledge is deep inside you. You just have to reach deep enough to find it."

"How do I reach it? Because nothing else I have tried so far has worked." Nyx pushed her long hair off her face.

"You just have to focus and learn to truly embrace your power. The answers will come to you in time."

Wonderful, more cryptic messages. She stayed with Lyra a while longer. It was too early to tell if the priestess would be any help or not. But part of Nyx hoped Lyra could help her find the answers she needed.

CHAPTER 13

Darius jolted awake as his senses warned him of danger. He couldn't have been asleep for more than a couple of hours and had been exhausted after a long day of patrolling the forest. Now what? He rubbed the sleep from his eyes and pulled on a shirt. It took him a moment to remember the spell he had cast around Nyx's room. It was meant to warn him if any strangers entered. She hadn't fallen asleep with him tonight. They had both agreed to be more careful around Ambrose so they could avoid further lectures from him.

Holy spirits, he never expected the assassin to come here. Ambrose's entire house was warded.

Darius ran down the hall towards Nyx's room. Runes glittered over the door. When he reached for the handle, heat seared against his skin. He yelped in alarm.

The assassin was more determined than he'd thought. Odd, they hadn't had any encounters with the assassin all day. Something crashed inside the room. Lightning flared between Darius' fingers, and he blasted the door apart.

A black figure had Nyx pinned on the floor.

He fired a lightning bolt straight at the assassin. Icy blue eyes stared back at him from behind a dark mask.

Nyx waved her arm and hit the assassin over the head with an oncoming swarm of flying books.

The assassin yelped and ducked out of the way.

Darius fired another lightning bolt. The assassin leapt onto the window ledge and jumped.

Nyx coughed and Darius hurried over to her. "Are you alright?" He knelt and touched her cheek. She had finger marks around her throat.

"How... did... they... get... in?" she rasped.

"I don't know." Darius went to the window, but the assassin was long gone. "This house is protected. Did they transport or climb in?"

"I didn't sense anyone transport in. My window was closed." Nyx rubbed her throat. "How'd you know I needed help?"

"I cast a spell around your room. Good thing I did. It woke me up." Darius went back to her and ran his fingers over her neck. "Why didn't you use your powers?

"I tried, but it didn't work. They were immune to me." Nyx rested her head against his chest, and he pulled her close.

"What's going on?" Ambrose appeared in the doorway. "What are you both doing?" Darius pulled away from Nyx. "I told you both to not become involved," Ambrose snapped. "You—"

"The assassin broke in and tried to kill her," Darius snapped. "And you are bothered by me trying to comfort her?" He couldn't believe his mentor was being so ridiculous.

Ambrose gaped at him. "Impossible. I set every ward in this house."

"She tried to strangle me." Nyx motioned to her neck. "My powers don't work on her."

Ambrose rubbed his temples. "How could they have got up here? Did they have wings?" He went over to the window and glanced down. "How do you know it was a female?"

She shook her head. "Not that I saw, but they can jump well. I don't know if it was a female, but they seemed to move like one."

"Did you get a good look at them?" Ambrose glanced between them.

"Blue eyes and a mask. But I got a glimpse of pointed ears, so they must be fae," Nyx replied.

"Did you use your touch on them?" Ambrose furrowed his brow. "No."

Ambrose rubbed his temples again. "I don't see how they could have gotten in here."

"It's not safe here. We should leave. Right now. Nyx, get your things so we can be ready to go. We can stay at my castle." Darius pushed past his mentor and stormed off to his room.

Ambrose trailed after him. "Surely that could wait until the morning? It's the middle of the night."

"It's better if we leave now. The assassin got too close to her. If I hadn't set the ward…" He didn't finish his sentence and didn't want to think about what might have happened.

Darius picked up his pack and everything in the room: books, weapons, maps, rushed inside. Nyx wasn't safe here. At least his estate would have much better protections. Darius dressed and headed back down the hall to find Nyx, now fully wrapped in a heavy cloak.

"Perhaps the castle would be safer since it has stronger wards. But keep your senses about you, boy. Don't let your emotions get the best of you," Ambrose warned.

"You can't leave." Ada came in. "Your castle isn't even ready to be lived in. Can't you—"

"No, we can't. If the assassin can break in once, they can do it again." Darius held out a hand to Nyx. "Ready?"

She nodded.

Darius traced runes around them, and light transported them out.

They reappeared in a pitch-black room. Darius waved his free hand to light candles in the room.

Nothing happened, and the room remained too dark for them to see anything.

"I can't see anything." Nyx gripped his hand tighter. "Where are we?"

"My castle. Why won't the candles light?" Darius conjured a glowing white orb.

It revealed the room to be empty.

"You have a castle?" Nyx arched an eyebrow.

"Technically, I am the Prince of Eldara. The territory, lands, and title belong to me. My mother saw to it I had everything Gideon has and more." He groaned. His mother! She did this. Damn her! He had already ordered this place to be cleared and ready, just in case he and Nyx had to move out. This was her way of forcing him back to the palace.

"You've never mentioned that before. Maybe we should go then," Nyx suggested. "I know things are awkward with Ambrose but—"

"No!" he said more forcefully than he meant to. "Besides, if we stayed, Ambrose would continue lecturing us about being inappropriate."

Nyx laughed. "Inappropriate?"

Darius looked away, too embarrassed to meet her gaze. "We—we should look around. Find somewhere to sleep for the night and deal with everything in the morning."

He had a look around, but all the rooms, save for his chambers, were empty. Unfortunately, it only had one bed.

Darius realised it had been stupid to leave in the middle of the night.

"Maybe we should go to the palace." Nyx didn't look happy at the idea.

He shook his head. "No, you'd have to sleep in the servant's quarters. Anyone could get you there. That's why I planned on bringing you here in case Ambrose's house proved to be unsafe."

"I can take care of myself, druid. You don't have to protect me." Nyx dropped her pack on the floor, pulled her cloak off and tossed it aside. "As long as you don't snore, I'm sure we can manage." She slipped under the covers.

Darius pulled off his boots. He used his magic to change into his bedclothes.

"Did I snore the other night?" He smirked at her.

"I was too tired to notice."

Darius slid into bed beside her. They lay there in awkward silence. The orb he'd conjured earlier hovered above their heads.

Nyx turned to face him. "Why is Ambrose so bothered by us?"

Darius sighed. "I don't know. He claimed it was dangerous because you're a mind whisperer, but your power can't hurt me. Mind whisperers can enslave people... by accident. They can't hold their power in when they... you know." He flushed.

"Oh, you mean when they lay with someone." Nyx's cheeks went red. "I never thought of that, but I suppose it makes sense given how I have to hold my power in."

"You've never been with anyone... like that then?" Darius couldn't believe he'd asked her such a question. What had he been thinking?

She laughed. "Of course not. No one ever came near me when I lived in Joriam. Everyone said I was ugly and cursed." Her smile faded. "That's why Harland cut my ears. He cut my wings too—or tried to cut them, but they kept healing. So he gave up."

"You're not ugly. You're the most beautiful person I've ever met." He reached out, his fingers finding hers.

Nyx squeezed his hand back and snuggled close to him. Darius wrapped his arm around her. "I don't want to lose you," he admitted.

"I'm not going to let an assassin kill me, druid." Nyx rested her head against his chest.

Darius waved his hand, so the orb went out. He would do everything in his power to make sure she stayed safe.

Darius woke early the next morning to get a better look at his castle. It was as empty as he feared. There wasn't a guard in sight. The guardhouse stood empty and disused. He supposed he should be glad. He didn't want resources wasted on an estate where no one was in residence.

He had told his mother he might be coming to stay here. She wouldn't have forgotten something like that. She had chosen to ignore him. Darius hated asking his mother for anything. He had his own wealth and title. Shouldn't he be able to control things like this for himself?

He headed to the great hall next to see if there was any furniture there. Or at least something for them to sit on.

Nyx was still asleep, so he hoped to surprise her given how much she wanted to return to Ambrose's house.

The great hall with its oak floors, grey stone walls, and high vaulted ceilings stood just as empty.

He remembered visiting this place years ago. It had been richly furnished. His mother must have removed everything as soon as he left to live with Ambrose.

Light flashed and Ada appeared. "Ah, my boy, I brought some breakfast." She held up a steaming pot. "Blessed spirits, why is there nothin' here?"

"That's a good question. One I'll be sure to ask my mother." He sighed. "I wanted to help Nyx with something. Instead, I have to deal with all of this." He motioned to the empty space. "Now I'll have to talk to my mother."

Ada set the heavy pot on the floor. "Nonsense, you leave it to me. I've been taking care of you since you were a babe. I'll see this place is put back to rights, don't you worry." She glanced around. "Where's the young miss?"

"She's asleep. Ada, I don't want to impose on you—"

Ada clucked her tongue. "You're never gonna learn to do as you're told, are you, boy?"

Darius smiled. "I suppose not."

"Now, go and wake young Nyx. I'll have breakfast ready for you soon enough." Ada scowled. "This place is a disgrace."

Darius bent and kissed her forehead. "I don't know what I'd do without you."

"Of course you don't." Ada ruffled his long blond hair and hesitated. "Ambrose wants an audience with ya. You need to set things right with him."

He scowled. Darius wasn't sure he was ready to talk to Ambrose yet. Not after last night. "That will have to wait. Nyx and I have something more important to do first."

Ambrose needed to accept he and Nyx were friends. Perhaps more than that. And he wouldn't give up on finding out what they could be, even if Ambrose disapproved. Rank never used to mean anything to Ambrose. There were no rules about why they can't be together. But his parents, especially his mother, would be livid. Darius didn't care.

Nyx was still asleep when he headed back to his chambers. "Nyx? It's time to wake up." He reached out to touch her. "Nyx?"

She muttered something and rolled over. Her large wings spread out before her.

"Nyx?" Darius shook her again. He ran his fingers along the length of her wings, noticing again how soft they were. "Guess I'll have breakfast without you then."

Nyx's eyes flew open. "You're cruel, druid." She scowled up at him.

He chuckled. "It woke you up, though. Come down when you're ready. Ada brought us food."

He headed back down to the dining hall, a small private one, and was surprised to find a table and four chairs there. It was covered with different dishes and cutlery.

How did Ada procure everything so fast?

Nyx, now fully dressed, dashed in behind him. "Where did all this come from?"

"I have no idea." Darius shook his head. "Ada only got here… before I woke you."

Ada came in carrying a pitcher of water. "What are you two gawking at?" the brownie demanded. "You look like you ain't seen food before."

"Where did you get all this?" Darius motioned to the table.

"I have my ways. Now sit." Ada motioned to the table. "Eat. I won't have you two starving to death whilst you're here."

Nyx sank into a chair. "Is she always like this?"

Darius chuckled and took a seat beside her. "Yes, it's best not to get in her way."

Ada came in a while later with more food. "The kitchen is disgusting. I'll be living here whilst you're here." She gave Darius a questioning look. As if she expected him to protest.

"What about Ambrose?" Nyx frowned. "I thought you were his housekeeper?"

"I've been with the young master here since he was in swaddling linens. I'll be with him to the day I die." Ada ruffled his hair. "About time you came to live here, boy."

"It's not going to be permanent," Darius pointed out.

"Why not? It's your birthright, boy. You should live here. It would make a nice place to raise a family too."

He gaped at her. "Ada, I'm not having children or getting married if that's what you're implying."

"Not yet. But you've got a fine young lady now. Perhaps all that nonsense about you not wanting to be with anyone is finally out of your head."

Nyx turned a shade pale as Ada wandered off. "Is she saying we're going to have children?"

Darius laughed. "She dreams of that. Holy spirits! And no, I don't want children. Ever."

Nyx arched an eyebrow. "Why?"

"It's not something I envisioned for myself. And I would prefer if the Valeran line died out." He shook his head. "Do you want them?"

Nyx shrugged. "I don't know. I'm too young to think about that yet."

"After breakfast we'll go to the Spirit Grove and get started on the mind sharing."

Nyx's mouth fell open. "I thought you said it was too dangerous?"

Darius hesitated. "It's not without risks, but you need my knowledge to help fend off that assassin. Are you sure you want to do this? You and I won't have any secrets from each other anymore."

Nyx bit her lip then nodded. "I'm sure. Are you sure? I thought you had secrets you never wanted to share with anyone."

He blew out a breath. "I'll do it. You need to be prepared for this, though. If this works, we will know everything about each other. A lot more than we know now. Things that you thought you might have buried deep in your past could come to light. You sure you want to risk that?"

Darius knew some of his darkest secrets would probably be revealed to her. Things he never wanted anyone to know. But if he had to share that with anyone, he would rather it be her. She had become his dearest friend in the time they had known each other.

Nyx jumped up from the table and threw her arms around him. She almost knocked his chair over in the process. "I'm sure. Thank you."

Darius returned her embrace.

Her cheeks flushed. "Oh, sorry, I shouldn't do that."

"I don't mind." He pulled her close and brushed his lips against hers.

Nyx deepened the kiss.

"Ah, now, none of that. You're letting good food go to waste!" Ada chided them.

Both he and Nyx flushed with embarrassment. She pulled away from him. "I was… just thanking him."

"Well, you can thank him later." Ada shook her head in disapproval but gave them a smile.

Darius hoped they wouldn't have to face Ambrose's wrath until much later. Besides, what could be so bad about him and Nyx being together?

CHAPTER 14

A pit of fear formed in Nyx's stomach when she and Darius reappeared in the Spirit Grove as the first rays of dawn sprinted in through the heavy canopy of trees. They had spent the last couple of days going over everything they would need to do for the mind sharing. Lucien and Ranelle had gone over everything and made preparations. She had never expected him to agree to the mind sharing. She wondered what had changed his mind.

Was it because they had grown closer? She still didn't know how to feel about that, or about him.

Neither she nor Darius had said much to Ambrose since they had moved out of his house. She had continued training with Lyra and didn't know what to make of the priestess. Nyx couldn't be sure whether the lessons with her were helping or not. Perhaps it was too soon to tell.

Darius had also given her a loose white robe to wear. He said for this kind of magic; they needed to be free. She didn't mind being naked underneath but hoped they wouldn't have to be naked during the sharing. Just because they had kissed didn't mean she was ready to be naked around him. She still didn't know what was going on between them. Were they still friends? Or more than that?

"How does the mind sharing work?" Nyx broke the silence between them.

"We have to be close. Recite the spell and go from there. If anything goes wrong, I will end it."

"But what happens? Will it hurt?" Nyx put a hand to her chest and the knot of fear grew.

Darius hesitated. "No, our minds will be completely open to each other, though. We might pick up on each other's emotions. And we will share different memories."

"I'll take that as a yes then." She frowned. "What do we do if something goes wrong?" She didn't like the idea of the mind sharing hurting. But she knew she had to try this. It might be the only way to retrieve her memories and find out where she had come from.

"I can't be sure what will happen, I've never done this before, but I'm sure I can end the spell if something does go wrong." He took her hand and squeezed it. "Not many people use this spell because they don't want to share their secrets with other people. I know some of the other druids tried to adapt the spell so we could just pass knowledge on, but I don't know if they ever achieved it."

Nyx nodded and relaxed. Maybe this would give her some insight into how he felt about her. And how she felt about him. They were friends—perhaps more—friends didn't kiss or share the same bed, though.

They wandered deeper into the Spirit Grove. Lights danced over their heads. Voices carried on the wind of spirits.

She had been apprehensive about the assassin when they had left the castle, but at least the assassin wouldn't be able to enter whilst they were here. She'd had a couple of close encounters with the assassin again. So far, they hadn't been able to enter Darius's castle. Nyx knew they needed to figure out a way to trap the assassin before anyone else got hurt. Or before they succeeded in killing her.

Nyx kept hold of Darius' hand as they continued to walk.

"This should do." Darius let go of her hand and traced a large circle deep in the earth, then drew runes.

Nyx joined him inside the circle and traced some runes of her own.

"What are those?" Darius furrowed his brow.

Nyx shrugged. "I have no idea."

"Well, what do they feel like to you?"

She bit her lip. "Safety, strength, blessing." She pointed to each symbol. "Or should I scratch them out?"

He shook his head. "Leave them." He sat cross-legged.

Nyx sat on the opposite side of the circle.

"You need to be closer." She shuffled forward. "No, closer. We have to be next to each other for this to work."

She moved nearer still, so their knees were touching. "Close enough?"

He took hold of her hands.

Nyx gripped his hands and nodded. "I'm ready."

"No matter what happens, whatever you see or feel, don't pull out of the spell," Darius warned. "Just let everything flow."

Together, they chanted the first part of the spell. "Mind to mind and spirit to spirit, let our thoughts intertwine." Orbs of light danced around them. "Open the door, pull back the veil, let our minds merge so we may exchange knowledge and spirit."

Nyx gasped as energy jolted between them. The glowing orbs grew brighter and spun faster. Closing her eyes, she pressed her forehead against his.

Thoughts, emotions, and blurred colours rushed between them.

Slowly, the images became sharper. She saw Darius running around as a young boy. The faces of a younger boy and girl: his siblings, Flora and Blaise. She had known he had siblings, but she'd never met them. Darius told her they lived in another realm with another druid family.

More years flashed by. Her heart ached to see him ignored or abused by both his parents and Gideon. His mother locked him up for days until he got things right. Both Gideon and his father beat him into submission. But despite that, they never broke his spirit.

She watched as the years flew by. His knowledge of magic and strength came through. All of it seeped into her mind. More memories came and went until the moment they ran into each other that night in Joriam. He hadn't wanted to like her, but there was an instant attraction there. It had grown into something deeper.

Nyx felt everything; his pain, his fear of losing control of what he was. The need to end the cycle of his family's violence and bloodshed and be different from them.

All at once, his memories faded. The images changed and blurred. Nyx felt her mind open further. She waited, ready for memories to come flooding out. The colours whirled faster, as if an image tried to form.

Why isn't it working? Nyx wanted to scream.

Don't force it, Darius warned. *Just let the memories come.*

She forced herself to relax. She had to make this work.

After a few moments, images took shape. She found herself alone under a large tree. Confused, with no memory of where she was or who she was.

She wandered through the forest. Her dress filthy and soaked with blood. Next, it changed to her being found by a trader and being pestered with questions. Questions she couldn't answer. Couldn't remember.

Nyx gritted her teeth. She wanted to pull back. Try something else.

Why wouldn't her memories come back? Had someone taken them?

Darius said this would remove any barriers and warned her to prepare herself for what might happen.

But gods, she was ready for this. She needed this.

More memories flashed by of her days spent on the streets, with Harland, protecting her sisters from his abuse. She had struggled with her gift. Her curse, as Harland had called it. Constantly being at the mercy of everyone's thoughts. Always searching for a way to make it stop.

Their emotions, their powers, joined together as light danced around them.

Nyx gasped for breath as the images faded.

"Are you alright?" Darius sounded out of breath, too.

"Why didn't it work?" Nyx took several deep breaths. "You said that would remove all barriers."

"It should have worked. Maybe your memories are inaccessible, or something stronger is blocking them."

Nyx let out a low growl. "There must be something else we can try." She scrambled to her feet, then her legs gave out.

Darius caught hold of her. "I said we had to ground ourselves before we leave." He pulled her onto his lap. "We should ground ourselves and head back to the castle. It might take a while to recover from the ritual."

"Did you get anything from me?"

"I saw from the point where you were found under the tree." Darius stroked her hair off her face. "You'll find another way."

Nyx sighed. "I thought it would be enough."

"It wasn't all bad, was it?"

She smiled, remembering how close they had felt. "I guess not. Now, will you shut up and kiss me? We both know you want to."

He chuckled and captured her mouth in a sweet kiss.

Nyx slipped her arms around his neck. She lost herself in the bliss of the moment until something wet dripped down her face. She pulled back in alarm, touched her nose and her hand came away bloody. "Druid, what's going on?"

"I don't know; this can't be good." Darius scrambled up.

More blood dripped down her face. "Why am I bleeding?"

Darius muttered a spell. This time she recognised the words that were meant to stop bleeding.

The mind sharing had worked—in part at least. But was this the cost?

Her vision blurred and shadows fell around her.

"I—I can't see. Druid!"

The world became swallowed by blackness. Nyx wondered what would happen next.

Would the mind sharing cause her to lose her sight, or worse?

CHAPTER 15

"Ambrose?" Darius yelled as he burst into Alaric's house and carried Nyx inside.

Ambrose and Alaric sat at a table. Both men shot to their feet.

"Holy spirits, what have you done?" Ambrose gasped.

More blood poured down Nyx's face, and she collapsed into unconsciousness.

"We—we did a mind sharing," Darius admitted. "Everything was fine at first. Then she started bleeding."

Ambrose swore. "Holy spirits, I warned you—"

"Just help her," Darius demanded. "You can berate me later." A knot of fear formed in his stomach, and his heart pounded in his ears.

"Bring her over here." Alaric motioned to the divan on the other side of the room.

Darius walked over and set Nyx down.

Alaric put his hand on her throat. "She is barely breathing."

"Did she have any other symptoms?" Ambrose demanded, as he came over. "What happened?"

Darius' mind raced. "She said she couldn't see anything not long after the bleeding started." He rubbed his temples. "Everything was fine during the sharing." He remembered how connected he felt to her. How they had almost felt like they were one being.

"What else? Tell me everything," Ambrose ordered.

Alaric carried on examining Nyx, then his hands glowed with white light.

"We saw each other's memories. Everything was fine."

"Did she remember her past?"

Darius shook his head. "Her earliest memory was waking up under a tree."

"What about after the sharing?" Ambrose paced up and down. "What did you do?"

His mouth fell open. "What?" His mind raced with thoughts. So much so, it was hard to remember what they had done.

"I need to know everything. So tell me."

"My powers are having no effect on her." Alaric frowned. "I don't understand it. I don't sense any kind of injury or trauma."

"We sat and talked afterwards. Everything was fine, then Nyx said she couldn't see anything, and she started bleeding."

"You have no idea what you've done," Ambrose growled. Faint symbols glittered across Nyx's skin. "Stand aside." Ambrose pushed past Alaric and placed one hand on Nyx's forehead and the other on her chest. His hands flared with light, and the strange symbols vanished. "You put her and yourself at risk. I warned you not to do a mind sharing. You have no idea what kind of consequences that kind of magic could have. She is a mind whisperer, and you are the son of the Archdruid. There's no telling what could happen if your powers fully connect with each other."

"Will she be alright?"

"She needs to rest. I suggest you don't go near her." Ambrose's jaw tightened. "You—"

"I knew the mind sharing was a risk, but I took every precaution possible." Darius crossed his arms. "She needs to know how to defend herself. If you think you're going to come between us—"

Ambrose's face turned to thunder. "This isn't about some infatuation. You and Nyx can never be together."

"Why? Because of who my father is? I won't give her up."

"You must. If she is part of the prophecy, then you are most likely the second half. If you were to be together, you could both turn dark. That's much more likely to happen, given how powerful you both are." Ambrose sighed. "Whatever feelings you have for her, put them aside. Or do you want to risk destroying each other?"

He stared at his mentor, dumbfounded. "Of course not, but—"

"Then you must let her go. Make sure she knows it too."

"But why… why can't I find another way? I can't be part of any prophecy. I'm not my father's heir; I don't have the kind of power it takes to be Archdruid. I care about her."

Darius couldn't believe Ambrose thought he and Nyx were part of the prophecy. He couldn't even be sure Nyx was part of it. But he *knew* he couldn't be. He didn't have the power. How could he and Nyx being together bring anything about? They were normal people who wanted to live their lives, as well as bring about a better future by working with the resistance.

Would their resistance work somehow cause complete devastation?

"If you care so much, walk away. Mind whisperers don't fall in love. They take people as their mates. Criminals, people they consider deserve to be enslaved. The only reason they do that is to continue their line." Ambrose gripped his staff. "One way or another, you will be parted soon enough. I'm only trying to save you future heartache."

"How do you know I'm part of the prophecy? Do you know something?" He arched an eyebrow. "Tell the truth for once."

Ambrose shook his head. "Now isn't the time for this conversation. And I have suspected it for a long time, yes. You and Nyx could be part of the prophecy. No one really knows for certain how the prophecy will come about because it's so old."

Darius sank onto the opposite divan and put his head in his hands. "What am I supposed to say to her?" He wouldn't end things with Nyx, but he was tired of Ambrose's lectures on their relationship.

"Tell her the truth. That your touch affected her."

He furrowed his brow. Something didn't feel right. His touch alone couldn't have affected Nyx like that. "What were those symbols? What aren't you telling me?" He rose to his feet. "Nyx and I have been sleeping next to each other every night since we left your house. She never had any effects after that."

"How can you be sure your touch didn't affect her? Neither of you probably would have noticed during the sharing. I think someone must have erased her memories or locked them away." Ambrose shook his head. "Which means you cannot risk trying to unlock her memories again."

"Why would anyone do that?" Darius watched Ambrose's expression.

"I don't know. We have no idea where she came from before she ended up in Joriam." Ambrose came over and put his hands on Darius's shoulders. "If you want to keep her safe, you need to act rationally. *You* can't keep her safe, not when you're being blinded by your feelings for her. You did the mind sharing because you care about her and look what it's done." He motioned to where Nyx lay unconscious. "This could have cost Nyx her life. Do you want to risk that happening again? I understand why you want to protect her. She is your friend, but you know better than to act like this."

"I think she'll be alright," Alaric spoke up. "Take her back to the castle and make sure she rests. Someone needs to watch over her in case she has any other side effects."

Darius nodded. "I'll take her."

Ambrose rose from his seat. "I'll come with you."

"No!" he said more forcefully than he'd meant to. "I—I need to talk to her. Alone."

He needed time to wrap his head around all of this. Had he really put Nyx's life in danger just because he had feelings for her? And if so, what would he do next?

Darius carried Nyx back to the castle. To his amazement, more furniture had already appeared, along with curtains and tapestries. Most of the place seemed furnished now.

"Ada?" he called out.

The brownie appeared and rushed over to him. "Ah, boy. I have—" She froze when she caught sight of Nyx. "Good spirits. What happened? Is she hurt?"

"She—never mind. She needs to rest."

"Take her to your bedchamber—all the furniture has been moved back in. Her chamber is still being cleaned out. The rest of the castle will be done soon enough."

"Good." Darius carried her to his room.

All his furniture had reappeared along with books, weapons, and other possessions. He would have been amazed had he not been in such turmoil.

He laid Nyx on the bed and sank onto the edge, burying his face in his hands.

"What is wrong, boy?" Ada came over and patted his hand.

"This is all my fault." He sighed. "I thought I…"

"It will be alright."

"How can it be?" he demanded. "I almost got her killed. All because I was trying to help." Darius had no idea what to tell Nyx. For a moment during the sharing, he'd felt connected to her in a way he'd never thought possible. He knew she had felt it, too. How could he tell her they couldn't be together? How could he even put it into words?

Holy spirits, why couldn't Ambrose have warned them from the beginning?

Yes, Ambrose had warned them not to become involved, but he'd never said how dangerous it was. Darius had never imagined he would affect Nyx's powers so much.

"Don't believe everything Ambrose says, my boy." Ada squeezed his hand. "Never seen you look at a girl the way you do with her. There's always hope."

Darius shook his head. "Not for this there is not."

"You'll find a way. I know you will." Ada wandered off.

Nyx stirred beside him. "Druid?"

"I'm here." He reached out to touch her, then remembered he couldn't. His touch might cause her pain.

Nyx blinked several times and grinned. "I can see again." She clutched her head. "Aargh, this doesn't feel as nice as the sharing did."

"You should rest awhile. I'll call Ada back." He rose and headed to the door.

Darius still didn't know how to process Ambrose's revelation, that he might be part of the prophecy. What did that even mean? What did it mean for them?

"Why are you avoiding me?" Nyx sat back up and narrowed her eyes. "What's wrong?"

"Nothing." He couldn't face her.

"Darius." She never called him that unless she got angry at him. The rest of the time, she called him druid.

Anger mixed with pain and confusion hit him. Her emotions.

Damn that mind sharing! He hadn't expected it to linger this long.

"Ambrose said something might have erased your memories or locked them away. That's why you had a reaction to the sharing."

She furrowed her brow. "Why would anyone do that?"

He shook his head. "I don't know. You need to rest."

"You're hiding something from me. I can feel it. You might be immune to my powers, but I can sense what you're feeling now."

Spirits, he hoped that didn't last. He didn't know if he could cope with being at the mercy of her emotions all the time. Or if he could put up with her feeling his emotions.

Darius drew away. "This was a mistake."

Nyx gaped at him. "What do you mean? The sharing?" She stood up and gripped the bedpost for support. "Or us? Ambrose told you something, didn't he?"

Darius went over and caught hold of her. "Would you please sit down?"

"No, not until you tell me why you're trying to block me out." Her eyes flashed. "It won't work."

He sighed. "I can't keep you safe if I'm too busy being blinded by my feelings for you. I almost got you killed today."

"I don't need you to protect me. Ambrose said something to you, didn't he? I know he was there after I collapsed," she snapped. "We both know he doesn't want us to be together. How can you believe him?"

"We have to be more careful and not be blinded by our emotions. I don't want anything to happen to you." He reached out and took her hand. "Did you remember anything else?"

She nodded. "When I lost consciousness, I remembered this feeling of being trapped somewhere. I think I was buried. Earth kept filling my eyes and my mouth." She shuddered. "I couldn't get out. I've had nightmares about that before, but this time it seemed so real. But I have no idea if it happened or when it happened."

"We will figure out a way to get your memories back." He pulled her in close and held onto her. He hoped he could help her do just that, but wondered what awful events she would remember if she did get her memories back.

CHAPTER 16

Nyx almost vomited when she reached the meeting room. Maybe leaving the castle hadn't been such a good idea. It had taken all her energy just to get dressed and call Ranelle with her mind. Her head throbbed. She knew the sharing would have side effects but hadn't thought it would be this bad.

Darius had left and told her to rest.

Her mind and body were still reeling from the sharing and his revelation.

The memory of being buried somewhere. Earth had surrounded her, filled her eyes, nose, and mouth. She couldn't shake off the awful image.

Ranelle rushed into the room. "Nyx, what's wrong? Did you remember something during the sharing?"

Nyx broke down in tears. Tears that she had been holding back.

Ranelle came over and comforted her while she wept.

She told Ranelle everything. Everything that happened during the sharing and after it.

"I think I was buried." Nyx sobbed. "I felt myself drowning in the earth." She shuddered.

"I'm sorry, this is my fault." Ranelle went pale. "I should never have suggested it."

She shook her head. "No, Darius warned me something bad could have happened." She sniffed. "That's all I saw. A glimpse in the blackness. I need to know more."

"We'll figure out what happened."

"I wish my sisters were here." Domnu and Kyri had always been there for her. At times like this, she missed them even more. Her search for them had yielded no results so far. Nyx would have given anything to have them there with her.

"You still have me, Darius, and Lucien. We're your friends."

Nyx wiped her eyes.

"I know. Thanks for being here."

"That's what friends are for." Ranelle smiled. "Besides, it's nice for me to have a friend rather than follow men around all the time. I will do whatever I can to help you uncover your past."

Nyx shivered. "I still keep thinking about being buried. What if someone tried to kill me when I was a child? Why would they do that?"

"Nyx, you don't have to torture yourself like this. Answers will come in time."

Would they? She couldn't help wondering. Even Harland hadn't been able to give any answers in the end.

Help me! Someone please!

Her head throbbed as someone screamed for help. Now what? She winced.

"You need to rest." Ranelle put a hand on her arm.

"No, I hear someone." Which proved being close to Darius hadn't neutralised her powers. "Calling for help. I need to find them." She headed to the window.

Help, please, someone! Please don't kill me!

"Nyx, wait. You're in no condition to fly," Ranelle called after her. "You're still recovering from the sharing."

Nyx unfurled her wings and jumped. Her head spun and her stomach recoiled. Yet her senses felt stronger and sharper than they ever had before. Like part of herself had awakened from a long slumber after years of being dormant. She glided around the castle but wasn't sure the sound had come from there.

She had heard people call for help before. Suddenly, images flashed through her mind of buildings surrounded by trees. The old city.

Why did it have to be that place again? Why did she keep being drawn back there?

Nyx flapped her wings faster and headed straight towards Varden Forest. Her first thought was to call Darius and tell him the news. Then she decided against it. She wasn't ready to face him again, yet.

"Wait for me," Ranelle puffed, flapping her dragon-like wings as she struggled to keep up. "Gods, do you have to fly so fast?"

"I've always been fast. The voice I heard is in the old city. Come on."

Ranelle shook her head. "Impossible. No one can get in and out of there."

"My powers aren't usually wrong," Nyx pointed out.

"Not sure if the Varden will be very welcoming towards me," Ranelle remarked.

"Why not? The druid said they are more welcoming of fae."

"I'm not just fae, though. Wyverns are kin to Dragonkind. They despise them."

"The person I heard must be around here somewhere. I have to find them." Nyx swooped lower. *Come on, where are you?* She knew the voice had to have come from somewhere.

She circled around and edged closer to the yellow stone tower that peaked out through the trees.

Wham!

The shield hit her so hard it knocked the air from her lungs.

Argh! Stupid shield!

Nyx searched her mind. The sharing had indeed worked. All of Darius' knowledge had passed to her. There were only a few ways she could try to bring the shield down, but she couldn't be sure any of them would work. Damn it, she needed to get through.

Light flared between her hands. "Let me through!" She pushed against the shield's power.

A warning rang through her mind, but it was too late. A bolt of energy shot from the shield and straight through her.

Nyx screamed as it knocked her off balance. She plummeted to the ground with a thud. Her body shuddered and reeled from the shock.

Ranelle swooped down and landed beside her. "Are you hurt?"

"Damn that shield." She gritted her teeth.

Lucien, carrying Darius on his back, blurred in beside them.

Darius jumped down and knelt beside her. "Holy spirits, I can't leave you alone for a minute. What are you doing here?"

Nyx growled at him. "I'm fine. Why are you here?"

"I felt your pain." Darius turned to Ranelle. "How long is this… thing between us going to last?"

Ranelle put her hands on her hips. "You're linked now. I warned you a sharing creates a link between people. That kind of magic always comes with a price."

Nyx scrambled to her feet. "As you can see, I'm fine." She brushed the dirt off her tunic. *Now go away!*

Darius winced.

Why had she wanted to do the sharing so much? His concern radiated through her, but she ignored it. Instead, she scanned the area with her mind.

"Do you still hear them?" Ranelle asked.

Ranelle and Lucien's thoughts echoed around her. Gods, had her mental shield stopped working? Had the sharing destroyed her shield?

"Hear what?" Lucien frowned. "Why are you out here? The Varden won't be very welcoming."

"I heard someone calling for help." Nyx increased the strength of her shield.

Darius grabbed her hand, and the chaos faded. *Better?*

No. She yanked her hand away from him. The last thing she wanted was to feel close to him.

"I'll fly around and see if I can spot anything. Come on, wolfsbane." Ranelle took to the air and Lucien blurred away.

Nyx crossed her arms. "I am fine."

"You were overwhelmed. How can I ignore that?"

"You going to tell me what Ambrose said to you earlier?" He refused to tell her much earlier and insisted she rest after the sharing. "You are feeling uneasy about something. So you might as well just tell me."

"Ambrose is doing everything in his power to make sure we're not together. I'm not sure I trust him. He's hiding something. When I saw those symbols on you after you collapsed, he didn't act surprised."

Nyx furrowed her brow. "Why would he be?"

He shrugged. "No idea, but the way he's been acting is odd. He knows more than he's telling us."

She bit her lip. "He was quick to shield himself from me, too. He said he used your blood, but it felt different somehow."

Help me! The voice came again.

"I still hear it. We have to get through that shield."

"I told you, there's no way."

She closed her eyes. "Wait, the presence isn't coming from inside the old city anymore. It's coming from Alaris. We need to go."

Nyx and Darius used a circle to transport back to the city and reappear inside the palace.

"Why would the voice be in the old city and then move here?" Nyx frowned. "Could they have transported somehow?"

"No one can get in or out of the old city. The shield prevents it. There has to be space for energy to pass through, otherwise transportation wouldn't work."

"This way." Nyx headed down a corridor. The voice grew louder. "In there."

"Nyx, wait," Darius hissed and grabbed hold of her. He pulled a glamour around them. *Don't make a sound.*

Why not?

The door swung open, and Isabella strolled out. She smiled at a man who came out with her.

What's she doing here? Nyx stared at the former queen as she strolled past them.

No idea. Darius pulled her tight against him. *If she sees us, she'll be suspicious.*

Nyx wanted to lash out and demand the priestess stop hurting people.

Maybe she could compel her to spill her secrets, but she knew she couldn't. Even if she did use her power, she couldn't be sure they would work on Isabella.

Isabella wandered off.

Nyx pulled free from Darius and grabbed the man. Power surged from her to him. Energy reverberated and shook the air around them.

"Why were you calling for help?" she asked him.

"What? I wasn't. The lady and I were discussing something."

Nyx scanned the man with her senses. His mind didn't seem to be in any turmoil as she had expected.

"Discussing what?" Darius prompted.

"She has commissioned me to design a new prayer book for the temple."

They questioned him further, then Nyx made him forget about seeing them. He knew nothing.

"I don't understand what happened," Nyx said once they were back at Darius' castle. "I heard him screaming for help."

"I don't doubt that. Perhaps Isabella's testing us somehow." Darius leaned back in his chair.

"To what end?"

He shook his head. "I don't know."

She hesitated. "About earlier. I know things are confusing between us. You're my best friend and I don't want to lose our friendship."

"Neither do I. Nyx—"

She took a deep breath and let it out. "Which is why we should stay friends. If we became more, our feelings would get in the way. What we're doing here is too important."

Darius sighed. "I won't let my feelings for you get in the way. I don't want to lose you either." He took her hand. "No matter what happens, we are in this together. It won't be easy, and we would have to keep it a secret. If people knew how important you are to me, they would use you against me."

"Then what do we do?"

"Go back to the way we were, I suppose. Can you do that?"

Nyx nodded and rested her head against his chest. All that mattered was they stayed together.

CHAPTER 17

Darius headed to the palace the next morning with Nyx. Ranelle might be able to watch things at the temple, but the Archdruid was away. That meant Isabella could worm her way back into power. He had to talk to his brother.

He told Nyx to wait outside when they reached Gideon's chambers.

"Darius?" Mercury rounded the corner. "What are you—"

He stifled a groan. "Mother." He forced a smile.

"What are you doing here?"

Planning to avoid you for one thing, Nyx thought.

Darius had to refrain from rolling his eyes.

"I have to see my brother."

"I heard you moved back into your castle. Why not come here and take up your rooms?" Mercury frowned.

"Because I hate it here." Darius pushed past his mother. "Now, if you would excuse me."

"Your general told me you asked for lighter duties. You can stay awhile." Mercury beamed. "Perhaps we—"

"Mother, I have other urgent matters to attend to."

"Is it really so hard to find time to spend with me?" Mercury scowled.

Nyx stifled her laugh with a cough.

Mercury glowered at her. "Must you drag that thing everywhere with you?"

Don't say anything, Darius warned.

The last thing he wanted was for Nyx to get into an argument with his mother. Most of the time, Nyx kept her mouth shut, but he knew it was only a matter of time before she answered back. He knew her too well.

"She's not a thing," he hissed. "It was your idea for her to become my servant. Hence, why she comes everywhere with me."

"You should send her off to the slave islands since her powers have proven useless." Mercury continued to speak as if Nyx wasn't there. "Why anyone would think she's part of the prophecy, the gods only know."

Nyx gritted her teeth and dropped her gaze to the floor.

The doors opened and Gideon frowned at them as he came out. "What's going on?"

He hadn't expected his brother to be back yet. But Darius knew he would need him to pull off summoning the council.

"Nothing. My mother was just leaving." Darius followed his brother inside and breathed a sigh of relief when the door closed behind them.

Druid, your mother is dragging me off with her. She says my clothes are unsuitable. Nyx sounded alarmed.

Why would she care about your clothes?

She says all servants have to dress the part. Her panic washed over him. *Do something to call me back. I can't be around your mother! Or I swear I will use my powers on her!*

She wants you to have new attire, you'll be fine.

What if she tries sending me to the slave islands?

Then call me and I will come and get you. But only call if it's an emergency. If not, see you later. Darius raised his mental shield and cut the connection.

He knew Nyx would be furious, but he had other matters to deal with.

"I need you to call a council meeting." He got straight to the point.

Gideon gaped at him. "Why would I do that?"

"Because whether you see it or not, your mother is plotting to overthrow Father and take the throne for herself." Darius crossed his arms. "You need to call a council meeting before she has the chance to."

Gideon scowled. "Why? She can't take the throne. I'm the heir."

"She will use you to rule through. Do you want to become her puppet?"

Gideon scoffed. "I haven't even spoken to my mother since her arrest."

"This is the first time Father has left since Isabella returned. You need to call a council meeting."

"I don't have the authority to do that."

"You have to. All you have to do is invoke Father's power." Darius put a hand on his brother's shoulder. "Call the meeting. Let the council know your mother has no authority over them."

Gideon narrowed his eyes. "You're up to something, Brother. What is it?"

"I just want to keep Father's throne safe. Your mother almost destroyed Andovia."

"You don't give a damn about Father's throne. Gods, you'd probably help the resistance if you could."

Darius forced his face to be expressionless. "Will you call a meeting or not?"

He needed Gideon to call the meeting to have all the council leaders in one place. Then Nyx could read them and find out what they knew.

Gideon still didn't look convinced. Darius needed him to do it. As the second-born son, he had no authority over the council. That was something even his mother wouldn't be able to change.

"I don't have any authority over the council." Gideon shook his head. "Only Father has control over them."

"So did your mother. You have her power now. Use it before she takes her place on the council again." Darius crossed his arms. "If you don't, people will think you're a prince in name only."

Gideon scowled. "Fine, I'll call a meeting. What do you expect me to say? I've never led anything. Mother always did the talking."

"Make it clear she has no power now. We were forced to spend years watching meetings. I'm sure you can come up with something." He followed Gideon to the council meeting hall, where a large wooden throne stood at the head of a rectangular table.

Isabella had always delighted in sitting on the Archdruid's throne. "I can't sit here." Gideon looked afraid to even go near it.

Darius remembered an incident when they were children. Gideon had dared to touch the Archdruid's real throne in the great hall and had been blasted across the room. The throne itself held power. No one could touch it but the Archdruid.

"It's not the true throne," Darius pointed out. "It has no power, and it can't hurt you."

"If Father finds out—"

Darius rolled his eyes. "Father isn't here, is he? I doubt he has someone reporting to him about his throne. You need to prove to Father you have power too, or you'll never earn his respect."

"Or he'll be furious and whip me half to death," Gideon grumbled. "It's alright for you gallivanting through the forest all day. I have to bear Father's wrath all the time."

"Prove to him you're just powerful as he is. He will never respect you unless you prove yourself."

"Are you mad? No one should ever challenge Father's power. He killed his own father to become the Archdruid. He might think I'm trying to do the same thing."

"Father knows he can't rule forever. One day, he will have to pass the mantle of power on to you. You need to prove yourself a worthy heir."

Darius had spent far more time with their father growing up. Mercury had dragged him everywhere with them. Fergus had included him at Mercury's insistence.

Gideon went over to the throne and gripped its arms. "High council of Andovia, I summon you before me."

They waited, but nothing happened. "You need to draw magic," he pointed out. "Father's power isn't contained in a makeshift throne."

"Oh. Yes." Gideon's hands flared with light. "High council, by my father's power I invoke you."

Still, nothing happened.

The doors creaked open, and Nyx came in carrying a tray of drinks.

Darius' mouth fell open at the sight of her. Her hair had changed to dark blonde, and her wings had disappeared. Now she wore a long brown dress accompanied with an apron.

Your mother did this to me, she growled in his mind. *You owe me for this, druid.*

Darius coughed to cover his laughter. *What happened to your wings?*

112

She used some magic on me and they retracted into my body. Look at me, I look ridiculous! Don't you dare laugh either!

He bit back a smile. He knew better than to antagonise her further.

Gideon muttered a curse under his breath. "Why is it not working?"

What is he doing? Nyx asked.

He's trying to summon the council.

"Try again," he told his brother.

Gideon sat on the throne. "Council of Andovia, I order you before me." No one appeared. Gideon stood up and threw his arms up in exasperation. "Why won't it work? I'm the heir." He scowled at Darius. "Or do you think Father did something to make sure no one summons the council?"

Darius shook his head. "I doubt it. What if there was an emergency, and they needed to summon him?"

"Then why won't it work?"

Darius sighed and drew magic. His eyes flared with light as he said the invocation.

A few moments later, each council leader appeared, one by one.

The council was made up of fae leaders. The Archdruid, the leader of the Silvans who had been represented by Isabella and her second, Irena. Alaric was the leader of the shifters and chief overseer. The fifth leader was Navi, an ice elf.

Irina, Alaric, and Navi all joined them at the table.

Gideon gaped at him. "How did you do that?" he hissed.

Darius shrugged. "It wasn't that hard."

Irena looked surprised when she caught sight of the Valeran brothers. "Who summoned us? The Archdruid is away from court."

Gideon opened his mouth, but no words came out.

"We did. My brother has something important we need to discuss with you." Darius nudged his brother. *Say something.*

Gideon shook his head as if to clear it. "Right. Everyone, take a seat." He sat down in his usual seat.

Darius repressed a sigh. Why was Gideon so afraid of that damned throne? He'd never make much of a leader if he was scared of it.

He wanted to talk to the council too, so he slumped onto the throne. Isabella's throne had been moved out, so he had nowhere else to sit. He had to admit it felt strange to sit there. Power slammed against his body, yet it didn't hurt him.

Gideon's mouth fell open. *What are you doing on Father's throne? There's nowhere else to sit. Get on with the meeting.*

The other three council leaders sent curious glances at Darius, but none of them said anything. That relieved him.

Curse it. Why hadn't he thought of getting another seat? He had no right to sit here, but he pushed away his unease.

Gideon would flay him alive for not only summoning the council but sitting on the throne too.

"This meeting is to discuss the matter of my mother—" Gideon began.

The doors burst open and Isabella herself came in. She no longer wore her black priestess robes. Instead, she wore an ivory-coloured gown trimmed with fur.

So much for serving penance.

Gideon's mouth fell open.

Darius groaned. Isabella must have known the perfect time to call the council.

"So good of you to announce my arrival, my son." Isabella beamed at him. She glowered at Darius. "Why are you on the Archdruid's throne? You have no right—"

Darius leaned back and crossed his arms. "I'm the Archdruid's son. You are nothing but a discarded mistress."

Once, he would never have dared say that to her. Now he didn't care. Her power was waning, and she knew it.

Isabella's face turned bright red. "How dare you—"

"Mother, you have been stripped of your titles. You have no authority on this council any longer." Gideon finally found his voice. "That's why I called this meeting. Will you all agree?" He turned to council leaders. "We will need to vote and sign this." A piece of parchment appeared in front of him on the table. "To make it clear, my mother has no authority. It's even signed by the Archdruid himself."

Isabella turned to glare at her son. "I am high priestess of the blessed. I—"

"No religious leaders are allowed to sit on the council," Darius spoke up. "It's one of the ancient laws."

"But the Archdruid—" Isabella protested.

"The Archdruid ranks over any leader, and he is the one who created the council of Andovia. You can't use him as an example." Darius leaned back on the throne. "You will never hold power in this realm again."

For once, he was glad of all the lessons his mother had forced him to endure growing up. It had given him a good understanding of how their laws worked.

"The boy is right," Alaric agreed. "As queen, you could be part of the council. As high priestess, you have no power here."

Isabella gripped the edge of the table. "This is absurd. Gideon, I'm your mother. I have been by your side—"

"Guards!" Gideon yelled.

Two armed guards walked in.

"Take her away," Gideon ordered, and the guards dragged Isabella from the room.

Darius bit back a smile. Maybe things were looking up.

CHAPTER 18

Nyx moved around the council meeting chamber and listened in on the thoughts of everyone there.

Only Gideon and Darius' minds remained closed to her. She could pick up on Darius' thoughts if she chose to, since they had a partial bond now. Gideon and the others rambled on and signed a piece of paper. She poured glasses of water for each leader and met Darius' gaze.

It felt odd seeing him on the Archdruid's throne. Yet he didn't look the least bit uncomfortable. Unlike Gideon, who had been terrified of it.

"We need to discuss something else of importance." Darius sat up straighter on the throne. "A couple of days ago, a high fae by the name of Thyren Ro was found dead outside the old city and a servant has also gone missing after being seen near there."

"Brother, we are—" Gideon snapped.

Nyx placed her foot on the hem of her dress, stumbled and sent the contents of the water jug splashing all over Gideon. She knew she might get in trouble, but she wouldn't let him interrupt Darius. Not when it was important to hear what the council knew. "Oops, I'm so sorry." She leaned forward as if to reach for him and tipped the remaining water into his lap.

Gideon shot to his feet. "Bloody stupid girl! Watch what you're doing next time!"

"Servants go missing all the time," Irena remarked. "They probably ran away. Or perhaps they were stupid enough to kill themselves by trying to get through the shield."

"No one can enter the old city, can they?" Navi asked.

"Exactly." Gideon gave a harsh laugh. "Which is why the idea of someone being murdered there is ridiculous. He more likely fell victim to the Varden. They will kill anyone they view as a threat when they enter their forest."

Nyx kept her senses focused on the leaders but didn't hear much from them. "The Varden don't stab people to death." The words were out of her mouth before she realised it. She kept her eyes on the floor and continued wiping up the water with her apron.

Gideon heated the air around himself to dry off. He glowered down at her. "No one asked for your opinion, slave."

Nyx shot to her feet and glared right back. "I was the one who found the man dying near the old city."

All eyes turned to her.

Nyx, I told you not to say anything, Darius warned.

She ignored him.

"And we are supposed to take your word for it?" Irena sneered and turned to Darius. "You need to teach your servant to keep her mouth shut. Maybe time on the slave islands would do her good."

"She's not going anywhere." Darius rose to his feet. "What do all of you know about high fae?"

Nyx probed each of their minds deeper. *Come on, what do you know?*

To her surprise, listening to each of their thoughts seemed much easier than usual. Perhaps all the training with Lyra had paid off.

Nothing.

Alaric's thoughts were harder to read. Too bad she couldn't hear anything from Isabella earlier. When she tried, she had been hit by a jolt of painful energy. Isabella had on an amulet that blocked a mind whisperer's powers. Nyx knew that because she and Darius had found one on a recent mission helping a pirate.

"Thyren was an ambassador for the council once," Navi spoke up. "But he retired over twenty years ago."

"So what did he do?" Darius asked.

Nyx focused her powers on Navi and scanned the elf's mind further.

Images of Thyren came to her, of mindless days at court and endless meetings. Nyx wondered how anyone could endure the monotony of it. Then a flicker of another image came to her of a crowd standing around a woman as she screamed for them to stop.

She was being executed. Pain stabbed through her mind.

Nyx grabbed the fallen jug and hurried into the antechamber. Why had her head hurt so much? Had Navi done something to her?

No, she hadn't sensed anything from the elf. Everything had been normal until she had seen that flash of memory.

Gods, she needed to focus. She had to help Darius, not run away. Nyx took a deep breath, used magic to refill the jug and headed back in.

"This meeting is over," Gideon announced. "Leave us."

Druid, Navi may know something. Waylay them.

Darius rose and turned to leave.

"Not so fast, brother." Gideon glowered at him.

I can't leave yet. Try to talk to Navi.

Alaric, Irena, and Navi headed out through the double doors.

Nyx trailed after them. She had to do something. But as a servant, she couldn't just ask questions. Navi might ignore her. Alaric was the only one who knew her.

Think, think, think.

Navi wore a pendant around their neck.

Break. Nyx focused her magic on the clasp, and the pendant fell. She focused her energy to slow its descent, so it made no sound.

Alaric and Irena went off in opposite directions.

The pendant flew into her hand. "Wait, you dropped this."

Navi's eyes widened. "I wondered if you would give that back." Navi held out her hand for the pendant. "Be more careful next time. If you want my attention, you should ask for it. Without resorting to trickery."

Nyx gaped at them. "How did you know?"

"The pendant is made from the finest Elven silver. The clasp does not come undone unless I open it. I felt you use your powers." They slipped the pendant back around their neck. "What is it you want, girl?"

Nyx hesitated. "To ask you about…" How could she say it? She couldn't admit she had been rummaging around their thoughts.

"Well, out with it. I'm sure you have more water to spill over the prince." Navi laughed. "I commend you for that. That boy has far less power than he believes."

"It's about an execution you and Thyren attended. An execution of a woman the Archdruid had killed. Do you remember that?"

All colour drained from Navi's face. They grabbed Nyx's arm. "Are you mad? You will expose yourself, mind whisperer."

"Please tell me what you know. I'm not a mind whisperer."

Navi gave a derisive snort. "Don't treat me like a fool. I sensed something earlier. What you saw was a long time ago and something best forgotten."

"Please tell me what it was. I need to know." Energy pulsed from Nyx's fingers into Navi.

Gods, what was wrong with her today? She always kept her power under tight control. She never used her influence unless it was necessary. It wasn't worth the risk. One thing in Andovia she could never be sure of was who her touch would work on.

Navi flinched. "No one in Andovia dares to speak of it. It was the queen's execution. I try my best to forget that day." They shuddered. "It was horrific—what the Archdruid did to her."

She gripped Navi's arm. *Focus on that memory,* she commanded. *I need to see more. Show me.*

The image became sharper. The guards dragged a woman in a loose robe out. Her face had blue and purple splotches from bruising and swelling over it. She looked unrecognisable.

Red patches streaked down her back from where she'd probably been whipped.

"See your queen. The fae queen. Now watch her burn."

They tied the woman to a pyre and Fergus threw a fireball at it.

Nyx drew back as pain seared through her head.

Why? What was it about that memory that hurt her so much?

"What's the matter?" Navi looked alarmed.

"Nothing…" She stumbled and clutched her head as the pain intensified. "Gods, did you do something to me?"

"Of course not." Navi reached out a hand, but Nyx drew back. "I'll fetch Darius."

Nyx sank to the floor and buried her head between her knees. She gasped for breath.

Something was there at the edge of her mind—just beyond reach.

Why couldn't she reach it? Why wouldn't it come to her?

"Nyx?" Darius hurried towards her. "What's wrong?"

"I suggest you get her out of here. There are eyes everywhere in this palace," Navi said.

Darius knelt beside her. "What's wrong?"

She shook her head and tears stung her eyes. *I don't know. Pain in my head…*

Darius traced a circle around them, so they reappeared in his chambers. "What happened?"

She took several deep breaths and laid against the cool floor.

After a few moments, she felt better and told him what she had seen in Navi's mind.

"Why would that memory cause me pain? It's like what happened yesterday after the sharing."

"I'll talk to Ambrose. Maybe he can come up with an explanation."

She frowned. "I thought you didn't trust him now."

"Like it or not, he's usually the only one with answers."

Nyx leaned back on her haunches. "Perhaps your father might know something." She rubbed her chin.

"You can't be thinking of asking—"

"No, druid. I meant the vault. Your father keeps his knowledge locked away somewhere, doesn't he?"

Darius gaped at her. "How—that sharing didn't keep anything secret from you, did it?" He sighed. "The answer is no. I'm not taking you there."

"Why not? We both know you can get in there. It might have information we need."

"Yeah, and if we get caught my father will kill us."

"I'll go myself then. Then you won't get into trouble." Nyx brushed off her skirts. "This awful dress will help me blend in."

Darius groaned. "You really are a bad influence on me. Fine, I'll come. If only to make sure you don't get us both killed."

CHAPTER 19

Darius couldn't believe he was taking Nyx, of all people, to his father's secret vault. Fergus would flay him alive if he ever found out. The Archdruid had only ever allowed Mercury in there and no one else.

Darius only knew the way in, as his mother had often used the place for his lessons over the years.

No one was supposed to know about the vault. He'd half hoped Nyx wouldn't gain that information either. He trusted her, but this was still dangerous.

This is a bad idea. Darius spoke in thought because he feared someone might overhear them.

Do you have any better ideas? Nyx arched an eyebrow. *Because we need some answers. Where else in the realm has centuries of magical knowledge? We didn't find anything when we went to the hall.*

No, but if we die because of this, I will never forgive you.

Nyx rolled her eyes. *We're not going to die, druid. If we get into trouble, we'll run away instead.*

And go where? Darius pressed the crystals set into the wall. Nothing happened.

She shrugged. *I don't know. We'll find somewhere. Doesn't matter as long as we stay together.*

The sequence to open the door to the vault had been the same for several months. Had his father decided to change it? It wouldn't surprise him. Fergus changed things every so often to avoid the vault being detected. That meant there would be no way to get in.

"It's been changed. I can't gain access unless I've seen my father do it. There's no other way to get inside." He shook his head. "If we use magic to try and find the sequence, it will trigger an alarm. Then my father would know someone is here."

"Why can't you just ask your mother to let you in? She used to bring you in here. She would probably let you in again."

She raised her hand and Darius caught hold of it. "I said don't use any kind of magic."

I was only going to see if I could sense anything from it. Nyx used her other hand and tapped different crystals. The wall slid aside.

"How did you do that?" Darius furrowed his brow. "No one can guess the combination. One failed attempt would trigger an alarm and trap anyone who tried to get in."

She shrugged. "It came to me. Perhaps my powers picked up on something."

Darius closed the wall, after making sure no one was around outside.

"We have to be very careful what we touch in here," he warned. "My father has traps in place on certain things. A lot of things are enchanted, so only he can touch them. It's another layer of security in place."

Nyx glanced up at the vault's high ceiling. Stacks of shelves filled with books, stones, crystals, and weapons were spread out. "This reminds me of the Hall of Knowledge. Why don't you have your own vault?"

"The knowledge in this place isn't meant to be shared. I think there's probably things in here that are best forgotten." Some of the darkest magics were recorded or stored in this place. Fergus used it as a refuge. Darius hated setting foot in the vault. Objects of power were kept here, too. He headed over to a shelf and picked up a book. "I'm not sure what to even look for." He furrowed his brow. "Why would I have my own? It's something only an Archdruid has. Although most druids have their own space where they store their knowledge; I have never seen the need to have one though."

"Maybe you should have one. We know the high fae were there at the queen's execution. The missing servant could have been there, too. Everything keeps leading back to the queen and the old city. If we could enter the city, it would help. I still say there's answers in there."

"Find information on the city of Varden," Darius instructed the book. The pages flipped open and moved on their own. "Including accounts of its destruction." He sat down on one of the cushioned divans and waited for the information to appear.

"What's that?" Nyx came over and sat beside him.

"It's like a keystone. You can find everything that's stored in the vault, and it will show you what you want to know. It will save us hours of searching through different books."

"That's better than the keeper, at least. That thing unnerves me."

Darius chuckled. "Here is an account of the day the shield went up. It's written in my father's hand."

I sent the Dragon Guard to round up any survivors from the city. The queen and her family are all dead. The Dragon Guard rounded up the surviving mind whisperers and burnt them. At last, I have succeeded in wiping out my enemy.

"Were the mind whisperers that much of a threat to him?" Nyx shuddered.

"Yeah, they opposed my father. The queen had an army, and most were loyal to her. She wanted the Archdruid gone and back in Almara. Before that, there weren't many islands under the Archdruid's control as there are now."

"Does it say anything about the shield?"

The shield has surrounded the entire city of Varden. No one can enter from land or air. No magic can pass through, not even mine. I do not know how anyone managed to activate the power source. I suspect the queen's mate, or someone close to her, of turning on the shield. But it will not stay up for long. I will bring it down.

"The power source?" Darius voiced his thoughts out loud.

"He must mean the crystal."

"What crystal?"

She shrugged. "No idea. You know things come to me sometimes. I don't know what they mean or where they come from."

He did know that but hadn't found any answers in the mass of jumbled knowledge she had shared with him.

He read further about how Fergus had made numerous attempts to bring down the shield using magic, dragon fire, and energy from Erthea itself.

"My father pulled power up from the earth. Using his connection to Erthea itself."

"How could anything withstand that? Everyone knows the stories about the Archdruid's power. Legend says nothing compares to it."

"Book, search for the power source in Andovia." The book closed and reopened in a different place. Darius read quietly for a moment. "My father said he's heard legends of the crystal. Something that protects Andovia, but it looks like he never found it."

"That must be what keeps the shield up. Too bad there's nothing in there to tell us how to get through it." Nyx sighed. "Is there anything in there about mind whisperers?" A small book flew across the room and landed in her lap. "Did I do that? I must be getting better at using my powers." She gasped. "Druid, this has records of dozens of mind whisperers and things about their powers."

"What does it say?"

"Looks like different accounts about mind whisperers and what they do. There is something here about dispensing justice. Lyra told me mind whisperers used to be the voice of justice and helped to protect the innocent and punish the guilty."

Darius? Ambrose's voice broke through his mind.

"Ambrose is calling me."

"What does he want?" Nyx glanced up from the book she had been reading.

What is it? Darius asked.

He still couldn't help but be angry at his mentor. They both knew Ambrose was hiding something.

Ambrose had been the one who'd stopped Isabella when she had tried opening the bigger rift into the underworld. Ambrose had never said how he had known how to stop her.

Yet Darius had never had a reason not to trust him. He had known Ambrose all his life.

Another body has been found, Ambrose told him. *Outside the old city. It's Thyren's servant.*

Darius groaned. *We're on our way.*

"I heard everything." Nyx sighed. "Damn."

"I'll call Sirin, and we can fly out there."

"Can I take this?" Nyx held up the book.

He shook his head. "If my father notices anything gone, he'll know we took it."

"It's one book."

"My father spells every single item in this place. I took something once, and it took me weeks to recover from the beating. Besides, you are the last surviving mind whisperer we know of. It wouldn't take him long to figure out one of us took it."

"But this has answers I need about what I am."

"I could cast a spell to duplicate it, but I wouldn't be surprised if my father has protections against that." Darius didn't want to take such a risk by using magic on the book. As much as he wanted to help her, he knew he had to be extra careful around anything in the vault.

Nyx traced different runes over the book and another one appeared that looked just like it. "Let's go."

They reached the outskirts of the old city a while later. The city's guard tower peeked out through the dense expanse of trees that surrounded the city.

Darius told Sirin to stay close by so the Varden wouldn't take issue with her being there.

They found Ambrose standing by a man slumped against a tree. "Good to see you both," Ambrose said. "One of the Varden called me to tell me about the body. This is the missing servant."

The man's dark hair was matted, his glassy eyes purple with bruising.

"It looks like he's been tortured too," Darius observed. "Holy spirits, I'd hoped we would find him before—"

"I'll have the body taken to Alaric, but I know you need to check everything before you report to your general."

"Where is the person who found the body?" Darius asked.

"She disappeared back into the forest when she was called away. It was Velestra."

Darius knelt to examine the body. *Lucien, can you come out to Varden Forest?* He reached out to his friend with his mind.

You know the Varden don't like me.

Never mind that. I need your help. Can you come or not?

I'll be there soon. Where are you?

South of the old city, near the guard tower.

Darius examined the area around the body. No sign of any marks or signs of a struggle.

He knelt and scanned the ground nearby. Nothing. No sign of tracks, no disturbances. "He wasn't killed here. We need to talk to Velestra since she found him."

"I'll go find her." Nyx spread her wings and took off.

"I miss having you and Nyx around," Ambrose remarked. "You didn't have to leave."

"It's safer if we do. Plus, I know you're hiding something from me."

Ambrose shook his head. "I told you everything I know. Why would you doubt me? Is it because of Nyx?"

"No, I trust my instincts. You taught me that."

"Yes, but you know I always have your best interests at heart. You are like a son to me."

Darius flinched. He had always considered Ambrose his father in every way that mattered. "Don't play with my emotions," Darius growled. "I can tell you're hiding something. You never even told me how you knew about Isabella."

Ambrose opened and closed his mouth. "I've been around a long time, boy. There are some things best left forgotten."

What was Ambrose hiding? What would it take to get him to tell the truth?

CHAPTER 20

Nyx glided around the trees and ducked to avoid being hit by branches. How did the Varden move around in here? This was denser than the forests she and Darius patrolled every day.

She darted around and spotted the outline of the tower up ahead. Nyx reached out and static rippled against her fingers. She hadn't slammed into the shield once.

Nyx scanned the area with her senses. The Varden had to be here somewhere.

Why couldn't Velestra have stuck around?

She circled around and spotted a white horse up ahead that stood within the trees. "Velestra, can I talk to you?" Nyx swooped down.

Velestra furrowed her brow, then nodded. "You've come to ask about the dead servant?"

Nyx noticed how Velestra used the word servant instead of slave, like everyone else. "Do you know anything about Thyren and his servant?"

"They're dead. Both appeared in a flash of light, but the servant was already dead when he appeared."

"Why didn't you mention that the other day?" Nyx frowned.

"You didn't ask. And no, I don't know either of the men." Velestra rolled her eyes. "Just because I used to live in the old city doesn't mean I knew everyone there."

"Wait, you lived there?" Nyx gaped at her. "Wouldn't that make you over a hundred years old? How are you still alive?"

She would have expected someone who had lived that long to look much older. But Velestra looked only about a decade older than her. Although she knew some Magickind could live for centuries, she hadn't realised they didn't seem to age. Perhaps they stopped at a certain point.

Velestra chuckled, and it sounded like bells. "Don't look so shocked, girl. You know we can live for centuries. Much like the tyrant who now sits on the throne."

"Do you remember the queen? The Andovian Queen, I mean."

The other fae's expression darkened. "Of course. What the Archdruid did to her was unforgivable."

"What did he do?"

She shuddered. "You don't want to know."

"You must know something. Have you seen anyone coming and going through the forest?" Energy shimmered beneath her fingers. It ached to get out. Nyx lowered her mental shield but couldn't hear anything from Velestra's mind. Something stirred at the edge of her own thoughts. "The queen placed shields around all the Varden Guard so they couldn't turn against her."

Velestra narrowed her eyes. "How do you know that?"

She shrugged. "I have no idea. Please tell me what you know."

Velestra sighed and climbed off her horse. "Come with me."

The other fae pushed through the trees as Nyx trailed after her.

Nyx wondered where Velestra was taking her and why they couldn't fly there.

Velestra said nothing, even though Nyx had asked a few questions on the way out, so she stopped trying after a while.

"Where are we going?" Nyx broke the silence between them.

"You'll see soon enough." Velestra pushed her way through the trees.

Nyx followed her. The great sandstone-coloured towers of the old city loomed ahead. Nature had reclaimed it over the last century. Tree branches and vines twisted around the towers.

"That is the old city and yes, I have seen someone lurking around the forest," Velestra admitted. "A figure clad in all black. But whenever me or the other riders got near, they fled."

That sounded familiar. Perhaps the assassin was connected to these killings, after all.

"Do you know anything else about them?"

"They move with great speed and disappear into thin air."

"It's an assassin. They've tried to kill me several times already. We think Isabella sent them after me." Nyx ran a hand through her hair. "Because of that stupid prophecy."

"You don't remember who you are, do you?" Velestra frowned. "And you allied yourself with an enemy."

"Wait, do you know who I am?" Nyx didn't know how that was possible. "And Darius isn't my enemy. He's my closest friend. I trust him more than anyone."

Velestra gave a harsh laugh. "How can you call him a friend? He's the son of the Archdruid. And no, I don't know anything about you, except you must be from the old city. One of the mind whisperers must have escaped or else you couldn't be here. You are far too young to be from that time period."

"The Archdruid swears he wiped them all out. I wish I could remember my parents—if I had any." She wondered why she had admitted such a secret to a stranger. Still, she felt a strange kinship to the Varden. Although she had no idea why. Nyx wasn't quick to trust anyone.

"You don't remember them?" Velestra frowned.

"I don't remember the first ten years of my life. Whenever I try to remember... bad things happen to me."

Velestra's frown deepened. "That can't be natural. No one erases memories unless there is something they wanted you to forget."

What had that been? Why had someone killed those two men? What did the Archdruid do to the queen?

"I know the Archdruid burned the queen alive. I think there's more to it than that. What else did he do?"

Velestra paled. "The Archdruid destroyed her. He cut off her wings, ravaged her body, then burned her whilst she still lived. That's why they search for her soul. She was the most powerful of her kind. She had power to match the Archdruid's. He tried to bind her spirit, but she escaped. I hope she's at peace now."

Nyx shivered. "If no one can get in and out of the old city, why were both bodies dumped near there? I doubt Thyren got far with the injuries he had."

"Someone must have transported him from somewhere else." Velestra leaned on her staff weapon. "But I found no trace of a circle."

That gave her an idea. "Thanks for your help. If you think of anything else, will you call for me? My name is Nyx Ashwood."

Velestra nodded. "I will, but you should leave. Living among the druids—being anywhere near the Archdruid, puts you in even greater danger."

"Where would I go? I'm a former slave and falsely accused of murder. If I'm not the druid's servant, then I'd be sent to the slave islands, or worse. Besides, I won't leave him."

Velestra's eyes narrowed. "You have feelings for him, don't you?"

Nyx opened her mouth to protest, then closed it. "That's not your business to know. Like I said, he's my friend."

She wished people would stop calling them enemies. Because they weren't that.

"Thanks for your help." Nyx spread her wings and took off in the opposite direction. Rising higher, the full extent of the old city came into view. It must've looked magnificent back in its time. Too bad no one could get in there now.

She flew through the trees and headed back to the spot where she had found Thyren a couple of days earlier. Patches of blood still covered the ground. She winced at the sight.

If Nyx and Darius had done the sharing sooner, perhaps she would have been able to save him. Perhaps not. There was no way of knowing now.

She knelt and traced runes on the ground to show signs of transportation. Just as she had seen Darius do.

The runes flared with light, then fizzled out. She muttered an oath. There had to be another clue here somewhere.

Darius and Lucien had swept the area where both bodies had been found but didn't discover anything either.

Too bad she couldn't have visions.

The thought made her miss her foster sister, Domnu, even more, and a sharp pang of sadness settled like a heavy weight in her chest.

Where were her sisters? Were they safe? Did they know she'd been looking for them?

She sighed and traced more runes on the ground. The runes flared with bright light this time. A glowing trail of energy appeared. Finally, a clue!

She considered calling Darius but decided to wait and see where it led her first.

Nyx followed the glowing trail until it ended a few feet away. She picked up a stone and threw it in that direction. The stone bounced and light flashed.

Damned shield!

Too bad that strange knowledge of hers wouldn't give her a way through the shield.

This proved Thyren had come from the old city, though. Somehow, he had got through. Now she had to call the druid and—

An arrow shot towards her.

Nyx raised her hand and directed it away. Another energy pushed back.

Here we go again.

So the assassin had returned.

This time, Nyx wouldn't let them get so close to her.

Nyx pushed back against the arrow with her mind but couldn't see any sign of the assassin. Where were they lurking?

Where are you? She traced a rune in the air and the arrow fell to the ground.

Nyx flapped her wings, shot into the air, and scanned the area with her mind. No sign of any thoughts or presences came to her.

The assassin was good at shielding herself.

She shot in the direction the arrow had come from, wings flapping hard as she fought to move faster. She spotted a dark shape perched on a branch.

Her mind raced with her wealth of knowledge.

A high magic spell for stunning an enemy came to her.

"Avock!" Nyx threw a bolt of energy as power thrummed through her.

She liked this spell. The mind sharing hadn't been for nothing after all.

The assassin screamed as they lost their balance on the branch and plummeted.

She grinned and searched her mind for a way to contain someone.

A web of energy seemed like it would do the trick. She pictured the glowing web with her mind, then raised her hand as she flew. A glowing blue web of energy formed around the assassin and trapped them mid-fall.

The assassin screamed. Odd, it sounded like a girl's scream. Maybe she had been right about the assassin being female. But why would they send a girl after her? Isabella was no fool.

"Hello again." Nyx flashed them a smile. "You really have a bad habit of following me."

Icy blue eyes stared back at her. No other features were visible behind the black mask. The assassin growled.

"So, who are you and why do you keep following me?"

The assassin thrashed against the web, hitting it with invisible blasts of energy.

She traced some runes around the web to make sure it held.

"We can hang around here all day, but I want answers. Now." Nyx reached through the web and grasped the assassin's arm. If there was any time to use her power, it would be now. Touch made it easier for her power to flow freely.

Nyx relinquished her hold on her power. Energy reverberated and impacted the air. At the same time, the assassin grabbed hold of her, and energy burst from them, too.

Both Nyx and the assassin screamed as energy exploded between them. The shock waves broke through the web and knocked Nyx off balance. They both screamed as they plummeted to the ground.

She hit the ground, hard. The air knocked from her lungs. Her head spun so much she struggled to keep herself balanced again.

The assassin landed a few feet away.

Nyx raised her hand and cast the web around the assassin again.

Had her power worked?

Nyx couldn't be sure since the assassin used some kind of magic too. Odd, it almost reminded her of her own magic. But that was impossible—wasn't it?

"Who are you and who sent you to kill me?" Nyx demanded and marched over to the glowing web.

The assassin seemed dazed for a moment, then thrashed against the web. "Let me out of here!"

Maybe her power hadn't worked. Or they would have started talking. "No, but you will give me some answers." She waved her hand, and the black mask flew off.

The girl appeared no older than Nyx. Pointed ears stuck out through her long, blonde hair. Her icy blue eyes flashed with anger.

She was not only fae, but possibly an Andovian. Nyx had learnt to recognise many kinds of fae, especially the enslaved ones.

She thought back to when the girl had used her magic. It almost felt like… like her power when it became unleashed.

"Let me out of here!" The girl pounded against the web with her fists.

"Are… Are you like me?" Nyx furrowed her brow.

The assassin scowled. "What do you mean? I'm nothing like you."

"Are you a mind whisperer?" Nyx couldn't believe it. All this time, she had wanted to find someone like her, and now she finally had. She had never expected it to be the person who had been sent to kill her.

"That doesn't matter. I will kill you!" She thrashed against the web again.

"That's why my powers don't work on you. Incredible. I thought I was the only mind whisperer left." Her excitement soon faded. "Who sent you to kill me?"

"I won't tell you anything."

Nyx sighed and muttered a curse. Under normal circumstances, she could make people talk. But how could she do that when her power proved to be useless? Talking had never been one of her strong suits.

She paced up and down after she reinforced the web again. "Isabella sent you to kill me, didn't she? You're not going anywhere, so you might as well tell me the truth."

"Why should I tell you anything?" the assassin snarled.

Nyx held out her hands and the assassin's knives flew into her grasp. Each blade had a strange triangle symbol carved into the hilt. She searched through her wealth of knowledge for a clue but found nothing. Darius had warned her not to expect instant results and that some knowledge would come to her over time.

"Fine, if you don't want to talk, I'll call my druid to come and take you in. I'm sure the Archdruid would love to know there's another mind whisperer in Andovia."

The girl's eyes narrowed. "I should have known you were a traitor. Working for the man who wiped out our race. Your parents would be ashamed of you." She spat at Nyx.

"I don't work for the Archdruid. I work with his son," Nyx snapped. "There's a difference. I don't know who my parents are." She turned away. *Druid? I need your help. I captured the assassin.*

"I don't know who my parents are either," the girl admitted, and her fists clenched. "Thanks to the Archdruid."

Druid? Nyx called again.

He still didn't reply.

"If you let me out, I promise to stop coming after you." The girl gave a smile that showed too many teeth, Nyx noted.

"I'm not a fool. Don't think you can trick me that easily." She resumed pacing. *Druid, why won't you answer me?*

Still, no response came.

Druid!

Nothing.

Darius!

She couldn't understand why he wouldn't answer. They were linked to each other through the sharing and had a much stronger connection now.

Nyx brushed dirt off her tunic and gasped. After her fall, she had been more focussed on the assassin rather than her surroundings. The static she felt earlier must've been the shield.

"We're in the old city," she remarked, more to herself than the assassin.

"You just figured that out?" The assassin scoffed. "You are pretty stupid for a servant."

Nyx narrowed her eyes. "What's wrong with that? At least I don't go around killing people for money."

The assassin fell quiet.

Nyx resumed pacing and searched her archive of knowledge for the best course of action. Several high magic spells came to her. Some darker than others. Now she understood why Darius was so reluctant to use them. Though Nyx didn't think she would struggle with self-control. Not with higher magic, at least.

Darius? Ranelle? Lucien? She called out for them with her mind. She waited, but still no one answered.

The web broke apart and the assassin sprang at her, knocking her to the ground. The assassin grabbed one of her fallen blades. "Did you really think I'd be that easy to contain?"

Nyx struggled as the assassin pinned her down. The dagger sliced into her throat and warm blood dripped down her neck.

She narrowed her eyes to move the assassin away from her. Energy rippled against the girl but did nothing. Nyx pushed back and shoved the girl away. Just because her powers didn't work on the girl, didn't mean she couldn't move and hit her with something. Nyx spotted a large fallen tree branch and willed it to move.

The branch shot straight at the assassin and struck her on the back of the head. The assassin stumbled and sank to her knees.

Nyx guessed she must have hit her harder than she thought. She waved her hand, so another glowing web of energy appeared. She reinforced it with runes to hold the web in place.

"This won't hold me." The girl smiled. "Besides, you will be dead soon enough, then there will be nothing to keep me trapped in here."

Nyx walked off and ripped off part of her tunic to press against her bleeding throat. At least the cut didn't seem too deep. She needed some help, and she knew it.

Bam! She slammed into the shield.

Curse it, she was trapped in the old city. It looked like she'd be stuck in there for a while.

Like it or not, she was on her own.

Nyx headed back towards the glowing web and stumbled as a wave of dizziness washed over her. "What did you do to me?" Something burned through her veins, but she had no idea what it was. She felt her knees buckle as her legs gave out.

"There's no escape this time." The assassin smiled down at her.

That was the last thing she saw before darkness swallowed her.

CHAPTER 21

Darius guided Sirin around the outskirts of the forest. A blanket of green, gold, and orange stretched out before them. One of his duties was to keep the peace in the forest and the way in and out of the three territories. Most people considered the forest guards to be little more than rangers, but they were so much more than that. Most of Eldara was covered by woodland. And populated by hundreds of Magickind. Someone had to keep things in order.

The true power in Andovia was the Dragon Guard, the Archdruid's fighting machine. The Dragon Guard not only reinforced the Archdruid's laws, but they razed entire cities to the ground within minutes.

Most of the other members of the Forest Guard didn't even have access to dragons. Darius had found Sirin as a hatchling, and she would have been killed if he hadn't saved her.

Her silver-white skin and smaller size didn't make her desirable as one of the Dragon Guard's steeds. Darius loved her. Her size and colour were perfect. He didn't want an uncontrollable brute of a dragon.

Down below, he spotted General Killian beckoning him.

Now what? He hoped no more bodies had been found.

He couldn't be sure the two recent deaths were connected to the assassin who had come after Nyx. But it wouldn't surprise him. If only he could get some answers and bring the person responsible to justice.

We'd better see what he wants, he told Sirin.

Where is Nyx? Sirin replied.

Sirin was a dragon of few words. Darius could only communicate with her because it was part of his gift. Nyx had never been able to communicate with dragons. It was a rare talent. He still had no idea where the ability came from. Perhaps his mother's ability to communicate with spirits had manifested differently in him.

She's gone back to Varden Forest.

Why? There's nothing there but dragon haters. Sirin growled.

Darius shrugged. "No idea. She said she wanted to look at something."

Sirin swooped down and landed beside General Killian. "What is it?" Darius asked.

"Someone new has been roaming through the woods. The dryads report seeing them on several occasions, and they attacked two of them when the dryads tried questioning them," General Killian replied. "I am issuing orders to everyone in the forest to be on the lookout for them. I won't have this stranger randomly attacking our people."

"I have a pretty good idea who you mean. An assassin has been coming after Nyx for the past few days. They have been following us everywhere."

The general's eyebrows rose. "Why would anyone want to kill your servant?"

Darius shrugged. "They think she is part of the prophecy. Someone wants her dead and hired someone very skilled to do it."

"Everyone has orders to detain them if the culprit is spotted."

He shook his head. "Capturing the assassin won't be so easy. We've already tried, and they always escape."

"Can't your mind whisperer use her touch on them?" General Killian held up his hand when Darius opened his mouth to protest. "Come now, we both know she's a lot more powerful than you let everyone believe. Why else would anyone be trying to kill her? Just deal with this problem. I won't have one girl putting everyone in the realm at risk."

He sighed. Although he understood the general's reasoning, he still didn't know how to put a stop to the assassin. Maybe it was time he used his own magic to capture them. Even if it meant using higher magic. The assassin was getting a little too close to Nyx, and he didn't want to risk anything happening to her.

"I'll do what I can to stop the assassin." Darius guided Sirin back into the air and they flew back towards Varden Forest.

Nyx had been gone for a while. He wondered why she hadn't called to let him know if she found anything.

Nyx? Darius reached out to her with his mind. With the assassin still on the loose, he wanted to make sure she was safe. *Nyx, are you alright?*

He waited, but she didn't respond.

Odd. She usually answered.

Nyx? He persisted. *Can you let me know where you are?*

Nothing.

Not even a "Be quiet, druid".

She's not answering me. We better head to Varden Forest to check on her.

Sirin gave a derisive snort. *What if they shoot us again?*

He scanned for Nyx with his mind. *I'll worry about that when we get there. The Varden seem to tolerate Nyx.* To his surprise, he couldn't sense Nyx's presence. That didn't make sense. They were linked. He should be able to sense her, no matter what.

"We need to hurry. Something is wrong."

Darius traced runes in the air. A glowing portal formed, and Sirin roared and dove straight into it.

They re-emerged above the sweeping canopy of Varden Forest.

Darius scanned for Nyx with his senses once again but couldn't find her. *Sirin, head straight towards the old city. Go to the spot where we found the first body.*

Sirin swooped lower. Below them, one of the Varden on a white horse beckoned to him.

Darius didn't want to deal with her prejudice again. Sirin hadn't done anything wrong to them or their forest. But he knew he couldn't ignore the Varden either, or it would lead to more unwanted trouble.

He sighed. *Sirin, let's go and see what she wants. But I'm not leaving here without Nyx.*

Sirin glided towards the fae rider.

"Velestra." Darius gave her nod.

"Valeran, we have a problem. Your servant has somehow infiltrated the shield. She is trapped in the old city with another fae."

Darius gaped at her. "How did she even get in there? No one can get through that shield."

Velestra grimaced. "I've no idea. No one has ever been through the shield. She and the other fae must have found a way through."

"How do you know she's in there? Do you know who she's with?"

"Another fae girl."

He wondered if he she meant Ranelle. Ranelle did look like a fae. *Ranelle, are you with Nyx?* Darius called to her.

No, why? Ranelle sounded confused.

Never mind.

"Where are Nyx and the other fae?"

"Follow me." Velestra guided her horse around and trotted off in the opposite direction.

Darius and Sirin flew behind her.

Velestra glared up at him. "Must you bring that beast here?"

Sirin grunted in disapproval, then roared, which made Velestra's horse rear up onto its hind legs.

Settle down, girl. Darius patted the dragon's side. "She's not harming anyone."

Velestra's horse stopped and pawed at the ground.

"She makes my mount nervous. We all remember what the Dragon Guard has done to us over the years."

"I'm not Dragon Guard and not all dragons terrorise people. We need to move faster." He urged Sirin onward. They headed straight towards the old city.

When they reached the edge of the border between Varden Forest and the old city, Darius jumped from the dragon's back.

Nyx lay crumpled on the ground, unmoving. His heart twisted at the sight of her. A blond-haired girl stood a few feet away, thrashing against a web of energy. He blanched when he recognised her clothing.

The assassin.

Darius hadn't expected it to be a girl. She looked only a couple of years younger than him. He thought it would be someone far older. "What have you done to her? Who are you?"

Her lip curled. "Why should I tell you anything? Your father killed my family and hunted my race to extinction."

Darius' jaw tightened. "How did you get through the shield?"

Velestra galloped over to him and dismounted her horse. "The girl looks like a true Andovian."

The assassin scowled. "This web won't hold me much longer. Once she's dead, I'll—"

"Do what?" He crossed his arms. "You're stuck in a city with no way out. Even if you get through the web, you'll most likely die in there."

He couldn't imagine how anyone could survive in the city, it was cut off from the rest of the realm. Food and other resources would have probably died out decades ago.

"If I can get in here, I can find a way out." The assassin raised her chin. "I can leave this awful realm once and for all."

"If you had a way out, you would have left her there to die already." He turned his attention to Nyx. "Nyx, can you hear me?"

She didn't respond.

The assassin snorted. "She'll be dead within the hour."

Darius turned to Velestra. "There must be a way through. Think. You know the old city better than anyone."

Velestra shook her head. "There isn't. No one has gone through in the past century."

"Clearly there must be a way." He motioned to Nyx and the assassin. "How else could they have got through otherwise?"

Velestra opened and closed her mouth. "How did you get through?" she demanded of the assassin. "No one has been able to get through that shield. Yet you somehow managed it."

"I didn't do anything. It's her fault, she trapped us in here." She motioned towards Nyx.

Darius paced up and down. Questioning the assassin would get them nowhere.

He needed to get to Nyx, or she would die. Then the assassin would not only succeed, but escape.

Only one person might be able to help now.

Ambrose? He reached out to the other druid with his mind.

What's wrong? His former mentor sounded concerned.

Nyx and the assassin are trapped in the old city. You have to come and help me get them out. Nyx has been poisoned.

Ambrose appeared beside him in a whirl of light. "How did they—"

Darius shrugged. "She won't say. Just help me get Nyx out of there."

"I—I can't. The shield's powers are too strong."

"We have to do something." He clenched his fists so hard, power crackled between his fingers.

Ambrose turned his attention to the assassin. "You're from the Order of Blood, I see."

The assassin scowled. "How do you know that?"

"I recognise the emblem on your blades." Ambrose motioned to the fallen knives. "How did you get through the shield? I would give us some answers if I were you. You will be arrested for your crimes once we get you out of there."

The assassin snorted. "You don't scare me, old man."

"Ambrose, stop talking and get us through the shield." Darius held up a hand when Ambrose opened his mouth to protest. "Just try."

"Very well." Ambrose sighed. He raised his glowing staff, and energy rippled towards the invisible shield. The shield flashed into existence. A glowing wall of bright blue light.

Ambrose raised his staff higher and pushed back against the energy.

A bolt of energy shot from the shield, struck Ambrose in the chest, and knocked him to the ground. Darius wondered how they were going to get Nyx out now.

One way or another, he would find a way to reach her.

CHAPTER 22

Nyx stirred and opened her eyes. Every muscle in her body ached. Her throat throbbed from where the dagger had cut her. It took her a few moments to remember where she was when she caught sight of the assassin.

She moaned and scrambled into a sitting position. "Druid?"

"I'm here." Darius stood a few feet away beside Ambrose.

"What happened?" She gasped.

"He tried to get through the shield. The shield's energy repelled him." Darius grimaced. "Nyx, you need to tell me how you got through. We don't have much time left."

"What are you talking about?" She rose, and her stomach recoiled. "Argh!"

"You've been poisoned."

The captive assassin smiled at her. "You can't keep this web around me forever. I'll soon be free."

"How are you going to get out of the old city without me?" Gods, she wanted to get up and wipe that annoying smirk off the girl's face, but knew she needed to conserve her strength.

"I'll find a way." The assassin's jaw tightened.

"I'm not sure how I got in here." Nyx turned back to the druid. "I used my influence on her. Or tried to. She used her touch against me at the same time. I think the force of our magics knocked us through the shield."

Darius' eyes widened.

Nyx guessed that could be the only thing that got them through the shield. Her power always released concussive blasts of energy.

"Perhaps you both need to do that again to get out." Darius rose to his full height.

Nyx scoffed. "Do you really think she's going to help?"

"I won't help." The assassin glowered at them. "It's her fault we ended up here."

"She won't help," Nyx agreed. "Maybe my power will be enough to get me through."

The assassin gaped at her. "You can't leave me in here."

She closed her eyes in an attempt to stop the swaying motion in her head. "It would serve you right if I did. You poisoned me."

As much as she wanted to leave the assassin there, she wouldn't do it. Leaving her to die would make her no better than the assassin.

"Using your power will weaken you further," Velestra warned. "Given your current state, it could kill you."

"Velestra, can you take Ambrose somewhere safe?" Darius asked. "And have a healer check on him?"

Velestra hesitated. "Isn't getting them out of the old city—"

"I'll figure it out. But I need him to be somewhere safe too."

"I'll have him checked." Velestra yanked Ambrose up and used magic to get him onto her horse.

"Maybe Ranelle or Lucien can help." Nyx wobbled and her head spun. "Or Alaric."

"You cannot invite everyone into our forest," Velestra said. "If you dare to bring your father or brother here, the full force of the Varden will come down on them." Velestra climbed up onto her mount. "I will return soon." She turned and rode off into the distance.

"I'll use my power again. The force of it must somehow disperse the shield's power."

The assassin laughed. "That will finish you off even sooner. You should know using your touch is draining."

Nyx hated to admit it, but she had a point. Using her influence would drain her energy. Her body already felt weak. What would using her touch again do to her?

"We need to know it will work before I waste precious energy," Nyx said. "Call Ranelle and Lucien."

"They're on their way. Are you sure your energy can break through? What happened when you touched each other?"

"I used my power on her. She used hers on me, then we fell through. It knocked us both over."

"Perhaps it just needs to be a strong force of energy then." Darius twisted his hands together and a tornado of energy swirled between his palms. His magic whirled around him, then shot towards the shield.

"Druid, be careful. What if—" Nyx got cut off as a bolt of energy shot out of the shield.

Darius dove out of the way. A bolt of energy struck the spot where he stood, scorching the ground.

"Attacking the shield head-on must make it retaliate." He scrambled up and sighed.

Lucien and Ranelle appeared in a whirl of light.

"Nyx, you're in the old city," Ranelle gasped.

"I already told you that." Darius frowned at her.

"Yes, but I didn't believe it." Ranelle ran a hand through her hair.

Nyx sank to the ground again as Darius filled them in on what happened.

"You won't be awake for much longer." The assassin thrashed against the web.

"Do shut up," Nyx snapped. "I'm not dead yet."

"That's only because the poison didn't have its full effect."

"Even if you escape, you will die if anything happens to her," Darius warned.

"Then I'll get to use my touch on you." The assassin smirked. "I'm sure having the son of the Archdruid under my control would be useful."

"Fool. He's immune to mind whisperer's powers," Nyx muttered.

"We need to figure out a way through. Right now." Darius paced up and down. "Hitting the shield head-on will strike anyone down. Ambrose is still unconscious."

"Let me try." Lucien blurred and shot straight towards Nyx. He cried out as he slammed into the shield and hit the ground hard.

"I could have told you that wouldn't work." Ranelle rolled her eyes. "Can we dig through?"

Darius shook his head. "No, it covers the ground, too. I can sense the vibrations."

144

Nyx rested her head against a tree trunk. Sweat beaded across her forehead.

"What poison was used? If we can cure Nyx…" Ranelle said.

Nyx only heard half of it before her vision blurred.

She found herself in a garden surrounded by flowers. A blonde-haired girl with pointed ears laughed with her as they chased each other. They were just children.

"I'll get you, Niamh."

Nyx blinked. More sweat dripped down her forehead.

Energy rolled around her as Darius, Lucien, and Ranelle used their magic against the shield.

"Niamh?" she murmured. "Where is Niamh?" Her thoughts were jumbled, and she expected to find the girl nearby.

It took her a moment to remember where she was.

"Why were you calling out my name?" The assassin frowned. "How do you even know it? I'm immune to your powers."

"I remember you. We were children. I chased you around…"

A burst of energy sent Darius and his friends flying through the air.

Niamh narrowed her eyes. "That's not possible. I don't remember anything before I was ten."

"Good gods." Ranelle scrambled to her feet. "You must be twins. I see it now. You look similar to each other."

Niamh scowled. "We're not sisters. She doesn't have pointed ears and I don't have wings. Look at her. We're nothing alike."

Nyx struggled to keep her eyes open and make herself focus. They were sisters? No, that couldn't be possible. Could it?

Or maybe it was. They were both mind whisperers. And who better to send to kill her than a mind whisperer? One of the few people in the world who was immune from her powers.

"Think about it. You look alike, you're both mind whisperers around the same age," Ranelle pointed out. "It would be too coincidental for you not to be related."

Niamh shook her head. "You're trying to trick me into saving her. I won't be fooled by this nonsense."

"Are we? Are you willing to take that risk?" Darius arched an eyebrow. "Are you going to let your sister die? Like Nyx, you don't have any family. You've spent your whole life wandering around, not knowing where you came from."

Niamh's hands clenched into fists. "You don't know anything about me!"

Nyx laid back on the ground. It was too much to stay upright.

"Nyx had pointed ears. They were cut off to make her more human," Darius told Niamh. "They tried to cut her wings off too, but they healed. Were you found under an ash tree?"

Niamh gaped at him. "How could you—"

"I know what happened to her. I know how much she wants to find her family. Well, you've found yours, Niamh. She will be dead soon unless you do something to save her."

The web around Niamh faded. Nyx's breathing grew ragged.

Niamh stood there, staring at her, and sank to her knees. "How can we be sisters?"

How the heck should I know? Nyx switched to speaking in thought. *I can't say I would pick you for my sister.* She closed her eyes.

"Nyx, you need to stay awake." Darius' voice sounded urgent.

She forced her eyes open once more. Darius pressed himself against the shield, his face etched with worry.

"Here. I have the antidote." Niamh fumbled inside her cloak.

"You used moon flower? Good gods, I'm surprised she's lasted this long." Lucien gasped. "It's too late for the antidote work."

"Do it anyway," Darius snapped.

Niamh hesitated. "How do I know you're not trying to trick me?" She glowered at Darius. "You love her; you'll do anything to save her."

Darius's jaw tightened. "She remembered your name. You must have some connection to each other. If you really want to find out who you are, don't let her die."

Niamh knelt, opened Nyx's mouth, and poured the nasty mixture down her throat. "If you are my sister, please don't die."

"Niamh, if you use your power, maybe it will be enough to force the shield open so you and Nyx can get through," Darius said.

"Come, sister." Niamh yanked Nyx to her feet and wrapped her arm around her to support her. "Brace yourself." Niamh pressed her palm against the shield.

Nyx wondered how this was possible. How could this assassin be her sister?

A concussive blast of energy shook the air around them as Niamh unleashed her power. A boom of thunder without sound reverberated around them. The shield flashed but didn't open. "It's not working." Niamh groaned. "Gods below, how else can we get through?"

Nyx gasped for breath. She knew her time had almost come. *No, I am not ready to die.*

Druid? She reached out to Darius with her mind. She didn't want to leave him either.

Bolts of energy shot from Darius' hands and the ground trembled around them as he attacked the shield.

Lucien and Ranelle stumbled backwards.

Niamh, use your power again, Nyx told her.

I can't. I haven't had time to recover. Niamh shook her head.

Nyx willed her hand to move. If she could reach Darius, she knew she wouldn't die.

Niamh, I need to reach the druid. Raise my hand for me.

What good will that do?

Just do it! She was not about to die. Not without saying goodbye to Darius first. She couldn't do that unless she got through the damned shield.

"Niamh!" she rasped.

Niamh took hold of her hand. Energy tingled between them. An odd recognition. She pushed Nyx's hand against the shield.

"Druid?" she choked out the word before the darkness dragged her under.

CHAPTER 23

Darius' chest tightened as he watched Nyx collapse into Niamh's arms.

His heart lurched. No, he couldn't lose her. He wouldn't.

Something inside him snapped, and he drew more power from the earth itself. Nothing on Erthea was going to stop him from getting through that shield.

Bring her back to me. His eyes filled with glowing light.

Whatever control he kept on his power broke. He let it flow free. Darius didn't care if he lost control. Didn't care if he tore the entire old city apart. Getting her back was the only thing that mattered.

"Darius, stop!" Ranelle cried. "You can't use high magic."

This wasn't high magic; this was something else. This power came from Erthea itself.

The glowing blue shield pushed and repelled against him. Sparks of energy shot in all directions.

"Darius!" Lucien reached for him.

"Stand back," he snarled.

Nothing would stop him from reaching Nyx.

"She's not breathing," Niamh said. "Gods forgive me."

His link with Nyx slowly slipped away.

Let. Me. Through.

He forced all the power he'd conjured up to hit the shield, forcing the entire barrier of energy to light up. The glowing wall of blue energy blazed like fire, then fell away.

148

An explosion reverberated through the air and thunder roared. The blast knocked Ranelle and Lucien to the ground.

Darius sank to his knees.

Niamh, still holding Nyx, staggered through.

"Lucien, heal Nyx. Hurry up!"

"I can't heal anyone," Lucien protested. "You know I don't have the ability yet. Even if I did, I can't heal anyone unless they were the person I was meant to be protecting."

"Heal her," he commanded, and waves of power pulsed through the air. "Now, overseer." He wouldn't take no for an answer. Lucien had the power inside him somewhere. If Darius had to drag it out of him, he would do so.

Lucien scrambled up.

Darius crawled forward and gathered Nyx up in his arms. He glared at Niamh. Sister or not, she had done this to Nyx.

Lucien held out his hands over Nyx, but nothing happened. "I can't heal anyone. I'll call—"

"Try again," Darius snapped, and gave his friend an imploring look. "Please. I can't lose her."

"To heal, you have to use your emotions. That's how healing magic works," Ranelle said, and touched Lucien's arm. "Stop thinking and feel."

Lucien closed his eyes and his hand glowed with golden light. The light washed over Nyx's body. She gasped for breath and her eyes fluttered open.

"Thank the spirits." Darius wrapped an arm around her and pulled her close.

"You're alive," Niamh gasped.

"Druid." Nyx smiled and rested her head against his shoulder.

Lucien stared at his hands in disbelief. "How did I—?"

Ranelle threw her arms around Lucien. "See! I told you, you could do it."

Lucien's eyes widened in shock, but he returned her embrace.

"She must be the one you're supposed to protect." Darius kept a protective arm around Nyx and kept his gaze on Niamh. If she tried anything, he would stop her. Sister or not, she was still a threat to them all.

"I'm—I'm sorry," Niamh murmured. She rose and ran off.

"Go after her," Darius snapped. Exhaustion weighed on him like a heavy cloak.

"No, don't." Nyx pulled away from him. "She's my sister. Let her go."

"She almost killed you. What's to stop her from trying again?" Darius gritted his teeth. "She was sent here to kill you. If she is from the Order of Blood, she won't stop until she completes her mission."

He hadn't encountered the Order of Blood before, but he knew of their reputation. They were a deadly order of assassins that were the best of the best. They never failed and kept on coming until their mission was complete. His father had used them in the past from what he heard from his mother.

"Perhaps she won't." Nyx pushed her hair off her face. "For now, let her go. I won't be so quick to trust her either."

"I'm not sure Nyx is the one you're meant to protect, wolfsbane." Ranelle pulled away from him.

"I'm not special," Nyx scoffed. "I doubt you're my overseer, Lucien."

Lucien continued to stare at his hands. "Darius, how did you know how to do that?"

He shrugged. "I didn't. It was an instinct, I guess."

"Or perhaps something else. I've never seen you use power like that before." Ranelle gave Darius an odd look.

He looked away. Ranelle would probably say he'd wielded the power of the Archdruid. Which couldn't be true. Maybe he could invoke it when he had to, but that didn't make him an Archdruid.

"Will you be alright?" He caressed Nyx's face and fought back the urge to kiss her. "I still say we should go after her. She almost killed you. I have orders to bring her in."

Niamh had said he loved her, and he hadn't denied it. Maybe he did, but his emotions felt too tumultuous to be sure.

Nyx shook her head. "I'll be fine. You can't do that. She's my sister." She gaped at him.

"Can you give us a minute?" Darius asked his friends.

Ranelle and Lucien walked off without saying another word.

"You can't bring her in," Nyx protested. "If people find out what she is—"

"Nyx, just because you found out you're related, doesn't make her less of a threat."

Nyx wobbled when she stood up, Darius caught hold of her. "You know how important finding out who I am is to me." She pulled away from him.

"I do, but she's our enemy. And I can't ignore orders." He never thought he'd have to argue with her over this.

Why did the assassin have to be her sister, of all people? Part of him wanted to deny such a thing was possible. But he couldn't. She and Niamh had the same eyes. Plus, two mind whisperers being found abandoned under an ash tree at the same time would be too much of a coincidence.

"But people will kill her if they find out what she is."

"Just because she saved you, doesn't mean she will stop coming after you," Darius snapped. "She's from the Order of Blood. They never stop until they take down their target. If she doesn't kill you, someone else will take her place. The Order will kill her if she fails."

"I haven't even had the chance to talk to her." Nyx's hands clenched into fists. "You can't just condemn her to death."

"I can't ignore my duty as a Forest Guard, either. Please try to understand." Darius reached for her, but she drew back.

"Maybe Ambrose is right. It doesn't work between us."

"This has nothing to do with us. It's about doing what's right."

"So condemning my sister to death is right?" She gasped.

"No, I didn't mean that." He rubbed his temples.

"Yes, you did. We're connected, remember? I feel what you feel."

Pain and anger flooded through him through their link. Along with betrayal.

"Nyx, I—"

"Just don't. Go do your duty then. Clearly I don't mean anything to you." She stormed over to Ranelle and Lucien without saying another word.

Darius sighed as Sirin swooped down beside him.

You made a fool of yourself, the dragon remarked.

Don't you nag me as well. He scrambled onto her back. *Let's go.*

Sirin roared and took to the air.

Putting distance between him and Nyx did nothing to ease the tension between them.

What would you have me do then? Darius demanded. *I can't ignore orders. If the assassin is hurting people—*

Nyx will never forgive you if you get her sister killed. And you would never forgive yourself, either.

Can we please not call her Nyx's sister? Just because they're related doesn't make them kin.

But they are kin. I can sense it. They're part of each other. You and Nyx are part of each other, too. Sirin craned her neck to give him a look. *You mustn't hurt your lifemate.*

Lifemate? Are you mad? We're not—

You love her. Even if you don't want to admit it yourself.

"Let's focus on finding Niamh, shall we?" He didn't want to think about his argument with Nyx. Or that lifemate comment. Hurting her didn't sit well with him, but what else was he was supposed to do? Darius had never gone against orders before.

Maybe Ambrose had been right. Were they over before they'd even begun?

He pushed those thoughts away and focussed his senses on the forest below.

I hear something, Sirin said. *I think the Varden has Nyx's sister.*

They do? Darius furrowed his brow.

Listen. Can't you hear people arguing?

Not really.

That's because you're feeling so conflicted about Nyx. Let's go. Before Darius could react, Sirin went headlong into a nosedive.

The trees reached up to meet them as Sirin drove through the thick canopy.

"Sirin!" Darius winced as branches thumped against him.

The dragon ignored him until they reached the ground and landed by Velestra. She had hold of Niamh. Or rather, tree branches had hold of Niamh.

"What are you doing here, Valeran?" Velestra demanded. "Shouldn't you be taking care of your servant?"

He ignored the question. "I'm here for her. I have orders to bring her in for trespassing and assault."

"I haven't assaulted anyone." Niamh wriggled against the branches wrapped around her body. "Let me go or I'll—"

"Your power won't work while imprisoned by the tree, mind whisperer." Velestra turned to him. "She tried killing someone on Varden land. I have to bring her before my elders and—"

"I haven't killed anyone!" Niamh protested.

"Nyx is fine, but you need to hand her over. The Forest Guard wants her as well."

"They have no authority here. You should know that better than anyone, Valeran." Velestra glared at him.

"She committed crimes outside of this forest—larger crimes than she did on Varden land." Darius made a scroll appear. "Read this, then hand her over."

Her eyes narrowed when she grabbed and read the scroll. "It's a decree that gives you the right to take anyone into your custody."

It had taken a lot of convincing on his mother's part to get his father to grant him such a thing. But it proved useful at times like this.

"How do I know this is real?"

"It bears my father's seal marked with his blood. Even I couldn't forge that."

Velestra gritted her teeth. "You can't—"

"This says otherwise." He motioned to the scroll. "The Archdruid's authority trumps even your laws. To put it simply, I'm going to take her."

"You are just like your father," she growled.

Darius flinched. No, he wasn't, but he'd do whatever he had to do to make sure Niamh didn't escape.

He went over and slapped a cuff on her wrist. Light flashed over her.

Niamh gasped as the branches released her. "What have you done to me?"

"The cuff renders anyone powerless. Don't bother running either. You're tied to me now." Darius held up his hand to show the other cuff.

Niamh turned and ran, then gasped as a wall of energy barred her way. "Do you really think this will hold me?"

"You're not as powerful as your sister." He grabbed her arm.

"What do you think she'll say when she finds out you arrested me?"

"She'll understand... eventually."

Niamh snorted. "She will never forgive you and you know it."

Darius dragged her away, ignoring her remarks.

He traced a circle. He, Sirin, and Niamh all reappeared near the guardhouse.

"You don't even know your sister. So don't pretend to know anything about her," he snapped.

"I haven't killed anyone since I've been in this realm."

"What about the two dryads you attacked?"

"They got in my way, so I stunned them."

"Oh really? What about the other deaths? Two fae have been killed in the last few days. The first one on the day you showed up." Darius gripped her wrist. "Do you expect me to believe you weren't responsible for that?"

"You can believe whatever you like. My orders are to kill Nyx, not anyone else. I don't kill unless I have to. That's how I work." Niamh raised her chin. "If you hand me over to those guards, we both know they'll kill me once they realise what I am."

"I won't let that happen. Maybe I can stop them from finding out you're a mind whisperer."

"How? If that doesn't kill me, being from the Order of Blood will."

"I'll figure something out." Darius tugged at her arm.

Nyx won't forgive you, Sirin remarked, *and you know it. Do you want to lose her?*

Darius ignored her. If he thought about Nyx, he'd never see this through. He needed time to come up with a solution for this mess.

"Please don't do this," Niamh said. "I spent years searching for someone like me." She gave a sad smile. "Now I have a sister and I finally have a chance to know her."

"You almost killed her. You won't stop until you finish the job."

"I—I can't finish it. Not now."

"Do you really expect me to believe that?" He scoffed. "You almost succeeded in killing her."

"Yes, and I hate myself for it. But I didn't know who she was."

Darius turned away and stiffened. He didn't want to believe her, but he didn't see any deception in her eyes. Nyx's pain still weighed heavily on his chest.

Handing Niamh over would mean certain death. Maybe he could protect her, maybe not. There were too many unknown risks. So many things could go wrong.

Darius blew out a breath. Spirits help him.

"If I let you go; will you swear to me you will never try to kill Nyx again? Make an unbreakable oath."

An unbreakable oath was a deal to never do something. It was binding by magic. If someone dared to break it, they would die as a result.

"Are you mad? I—" Niamh gulped when he glowered at her.

"I'll do it." She grasped his arm to seal the oath.

Energy jolted between them.

"Good, now you will leave this realm and never return."

"But—but my sister—"

"Leave. You're not safe here. Nyx doesn't want you dead. You're free to go. If I find out you lied about anything or you become a threat to us, I'll kill you myself." Darius yanked the cuff off her wrist.

Niamh hesitated. "You really love her, don't you?"

"What's that got to do with anything?"

"Most men wouldn't do such a thing. I won't forget it." She turned to leave. "Nor will my sister, either."

"Find sanctuary among the Varden. Take this." He handed her a small scroll. "It's a pardon written by my father. It should keep you safe for a while."

"Thank you." Niamh nodded. "You can believe me when I say I am not about to let anyone hurt my sister either." She then disappeared into the trees.

Darius hoped he wouldn't live to regret his decision.

CHAPTER 24

Don't mind him. He just wants to keep you safe.

Nyx jumped when an unknown voice rang through her mind. She turned around as Darius climbed onto Sirin's back.

She won't forgive you, the voice told him. Good gods, could she hear Sirin now?

Talking to dragons was Darius's power, not hers.

So how had she heard the dragon? Was it because she and Darius were linked now?

She would have been excited, if she didn't feel like death. Anger at Darius heated her blood.

Nyx couldn't believe he'd taken Niamh into custody, knowing what happened to her. She hadn't even had a chance to talk to her sister yet. She didn't know how to feel about Niamh either. Or the fact Darius had chosen duty over her.

She shouldn't have been surprised. He was part of the Forest Guard, but it still hurt.

"Nyx, are you alright?" Ranelle put her hand on her shoulder.

She shook her head. Part of her wanted to cry, but she wouldn't break down. Not here.

"You need to rest—you came pretty close to death. It will take you a few days to recover," Lucien said. "I'll carry you back."

"Days? But I—" She gritted her teeth. "I don't know what Niamh is capable of."

Ranelle glanced around, uneasy. "Let's get out of here. The assassin could come back."

Nyx stumbled and Lucien picked her up. "Put me down. I'll be fine. You don't need to worry about Niamh. I don't think she will hurt me—not now she knows who we are to each other."

"You should be dead right now. Let's just head back to the castle," Ranelle replied. "Good gods, I've never seen anyone use power like Darius did. No one except the Archdruid."

"Archdruid? Wait, was that the power I felt?" She furrowed her brow.

Lucien and Ranelle glanced at each other.

"I think so." Ranelle nodded. "Which means Darius could be the next Archdruid instead of—"

"Be quiet," Lucien hissed. "We shouldn't talk about this out in the open. Draw a circle so we can transport out of here."

"No, wait." Part of Nyx wanted to stay and look for Niamh again. "Lucien, do you think you could track Niamh?"

Lucien hesitated. "Are you sure you want to find her?"

Nyx bit her lip. Did she? She didn't know how to feel. Her only sisters were her foster sisters. And she'd already lost them. She had never imagined having a blood sister. Much less a possible twin.

"I need to talk to her. But maybe that would be better done when I don't feel like death."

Ranelle traced a circle and runes on the ground.

Nyx didn't enjoy being jostled around as Lucien carried her into the castle.

"We should call Ada to come and help you," Ranelle remarked.

"I'm not an invalid. I can take care of myself."

Lucien carried her up to the room she directed him to. It was right next to Darius'.

Ranelle gasped. "Darius gave you this room?"

Nyx frowned. "Yes. Why?"

"This room is usually reserved for the princess of the castle."

Nyx didn't know much about castles. Rooms were rooms to her. She snorted. "I'm no princess. The druid gave it to me in case the assassin somehow got to me again."

Darius didn't care where she slept. Nor did he treat her like a servant, either.

"Come, Nyx. You know he has feelings for you." Ranelle gave her an incredulous look.

Nyx grimaced. "Please don't say that. We are not a couple."

"I'm sorry about your argument," Ranelle remarked. "He's in a tough position."

"It's fine." Nyx looked away. Just another reminder given she and the druid weren't meant to be. That they could never be together. She didn't want to talk

157

about their argument, much less think about it.

Lucien scoffed. "Tough position? He's only doing his duty and what he feels is right."

"So, it's right for him to sentence Niamh to death then?" Nyx's hands clenched. "I thought I meant more to him than that. This just proves it can never work between us. I guess I should accept the fact I'm doomed to be alone forever."

"I didn't say that."

"It doesn't matter. Mind whisperers don't get to fall in love or be with anyone romantically."

"That's not true. You and Darius are perfect for each other." Ranelle squeezed her shoulder.

"Most lykaes can't be with anyone other than their kia either," Lucien supplied.

"Kia? What's a kia?" Nyx slumped back on the soft bed.

"It's the lykae's term for a destined mate." Ranelle rolled her eyes. "Lykaes believe they need the other half of their soul so they can control their inner beasts." She snorted.

Lucien scowled at her. "A kia is the light to our darkness. Don't you dragons believe in destined mates as well? Or do you just force anyone you want to interbreed with you?"

Nyx closed her eyes as they continued bickering. Exhaustion weighed heavily on her.

"Nyx, how did you recognise Niamh?" Ranelle wanted to know.

Nyx opened her eyes again. "I remembered something. I saw her as a little girl. I got confused due to the poison." She yawned. "How can I have a twin, though?"

"It's odd she doesn't remember her past, either. Do you remember anything else?"

Her eyelids fluttered, she didn't have the strength to keep them open.

"Let her sleep," Lucien whispered. "I'm not sure how she survived. She should have been dead before she got through that shield."

"I think the sharing created a strong link between her and Darius." Ranelle sighed. "I shouldn't have suggested it."

"Why not? It worked."

"Yes, but it made them both realise they have feelings for each other," Ranelle hissed.

"How can Darius have feelings for her?"

A harsh sound shook the air.

"Ouch! What was that for?" Lucien growled.

"Because you're judging her for being fae," Ranelle snapped.

"I'm not. I have nothing against the fae."

"No, you just judge my race instead." Ranelle sounded angry.

"I never—" Lucien sighed. "I'm not judging. I just meant Darius never falls in love with anyone."

"You don't have to be married to fall in love or have children, wolfsbane," Ranelle snapped. "I'm not surprised. I've never seen Darius with anyone the way he is with her. She accepts him and he accepts her."

Nyx drifted off to sleep and didn't hear anything else they said.

This time she found herself back in the garden, running with Niamh. She looked to be around ten. The same age they had been when they were abandoned.

Then an image of a burning woman appeared.

Nyx jolted awake. Her room stood in darkness, only thin slivers of moonlight coming in through the window.

The bed felt big and unfamiliar. She'd spent the last few nights in Darius' bed. It felt strange not feeling his warmth beside her.

Nyx turned over on her side. She wouldn't sleep next to him again.

Maybe Ambrose had been right. In what world could they be together? He'd already shown her it wouldn't work between them.

After a while, she climbed out of bed. Was Niamh in custody? Had they already sentenced her to death?

Talking to Darius didn't appeal to her, so she had to be careful she didn't wake him. Curse their link.

She hadn't meant to sleep for so long, though.

Putting on her boots, she traced runes on the floor to transport herself outside. The runes flared with light, then fizzled out.

Curse it, why wouldn't it work? She needed to get out of the castle for a while. To think and clear her mind.

Nyx scrambled onto the window ledge. Her limbs moved like heavy weights.

Shouldn't the poison have worn off by now? They said she had been cured, but it had sapped her of all her strength. She wanted to go and find her sister. At least then they could talk.

Nyx took a deep breath then leapt from the window. Her wings flapped hard and fought to keep her airborne but had no strength in them.

Damn that poison!

Something big flew under her and caught hold of her. Nyx winced as she landed against hard scales.

"Sirin?" she gasped.

Silly girl, you're too weak to fly.

"Why can I hear you now? I've never heard you before."

Your bond with Darius is becoming stronger.

Nyx scoffed at that. "We don't have a bond. We're just linked because of the mind sharing."

I know what I feel when you do have a bond. It's stronger than you think. Where are we going then?

She shrugged. "I don't know. I just need... to get out of here."

I can do that.

She furrowed her brow. I thought you didn't like me?

I never said that.

Sirin glided over the forest like moonlight.

It felt odd to be the only one riding her. Nyx was so used to Darius being in front of her.

"Sirin, go towards the old city."

What about the Varden? They'll be angry after yesterday.

Her frown deepened. Angry over what?

Because Darius refused to let them keep your sister in their custody.

Yes, I already know he arrested her. On second thought, take me to the guardhouse. I need to talk to her.

He didn't take her there.

Her mouth fell open. "What do you mean? You said he took her from the Varden."

Yes, but he let her go.

"He what?"

He did it to help you. You mean more to him than you know.

Nyx winced and her heart skipped a beat. "Maybe it's better for us to stay friends."

You don't believe that.

She sighed. "I don't know what to believe anymore."

You belong with Darius. You know that in your heart. In the end, he did the right thing.

Fly over the old city. I need to find Niamh. Something tells me she will be near there.

Sirin flapped her wings harder.

When the old city came into view, they circled around. But Nyx couldn't sense Niamh anywhere. Had Niamh already left?

160

CHAPTER 25

Darius spent the rest of the day patrolling. He called his mentor in thought to check on him. Ambrose confirmed he had gotten home but had an awful headache.

Darius checked in on Nyx too, but she hadn't been in her room. As much as he wanted to go and be by her side, he had to spend the next day performing his usual guard duties.

Finally, we can go home. Darius sighed to Sirin.

Sirin snorted. *You want to see your fae again.*

He gaped at his dragon. *She's not my anything.* He frowned. *You're not jealous, are you?*

It had been him and Sirin for so long. Darius knew dragons could get jealous if their bonded rider spent a lot of time with someone else.

Sirin snorted again. *No, I like Nyx. I didn't at first, but she is kin now.*

Kin? Darius arched an eyebrow.

She's a part of you. That makes her kindred.

Darius gaped at her. "What? How? She's not—" He rubbed the back of his neck.

We both know you're in love with her. So don't bother denying it.

"I am not!" he snapped. "I can't be. And you should know why."

You'll find a way. I never thought the next Archdruid would be my rider. Sirin bowed her head.

"Next what?" He burst out laughing. "I'm not the heir."

Sirin huffed. *You used the Archdruid's power. We all felt it. And sharing your power with Nyx created a bond between you.*

"I didn't share—" Darius didn't have time to ponder what the dragon meant.

Ambrose appeared in a bright flash of light. "Two more people have been found dead."

Darius turned away from the dragon. "Who? And where?"

"Another servant and a high fae lady. Both at the palace."

"Aren't the palace guard investigating?" He hated going to the palace. It would be near impossible to perform his guard duties there.

"One of them contacted me. We need to hurry. If the palace guard looks into this, news will spread fast, and that could give Isabella the chance to spin a web of lies."

"I am in the Forest Guard. I have no authority in the palace—" he protested.

"As the Archdruid's son, you do. Time to put your rank to good use." Ambrose motioned for him to join him in the circle.

Darius groaned. It had been a long day already. But Ambrose had a point. He didn't want Isabella, or even his mother, covering anything up.

"Sirin, fly home. Keep an eye on things there."

I'll check on Nyx, too.

Darius and Ambrose reappeared outside the palace and made their way inside. The guard at the door gave Ambrose a nod, then stepped aside.

Darius followed his mentor in. Two bodies lay slumped on the floor. One woman lay propped against the bed. A glassy eyed man lay only a few feet away.

"Why did the guard call you?" Darius furrowed his brow.

"Because he has orders to do so. It's useful in times like this." Ambrose went over to the first body. "They look like they were killed here. Not transported from somewhere else like the other two were."

Darius knelt by the servant. "There's no signs of torture. Just blood around their noses."

"We'll have to get Alaric to check. Too bad Nyx is not up to using her powers."

"What good would that do?" Darius raised an eyebrow. "Her powers only work on the living."

"Perhaps she would sense something." Ambrose rubbed his chin and tapped his staff on the floor. The room shimmered with bright blue light. "No sign of any spells being used."

There were faint marks visible on the bodies. Darius frowned in concentration. Something about them seemed familiar to him somehow. Like he had seen them before. "Holy spirits," he muttered and rose to his feet. "These are the marks of a mind whisperer."

Ambrose clutched his staff. "You mean Nyx?"

He shook his head. "No. Yes. I mean, this is like how she defended herself from those fae several months ago." He motioned to the bodies. "Do you know of anyone else who could have killed this way?"

"Death magic can manifest itself in many different forms."

Darius shook his head again. "Alaric can check, but I doubt he will find any other marks. Nyx couldn't have done this. She is too weak. Judging by the time of death, she would have been trapped in the old city when they were found."

"The assassin, perhaps then. Since we have another mind whisperer in our midst."

"Why kill these people? What connection do they have?" Darius knelt by the servant and pulled back his hair. "An Andovian." He headed over to the woman's body. "Her ears have been clipped."

"Two Andovians. I think you need to find the assassin."

"She's Nyx's sister."

Ambrose gave him a hard look. "Does Nyx have you under her power now?"

"Of course not." Darius scowled. He couldn't say he trusted Niamh, either. Not after what she had done.

"Good, then stop letting your emotions get the best of you."

"But she was trapped in the old city, too. She used her power to get through the shield. Wouldn't she have been weakened?"

"All mind whisperers are different. Some recover quicker than others."

"This is why I don't trust you anymore." Darius's fists clenched. "How can I work with you when you don't give me any answers? If you know something about mind whisperers—"

"I was bound to one once, but it was years ago." Ambrose's jaw tightened. "Before you ask, no. The one who bound me to her died a long time ago."

Darius gaped at him. "Why didn't you say anything?"

Ambrose had always been a private man. He shared his

experiences with magic, but never much else about his life. He never married or had children, from what Darius knew.

"Because I blocked out most of that time. It's best forgotten."

"Bound? Do you mean a soul bond?"

People could take the joining vows and their souls would become bound to each other forever.

Ambrose gave a harsh laugh. "I was enslaved by her power. That's why I warned you not to become involved with Nyx. Even if you think you love her, your feelings for each other will destroy you both."

Darius looked away. "We are not involved. She's my best friend, that's all."

Ambrose snorted. "I saw the fear in your eyes today. You're letting your emotions cloud your judgement, boy."

"Can we focus on this?" Darius motioned to the bodies. "Is there a way to prove a mind whisperer did this?"

Ambrose rubbed his chin. "Perhaps, I don't know everything about them."

After he had done a sweep of the room, he had the bodies taken off to Alaric for some more testing. Darius questioned both guards and servants, but no one had seen anyone go in or out of the lady's chambers. He breathed a sigh of relief when he finally got to the castle. It looked a little homier. Ada had filled the place with furniture, tapestries, books, and much more. He had no idea where it had all come from. He went up to Nyx's room to check on her. Then he could drag himself to bed.

"Glan," he muttered the word for clean just to freshen himself up.

He couldn't remember the last time he'd been so drained. When he got to her room, he found it empty.

Darius scanned the castle with his mind and sensed her outside.

He headed down to the grounds behind the castle. The garden had become barren due to the lack of cultivation.

Nyx sat on the ground talking to Sirin.

"You're talking to Sirin?" He arched a brow. *What have you told her?* he asked his dragon.

Many things, Sirin chortled.

"It's cold. Shouldn't you be resting inside?" Darius cut her off. He didn't want to discuss any embarrassing memories.

"No, I had to feel grounded. Being close to the earth rejuvenates energy." Her feet were bare and her long pink hair hung loosely around her shoulders.

"Night, Sirin." Darius patted his dragon.

Sirin roared and took off.

"Since when can you talk to her? I thought you couldn't hear her."

"So did I. Now I can. You said she didn't talk much."

"She doesn't."

"She does to me." Nyx gave him a smug look. "Maybe she needed a girl to talk to."

Darius rubbed the back of his neck. "Listen, there's things I need to tell you. But first—"

"Sirin told me you let Niamh go. Why?"

"You know why. I care about you."

Nyx shook her head. "We can't do this, druid. Not anymore. We would be better off as friends, so we should stay that way. Anything else that has happened between us has to end now."

He gaped at her. "Why? Is this because of what happened with Niamh?"

"In part, yes. Today you had to choose between me and duty."

"I didn't just save her for you. I did it because it was the right thing for all of us."

"You shouldn't have had to make that choice. Which is why we need to stop this thing between us before it goes any further."

Darius couldn't believe what she was saying. "I want to be with you."

"I don't want to be with you. Whatever feelings we have for each other ends now." Nyx stepped away from him. "I'm tired. I'm going back to bed."

She walked away before he had a chance to say anything else.

CHAPTER 26

Nyx woke early the next morning. She got up, washed, and dressed.

Ada already had breakfast laid out in the small dining hall, so she helped herself to food. She raised a hand and the bowls of food levitated into the air. She still felt weak, but she had to find Niamh.

Still, she wouldn't go unprepared. She slipped on her sword bracelet. She didn't want to fight her sister, but she knew she needed to be prepared for anything.

Lucien stopped by last night and left a jar of poison antidotes. Including the poison Niamh had used on her yesterday. Nyx slipped some of the herb into her pocket. She looked more ready for battle than for meeting her long-lost twin.

Sister or not, Niamh might still decide to finish the job and kill her.

Nyx didn't know how to feel about having a biological sister. Part of her wanted and welcomed that missing link. Another part wanted nothing to do with Niamh, but she wouldn't judge her for being an assassin. She had no idea what Niamh had been through.

How had they become separated? Twins were supposed to have a special connection, weren't they? What had torn them apart? Why couldn't either of them remember their past?

Nyx headed outside and called for Sirin with her mind.

The dragon appeared a few moments later.

"I need your help with something," Nyx told her. "Can you take me out to Varden Forest? I'm too weak to fly that far."

Sirin crouched so Nyx could climb on. *Does Darius know?*

He won't mind. At least she hoped he wouldn't mind. *We'll be back before he wakes up.* She scrambled onto the dragon's back.

Varden Forest stretched out before them like a blanket of darkness in the early morning light.

Nyx pulled her wings around herself and shivered. She should have brought a cloak with her. But she needed to move and fight if Niamh turned on her. A cloak would hinder her.

Nyx had no idea where Niamh might be. Nor could she sense her presence.

Niamh could be anywhere.

Niamh? Nyx called out with her mind. *Niamh, I need to talk to you.*

She guessed Niamh would hear her. Their minds were open to each other on some level.

Sirin flew over the entire expanse of forest, but Nyx didn't sense anything.

There is no one here except the Varden and the other forest dwellers, Sirin remarked. Perhaps the assassin left.

She is in this realm somewhere. I know it. Maybe we should go back closer to Ambrose's house or to Alaris.

Orbs of gold light rose from somewhere in the forest. The lights danced around Sirin's head.

The dragon growled.

The orbs swirled around Nyx. She laughed as they tickled her face. "That's her. I'll fly—"

Sirin made a disgruntled sound. *No, I'm not leaving without you. Darius wouldn't be happy if I did.*

Darius and I are just friends. No matter how much she wished they could be more. She shrugged. *You don't need to worry about me.*

Sirin ignored her and dove headfirst into the canopy of trees.

Nyx yelped as branches bashed against her.

A few moments later, they landed with a thud. The dragon roared, her snout close to Niamh's face.

Niamh flinched but didn't back away. "You have a dragon."

Nyx laughed. "No, she is a friend. The druid is her rider."

Sirin lowered her head to the assassin and gave her a wary sniff. *This is not kindred.*

She's my kindred. Believe me.

"Could you please stop huffing at me?" Niamh grabbed the

167

dragon's snout.

"It's alright, Sirin. She won't hurt me, will you, Niamh?"

Niamh backed off and raised her hands in surrender. "Of course not."

"Go, Sirin. I'll call if I need you. You should leave before one of the Varden comes to warn you off."

Sirin snorted and drew closer to Niamh. *Do not harm my kindred, mind whisperer,* she warned loudly so Niamh would hear.

Niamh flinched. "Gods below, it can talk."

Sirin huffed, then took to the air.

"Of course she does."

"Why did she call you kindred?"

"Dragons only do that people who are important to them. Darius is her rider, not me." She ran a hand through her hair. "We need to talk."

"Indeed, we do." Niamh's icy blue eyes narrowed. "I don't remember you. So how do you know me?"

"You know what your heart tells you, don't you? I only caught a brief flash of memory."

"I'm not ruled by my heart." Niamh scoffed. "I prefer logic and instinct."

"You truly don't remember anything from your childhood?" Nyx furrowed her brow.

Niamh shook her head. "I remember being under a tree. The druid told me you were found under one too."

She nodded. "I was alone when they found me in Joriam. Where were you found?"

"In Ereden—in the Elven lands. You seem to have fared far better."

"Hardly. Before I came to Andovia, I was sold into slavery. I grew up as a thief until last year. Darius saved me from execution, and now I'm his servant. Well, sort of."

Niamh's expression darkened. "How can you work for him? His father—"

"He's nothing like his father, believe me."

Her newfound sister didn't look convinced. "I'm still not sure I believe this. How can we be sisters?"

"What do your instincts tell you?" She crossed her arms.

She'd always expected finding family would be a happy event filled with tears and love. How naïve she had been to think that. That had been a child's fantasy. Nothing more.

"Maybe I can show you the memory I saw." Nyx held out her hands. "Perhaps it might trigger your memory too."

Niamh hesitated. "I still have orders to kill you. You have no idea of some of the awful things I've done."

"I'm not perfect either. I—I used my power to kill too. But I didn't mean to." Nyx raised her chin. "You won't kill me."

"How can you be so sure? I've never failed my Order. They raised me to be the perfect killer, and that's what I am."

"Just take my hands and I'll show you the memory."

Niamh flinched, then grasped Nyx's hands. Energy jolted between them. Their eyes met and the memory unfolded.

Nyx chased her around the garden. They both giggled. "Niamh?" Young Nyx called out. "Niamh, where are you?"

Niamh pulled back. "That's all? Why can't we see more?"

She shook her head. "I don't know. No magic I've tried so far can show me anything more."

"I do believe you." Niamh frowned. "How did you remember us in the garden?"

"I don't know. I felt so confused by the poison."

"Maybe the poison triggered it. I could take it and—" Niamh sighed. "Although I doubt it would do much good. I have immunity to it."

"How?"

"You don't want to know."

"Yes, I do. I want to know you."

Niamh drew away. "If I don't complete my mission, the Order of Blood will kill me."

"No, they won't. We're sisters. We can look out for each other." Nyx paused. "I need you to tell me the truth, though. Have you killed anyone in Andovia since you arrived here?"

Niamh yanked her hands away. "So much for sticking together. You do think I killed those people."

Nyx repressed a sigh. Why did her twin have to be as hard-headed as her?

"I'm asking you, yes. But in truth, no. I don't think you did." Like Niamh, she trusted her instincts, too.

"Good, because I was sent to kill you, not anyone else. I don't waste my time killing people who aren't important."

She put her hands on her hips. "Then who did? Because two of those deaths were caused by the touch of a mind whisperer."

Niamh's eyes widened. "I never use my touch to kill people. I know better than to leave a trace."

"Then we need to find out who did." Nyx tossed her plait over her shoulder. "Maybe we should go and see my friend, Lucien. He might be able to run some tests and see if the killer is a mind whisperer or not."

"What kind of tests?" Niamh narrowed her eyes.

She shrugged. "I don't know. He uses all sorts of concoctions with herbs and blood—"

"Blood? I'm not giving my blood to anyone. That would give them power over me."

"Will you just agree to come with me?" Nyx rubbed her temples. "This realm isn't safe for mind whisperers, so we need to be careful."

"Then why are you here?"

"Because I convinced people I'm not very powerful."

Niamh snorted. "I felt your touch. You're strong—stronger than me."

"I doubt that. You're strong too. Have you ever met another mind whisperer?"

Niamh shook her head. "The Order told me they were all wiped out a century ago."

"There has to be one left. Or at least there was. How else did we get here?"

"But why were we left? Why don't we remember anything?"

"I wish I knew. I know somewhere we might get some answers. Come on." Nyx traced a circle and runes on the ground then stepped inside it.

"You're using druid magic?" Her sister furrowed her brow.

"Er... Darius taught me." She didn't want to tell Niamh about the mind sharing, she doubted Niamh would react well.

"How did you end up as a servant? I'm amazed he didn't kill you, given his father's work."

"He's not like his father. He is different. I ended up here after—"

"They told me you killed a man in Joriam. Is it true?"

Nyx winced. Did Niamh want it to be true? How many people had she killed? She pushed those thoughts away. She didn't want to think about that.

"No, it's not. A darkling killed him. But I killed two fae last year with my power." She shuddered. "I didn't mean to. They tried to kill me first." Sometimes she still saw their eyes in her dreams. "You said you don't use your power to kill?"

"Of course not. It leaves a trace. Weapons are cleaner. Poison is good too."

Nyx shuddered again. "Yeah, I'm familiar with that."

"I already apologised for what happened."

"How much do you know about me?" Nyx put her hands on her hips and stepped out of the circle.

"Not much. Your name, that you're Valeran's servant. No one said…" Niamh cursed. "Gods below, they knew. They had to."

"Who? Who sent you to kill me?"

"The Order of Blood. That's all I know. I don't ask why I'm being sent somewhere or why they want someone dead."

"Why not? I would ask."

"Because I don't question my orders. They only told me a few details about you." Niamh shook her head.

"So, what happens now? If you don't kill me?"

"I won't kill you. I made an unbreakable oath to your druid, he made me do it so I can't harm you in any way."

Her mouth fell open. She knew about unbreakable oaths from Darius's knowledge, but she never imagined he'd do that.

"He's not *my* druid. We are… friends. Heck, I'm not sure what we are anymore."

"You haven't used your touch on him?"

"Of course not. Well, I tried to when we first met but he is immune to it."

"Odd. I didn't think anyone could fall in love with a mind whisperer."

"Why does everyone keep saying that? He doesn't love me."

Niamh snorted. "Yes, he does. I can see it in his eyes."

"Maybe we should try a spell to see if we can remember anything else." She didn't want to talk or think about Darius for a while.

Niamh hesitated. "I know some Elven magic, but I don't know any spells to retrieve memories. It wasn't part of my training."

"I know a spell and somewhere safe we can cast it."

They used the circle to transport to the ring of standing stones.

"Isn't this a place for druid magic?" Niamh furrowed her brow.

"No, any magic can be used here. But I can only use druid magic. I've never tried Elven magic."

"I thought only druids could use it?"

"Druids have one of the easiest and most versatile magic systems since their power comes from nature. It makes it easy to learn."

She and Niamh sat down in a circle and faced each other.

"I've only tried this once, and it didn't work all that well," Nyx admitted. "Maybe the two of us need to do it."

"How come you remembered me yesterday? I've never remembered anything from before I woke up under the tree."

Nyx shrugged. "No idea. Maybe because my mind was more open to it. But it proved my memories—our memories are still locked inside us somewhere." She held out her hands. "Ready?"

Niamh took them and nodded. Light flared between them the moment their fingers touched. Odd, they didn't know each other, yet on some level Nyx's power recognised her.

Maybe they had known each other until something had parted them.

Together, they chanted the spell.

Light flared around them, then knocked them apart.

Nyx winced as pain sliced through her head.

"Why did that happen?" Niamh rubbed her forehead.

Nyx blew out a breath. "Because something is preventing us from reaching our memories."

"Maybe we should try again."

"It won't work. It will only cause us more pain." She groaned and searched her mind for more possible spells.

Nothing came to her.

What would it take to get the answers they needed?

CHAPTER 27

Darius headed home. He'd spent all day trying and doing everything he could think of to get answers about the recent deaths.

So far, he found nothing. No connection. Other than the fact they had to have been there the day his father executed the queen. But they all seemed so random. Isabella hadn't made any more moves, either. But with his mother in charge at court, he doubted she would make a move for the throne right now.

Odd, the day they had seen Isabella in the council meeting chamber, she seemed like her old self. Yet today, when seeing her in the temple, she looked as demure as the night he saw her in her room.

He hadn't seen Nyx all week. She hadn't joined him on patrol or called to say where she was. He hated the growing distance between them. Worse still, he couldn't ignore the constant need to feel her presence. It had been there since they had done the mind sharing.

Darius reached out to her a few times with his mind, and he had been met by a wall of silence. That irritated him even more.

When he got to the castle, he found it in darkness. No sign of Nyx or Ada anywhere. The place felt big and empty. He wondered if it would ever feel like home the way Ambrose's house had.

Pacing up and down in front of the empty fireplace did nothing to ease his tension. Going to the Spirit Grove hadn't yielded any results, either.

Maybe it was time to resort to more drastic measures.

Darius headed outside through the gardens until he reached a small growth of trees. Moving past the trees, he came to a concealed entrance for a cave and headed inside. The cavern walls glittered with crystals. He stripped off his shirt and boots.

After a few moments, glowing touches appeared over his arms, shoulders, and torso. Each mark represented the levels of training he mastered, both as a druid and higher magic sorcerer.

Most of the time, the marks stayed invisible, and he preferred it that way. If people saw the advanced higher magic, he knew some would fear it was dark magic. Then he'd be no better than his father.

Besides, it wasn't as if he'd had a choice in learning it. It was either that or endure days of abuse from his mother.

Darius pushed the thoughts away and raised his arms. Letting go of his grip on his magic.

Lightning arced above him, sending bolts straight through his body. Lightning was his element and flowed through him as easily as breathing. More lightning flared between his fingers.

Darius motioned with his hands and muttered words of power. A swelling portal formed between his fingers. It expanded as he released it.

He hadn't used spirit magic in months. This was his mother's gift, and he hated using sorcery. Yet he couldn't deny it was part of him. And now it might be the only way to get answers.

The portal swirled with mist and light until tendrils of smoke poured out.

The smoke coalesced into a humanoid figure with glowing amber eyes.

"Zephyr," Darius addressed the spirit by its true name.

Spirits could only be controlled by their true names, especially dark spirits. They moved around from the underworld and this world but could never stay here for long.

"Valeran." The spirit's voice grated like nails against stone.

"People are being killed here. Close to the old city. I need to know whose causing it." He motioned to one of the bodies. They were preserved by magic with the help of Lucien. They hadn't burned them because Lucien had been experimenting to see if he could glean anything from them.

Darius didn't usually keep dead bodies lying around and hadn't told anyone else about them, but these were exceptional circumstances.

"Inhabit one of these bodies and tell me what you can find from them."

Smoke billowed into the body of the first victim and convulsed as Zephyr took control.

"Well?" Darius demanded. He wanted this over with. He hated this magic. Hated how part of him enjoyed the icy feel of its touch and the control and dominance that came with it.

"Who killed these people?"

"She who hides in shadow will soon rise again."

"Who lurks in shadow?"

"She who walked among the immortals. She who hides in shadow."

Darius gritted his teeth and raised his hand. "Enough riddles. Give me a name."

"We cannot speak her name. For she hides in shadow. Only when she rises will her name be spoken again."

He closed his hand into a fist, making Zephyr screech in agony as his power gripped the spirit. "Give me name. Now!" More lightning burst around him. When he opened himself up to this magic, he opened up to everything. Including his lightning. More energy shot around him.

"I—I can't..." the spirit growled.

"Then go. Find the killer and report back to me. Go!"

Zephyr vanished and Darius motioned for the portal to close, but it wouldn't. His magic wanted to stay free. It was *glad* to be free from the tight hold he kept it under. More lightning pulsed through him. "Close, damn it," he cursed, and willed the portal to disperse.

More tendrils of smoke poured out.

No, more spirits.

If he didn't know their names, he couldn't control them. Darius raised his hands. Lightning shot in all directions. Maybe the bodies and potential of empty vessels drew them.

He kept one hand on the portal and used the other to direct the lightning at the bodies. In a burst of light, the bodies evaporated.

Come on, close.

"Leave," he growled.

One by one, the spirits dispersed, but the portal refused to close. More lightning blasted around him, disintegrating rocks in the process.

"Druid?" Nyx appeared in the cave entrance. "What are you doing?"

"Nyx, get out of here." He pushed more power against the portal.

Nyx ran over and stared at the portal, wide-eyed. "Spirit magic," she gasped.

"Nyx, go. Now!" Sweat broke out over his forehead and he sank to his knees.

The portal grew even bigger, but Nyx didn't budge.

"Nyx, please go. If I can't stop this, I won't have you getting hurt."

Nyx bent over and kissed him, hard.

Darius's eyes widened. She gasped as the lightning surged through to her.

Darius put his hands out to shove her away. Was she mad? She had to know how dangerous absorbing his lightning would be.

Even so, Nyx pulled him closer, taking more of his power in. Light flashed around them.

He gasped for breath when the power finally faded. "What are you doing?"

Her eyes flashed both with lightning and anger. "What am I doing? What are *you* doing? I can't believe you were using spirit magic! Or that you kept those bodies here."

Darius took several deep breaths. "You have no idea what kind of danger you put yourself in."

"Me? Your power doesn't hurt me. I can't believe you were stupid enough—"

"How did you know about the bodies?"

"Because your mind was open to me. I felt and saw everything. If you hadn't been blocking me all week—"

"You haven't said two words to me either."

"Why would you open a portal like that? You might think you hid parts of yourself during the sharing, but you didn't." Nyx glowered at him.

"I had to do something. Nothing else is working."

"You put yourself at risk, not to mention others. I know how much you struggle with sorcery."

"What else did you expect me to do?" Darius crossed his arms.

"You could have asked me for help!"

"That's hard to do when you haven't spoken to me all week."

"That's…" Nyx sighed. "True enough. But you could've asked me, and I would've helped you."

"Would you? I know you're thinking about leaving."

"I'm not leaving. Just don't do something stupid again." She gave him a shove, then ran her hand over the marks on his chest. "Is this why you never let me touch you?"

Darius looked away. "I tried everything I can think of to get rid of them, but they never fade. So I keep them glamoured."

"You don't have to hide anything from me." She stared at him for a moment longer, then turned to leave.

He caught hold of her hand. "I miss you. Talking to you. I just… miss you."

She blew out a breath. "Please. Don't. It doesn't work between us. It can't."

"Why not? Because of what happened with Niamh?"

"That's just one of many reasons. I'm not leaving. We still have to work together. It's better if we don't fall in love. It'll just make things more complicated."

"But I do—"

"Master!" Ada rushed into the cave. "Master, come quick!"

"What is it?" Darius grabbed his shirt, conscious of his marks being on display.

"It's Master Ambrose. He's been attacked!"

CHAPTER 28

Nyx and Darius hurried to Ambrose's house.

She had no idea what to expect to find there. Ada hadn't given them any details about what happened. Just that she'd found him unconscious.

"Ambrose?" Nyx called out.

"In here," Ada called back.

Ambrose lay crumpled on the floor, his eyes blank and wide open. Nyx put a hand over her mouth. "Is he…?"

"No, he's breathing." Darius knelt by his mentor. "He's been stunned by magic. I've never seen anything like this, though. Ada, how long has he been like this?"

"Since I came to get you. That Varden woman brought him back on her white horse."

"That must be Velestra," Nyx remarked. "Is she still here?"

"No, she left after she dropped Master Ambrose off." Ada shook her head.

"Did Velestra say anything else?" Darius asked the brownie.

"She said she found him outside of the old city. But she didn't see who attacked him."

Nyx gasped when a shadow moved in the corner of the room. She stepped back. "What's that?"

Darius rose and his face hardened. "It's the spirit I summoned. Zephyr, I sent you to find the killer, not to—"

The spirit's icy energy washed over her. Cold and unnatural.

"I did as you commanded, master. I found the killer." Zephyr's voice came out harsh and gravelly. "He lies before you."

Darius glanced down at Ambrose, then back at the spirit. "That's impossible."

"I think it's telling the truth." Nyx moved to Darius' side.

"Ada, fetch Alaric," Darius told her. "Speak of this to no one."

"Yes, master." Ada scurried away.

"I don't sense any deception from that… spirit." Nyx looked away when the glowing eyes turned on her.

"Listen to the mind whisperer. She can see the truth."

"But—but he wouldn't—I've known him my whole life. He wouldn't kill anyone."

"Wouldn't he? He's very powerful and there's so much we don't know about his past," Nyx pointed out.

"It makes no sense, though. What reason would he have to kill those people?"

"He probably wants to stop the rising," Zephyr growled.

"What?" Nyx narrowed her eyes. "What does that mean?" She scanned the spirit with her mind but didn't get much from him except the feeling of strong energy.

"The rising will come soon. She who hides in the shadows will soon reappear."

"Zephyr, can you find out who did this to Ambrose?" Darius motioned towards his unconscious mentor.

"I will try but she hides in shadow."

"That doesn't matter. Find whoever it is, but don't get too close. Just find out who they are." Darius waved his hand, and the spirit faded. "Holy spirits, how could this happen?" He paced up and down. "It makes no sense."

"Maybe I can read him." Nyx knelt and reached out to touch Ambrose.

"Don't! We don't know what kind of magic we're dealing with." Darius ran a hand through his hair. "Why would he do this?"

Nyx couldn't believe it either, but she'd only known Ambrose for about a year. He wasn't a father to her like he had been to Darius.

"Maybe… maybe he had a reason."

"There's never a good reason for murder, Nyx."

"It was murder, yes. But we don't know what happened."

She got up and put her hand on his shoulder. "We'll figure this out."

Alaric appeared in a flash of light. "What happened to him?"

"We don't know," Nyx answered. "The Varden found him outside the old city."

"Have you called the Guard?" Alaric glanced between them.

Darius stopped dead in the middle of pacing. "No, we—"

"We were too shocked to think about that. I'll call them." Nyx squeezed Darius's shoulder. "Will Ambrose be alright?"

Alaric knelt and held his hands over Ambrose. Light washed over the druid, but he didn't stir. "This is bad. It can't happen."

"Do you know what caused it?" Darius demanded.

"Sorcery, from the look of it. And something more. He's been touched by another magic."

"What?" Nyx frowned.

"I'd say a mind whisperer."

"Nyx was with me when the attack happened." Darius glanced over at her.

"Niamh was with me in the Varden village before that. She couldn't have done it either."

"Can you be sure?" Darius narrowed his eyes.

"Yes, she wouldn't do this. She wouldn't have had time to do anything." She shook her head. "If you don't believe me, I'll ask her. One thing I have learnt over the past few days is mind whisperers can't lie to each other." She waved her hand and Niamh appeared in a flash of light.

How did you do that? Darius asked.

I can move things with my mind, remember? Don't be so quick to accuse her. She fought the urge to glare at him.

"What's going on?" Niamh furrowed her brow.

"Did you do this?" Darius motioned to Ambrose.

"No, I was in the Varden's village with Nyx—until she left and then summoned me here."

"She is telling the truth." Nyx touched his shoulder and left their link open. *If you can't trust her, at least trust me.* She hoped he'd sense the truth through their link.

"I still can't see who else would do this. If he has been touched by a mind whisperer and it wasn't either of you…" He trailed off.

"There is another mind whisperer here." Nyx gasped. "But how…?"

"There's another mind whisperer?" Niamh's frown deepened. "Where?"

"Alaric, get Ambrose taken care of," Darius told him. "We'll see what else we can find out."

Alaric nodded. "I'll take him to my house. He'll be safer there." He and Ambrose vanished in a flash of light.

"How do I track a mind whisperer?" Darius resumed pacing again.

The sisters glanced at each other.

"I don't know." Nyx shrugged. "I can only sense Niamh because we're sisters."

"She's right. I can track people with my mind, but not another mind whisperer. Their thoughts would be shielded from me."

"You grew up with the Order. They trained you and disciplined you." Darius stared at Niamh, incredulous.

Niamh glowered at Nyx. "Do you tell him everything we talk about?"

"No, I haven't told him anything. Druid, stop wandering around in my mind," Nyx snapped. "If you want to know something, ask. Gods, I wish we never did that mind sharing."

Niamh gasped. "You did a mind sharing? Are you mad?"

Nyx and Darius shared a look.

"Never mind. You're in love." Niamh rolled her eyes.

"We are not," she and Darius said in unison. Pain stabbed through her chest at Darius' denial, but she pushed it away. "Niamh, can you find out who sent you to kill me?" Nyx asked.

"I suppose so. I have never had to ask before now."

"Good. It might help us find the killer. Go." Nyx waved her hand and Niamh vanished. "Druid?"

Darius had sunk into a chair and put his head in his hands. "I will call the Guard."

"No. Leave them out of this." He looked up. "I can't explain to them about Ambrose. It will lead to too many unwanted questions. Things we can't answer."

"Maybe we should look around and see what we can find in the house."

They headed into Ambrose's bedroom. Everything appeared neat and organised. The fourposter bed hung with heavy red linens. Books lined the table and desk.

"I've never been in here," Darius admitted.

"Never?"

"No, Ambrose is a very private man."

Nyx rifled through the books and papers on the desk. Darius turned his attention to the bookcase. She opened a book and a piece of paper fell out. "Druid?"

"What?"

"Look." She held out the paper. "It has all the names and more."

"These are the victim's names. I don't know who half—holy spirits," Darius cursed.

"What's wrong?" His panic washed over her as she realised she hadn't raised her shield again.

"I need to leave. Now." Darius dashed down the hall.

"Druid, wait!" Nyx called after him.

She found him outside on the platform that led down from the tree house. He whistled for Sirin.

"Where are you going?"

"I know who the next victim is. I have to get to her before anyone else does."

Nyx grabbed his arm. "Then I'm coming with you."

Darius hesitated. "What about Ambrose?"

"Alaric can take care of him. Saving the next victim is more important."

CHAPTER 29

"Are you going to tell me where we're going?" Nyx asked a few hours later. "Or who we're going to see?"

Open sky stretched out before them as Sirin flew over the rugged wilderness of rolling green hills. They hadn't seen a village or any sign of a settlement for miles. Normally flying brought Darius a sense of peace, but it did little to ease his churning thoughts now. "Promise me you won't reveal this place to anyone?"

Nyx scoffed. "Why would I?"

"I mean it, Nyx. No one can know where she is. If my father or anyone else found her, they would use her against me." He hadn't told her anything about where they were going and had been ignoring her questions since they had left Ambrose's house.

He did trust her, but this was one of his most closely guarded secrets. Even more closely guarded than the runes and other magic etched into his skin. But she already knew about those now, and she hadn't been repulsed by him in the way he'd expected.

"I promise."

Darius breathed a sigh of relief. "Good, we're almost there."

They flew several more leagues in silence. He was glad she didn't ask him any more questions about who they were going to see. Not like he'd expected her to. Nyx was curious by nature.

Sirin glided lower as mountains loomed below them. A small castle sat nestled between the icy caps.

Nyx gasped. "Why didn't we see that earlier?"

"Because it's protected by magic." Darius scrambled off Sirin and helped Nyx down. "I hope she's well today."

"She? Who are we going to see?" She frowned. "I don't know why you don't just tell me why we are here."

"I'll... show you." He took her hand and led her through the castle.

The guards bowed their heads as they passed.

A woman came out. "Lord Darius." She bowed her head. "What a pleasant surprise."

"Elizabeth, how's my grandmother?" A pang of guilt weighed in his chest. He hadn't been to visit his grandmother in the last few months since meeting Nyx.

"Quiet today. I can't say she'll recognise you," the woman replied. "She's in the garden."

"Thanks." Darius led Nyx down a hallway and out to a small garden.

A pit of dread formed in his stomach. He was used to his grandmother not recognising him. They had been close when he was younger, when she had still lived around his father. He had been the one to move her away from court and out of his father's grasp. It had taken a lot of effort to convince his father that his grandmother had left on her own.

A woman with long white hair dressed in a velvet green gown sat on a bench, trimming flowers.

"This is my grandmother. Rhian Valeran."

"That woman gave birth to your father?" Nyx put a hand over her mouth. "Good gods, how old is she? Hasn't your father been the ruling Archdruid for at least two centuries?"

"She's nothing like my father and yes, she is old. My grandfather went mad, but she kept the family together. At least until my father came of age." He grimaced. "I think all the terrible things she watched them do fractured her mind. Some days she doesn't recognise anyone and still thinks she's married to my grandfather. She would have been there when they executed the queen. My father made her watch—like he wanted her to be proud."

He didn't want to think about the kind of terrors his grandmother must have been forced to endure during the decades she had been married to his grandfather. He was surprised she had lasted this long, and that her fractured mind hadn't destroyed her long before now.

Nyx shuddered. "What if she can't remember? I don't know how my power will affect her. I can't force her to remember something that isn't in her mind anymore."

"That's where you can use your power. Help her to remember."

"Druid, I have never used my power on a fractured mind. What if I make her worse?" Nyx put her hands on her hips. "She could lose whatever sanity she has left. Do you really want to take that risk? The mind isn't a book that you can open whenever you want to. It's a lot more fragile than that."

Darius hesitated. He didn't want to risk his grandmother becoming any worse, but she was the only one with potential answers. Especially now Ambrose was gone, possibly for good. "Can you at least try?" Darius didn't want to subject his grandmother to Nyx's power, but they needed answers. "Gran?" Darius approached her and held on to Nyx's hand.

The old woman looked up. "Fergus, there you are, boy." She smiled. "Shouldn't you be in the tower studying?"

"No, Gran, it's me. Darius. I'm Fergus's son." He cursed himself for being away for so long. The longer he went with her not seeing him, the less likely she was to remember him.

Her brow knitted in confusion. "That can't be right." Darius cursed himself. The healer always warned him against confusing her. "I mean, yes, Mama. I'm here." Darius touched her shoulder. "I've missed you."

"I swear you grow more handsome every day, my boy." She pinched his cheek and stared at Nyx. Her eyes went wide. "Holy spirits, why have you brought that creature with you? She's dead— they're all supposed to be dead." She started screaming. "Why is that creature here? Spirits, so much death. I knew they would all come back to haunt us!"

"Gran, calm down."

"Why did you do it, Fergus?!" she screamed. "Why did you kill her? Why did you kill all of them?" She sank to her knees, tears streamed down her face. "Why did you kill them?! So much screaming."

Nyx came over and put her hand on Rhian's shoulder. "Calm down, no one is here to harm you." Her voice sounded almost soothing. "Why are you so afraid?"

185

"Because the queen and all the other mind whisperers swore vengeance on my family. I remember. You, Fergus, you murdered them all."

"Who? Who do you think I am?" Nyx frowned.

"You look just like those other mind whisperers. I'm so sorry. If I'd known, I'd never have let him harm all of you."

"What vow?" Darius asked. "What did the queen vow?"

"You were there, Fergus, you should remember."

"Tell us anyway," Nyx urged.

"She vowed vengeance. She said death itself wouldn't be able to hold her or the other mind whisperers." Rhian shuddered.

Darius turned to Nyx. "That must be why Isabella wants her spirit. She wants to use the queen against my father."

"That might explain why Isabella was killing people last year. But how does that help her find the queen?" She furrowed her brow.

Darius rose and rattled off a list of names. "I still don't see how they're connected."

Nyx soothed Rhian, who rocked back and forth.

"They were all there." Rhian stared at them. "All of them, you cleared them, Fergus."

"Cleared them of what?" Darius' brow creased. "What do you know about those people?"

"Please tell us," Nyx urged.

"You cleared them. They were close to the queen. You thought they helped to get her body out of the city before that shield went up." Rhian sniffed. "How is she here?" She motioned to Nyx.

"I'm not the queen. I'm just a mind whisperer."

Rhian snorted. "You look just like the other mind whisperers. You have their eyes—they haunt my dreams."

"Gran, do you know what happened to the queen? After she died?" Darius persisted.

"They took her body—her followers. To make sure no one, including you, desecrated it, Fergus." She shuddered again. "Her husband must've done it. I know you tortured him, and he never gave you anything."

"Her husband? He was there?" Nyx arched an eyebrow.

"Ambrose, of course. He never did reveal what he did with the bodies of the queen or the other mind whisperers."

Darius's blood ran cold. "Ambrose said he was bound to a mind whisperer. Holy bloody spirits."

"Druid, what if the queen's spirit didn't move on, or ended up trapped somewhere like we thought?" Nyx gripped his arm. "What if she's possessing someone and is still in Andovia? We need to get back there, fast."

"Wait, I can't just leave my grandmother. What if she is still a target?"

"Then you stay here and protect her, and I will go back."

"But—but what if something goes wrong and you need help?"

"Then I'll have my sister to help me."

CHAPTER 30

Nyx didn't like leaving Darius behind, but she understood why he wanted to stay with his grandmother to keep her safe. She needed to talk to Niamh and see if her sister had learnt anything. As well as check on Ambrose.

She reappeared in Alaric's sitting room and found Lucien there. "How's Ambrose?"

"The same. Alaric doesn't know what kind of magic has been used on him," Lucien replied. "Where have you been?"

"With Darius. We found the next victim. Darius stayed with her to ensure she's safe." Nyx approached the door to the spare bedchamber. "Maybe I should read Ambrose."

"Are you sure that's wise? What if the magic affects you?"

"I don't have to touch him to read him." She headed to the chamber and found Ambrose lying in the four-poster bed. His eyes were shut now.

Nyx stopped by his bedside and hesitated. She couldn't believe the man she thought of as a mentor could have killed those people.

She took a deep breath and let her power roam free.

What are you hiding from me, Ambrose? She released her power into his body.

A wall of resistance met her.

No thoughts or images came to her.

Pain stabbed through her head as her senses pushed against his mental block. She pushed harder, but the block wouldn't budge.

Nyx reached out. Would the magic that had stunned him do the same to her if she used her touch on him?

Then again, she didn't have to touch him to use her power. Maybe having another mind whisperer to help would be useful.

Niamh, I need you, she called out.

Niamh appeared in a whirl of green light. "Do you have to keep summoning me without asking?" She put her hands on her hips.

"Sorry, I do it without meaning to. Did you find anything out?"

Niamh shook her head. "Nothing. No one from the Order will respond to me, which is odd. Master Oswald always contacts me if I take too long to complete a mission."

"I need you to help me read Ambrose. Maybe we can see who attacked him." Nyx gave her sister a quick rundown of everything that happened when she had gone to see Darius's grandmother.

"I still can't believe there might be another mind whisperer out there," Niamh remarked.

"If there is, I'm not sure I want to know them. They're probably the one who sent you to kill me."

Niamh scowled. "You're right. I… I just wish we knew more about our origins."

Nyx nodded. "I know, but right now we need to find out who attacked Ambrose."

"Yes, we do." Niamh took her hand. "He has a mental block like your druid."

"Darius has natural immunity. Ambrose did something, I have read him before. Maybe together we can get through his block."

"I have never done that before. But then, most people aren't immune to my touch. Or at least they weren't before I came to this realm."

"Let's just see what we can get from his mind." Nyx let her power wash over Ambrose again and felt Niamh do the same.

Ambrose's block hit them like a solid wall of resistance.

"Maybe we need to physically touch him," Niamh suggested. "Touch makes people easier to read."

"What if the magic that ensnared him affects us? He's comatose."

"We're stronger than the other mind whisperer. We can do it." Niamh gripped her hand tighter.

They reached out with their free hands to touch Ambrose. The air reverberated around them as their magic flowed freely. An image of

Ambrose closing the shield came to them. Then a blast of energy knocked them backwards.

"What was that?" Niamh gasped.

"A memory, I think. Ambrose can get in and out of the old city."

"Is that why we haven't been able to get back in there?" Niamh frowned.

She and Nyx spent the past few days trying to get back through the shield. Nothing they had tried worked.

Nyx bent over and picked up Ambrose's staff. "Maybe we have a way of getting in now."

Nyx and Niamh transported to the edge of the old city. She hoped Ambrose wouldn't mind them taking the staff. She didn't even know whether she trusted the overseer now, but Lucien said he'd keep an eye on things.

"How does that work?" Niamh motioned to the staff.

"I'm not sure. Most druids don't use them. The crystal must channel or focus Ambrose's power somehow."

Nyx tapped the staff on the ground as she'd seen Ambrose do dozens of times. Nothing happened.

Niamh reached out, and the shield flared into existence. "How does Ambrose make it work?"

She shrugged and searched through her druid knowledge. It made her wish Darius was with them. Normally she had Darius or Ambrose to turn to for answers. Now she had neither of them.

Nyx scanned the crystal with her senses. It pulsed with energy, yet it didn't feel like Ambrose's magic, as she'd expected. "This doesn't hold Ambrose's power."

"What does it hold?" Niamh frowned. "I'm better with weapons than crystals. Elves don't use them and neither do the Order."

"I'm not sure." Nyx held the staff up as she'd seen Ambrose do.

Light flared through the crystal and the shield blazed to life around them.

Nyx moved closer, and an opening formed in the glowing wall of light. "Come on." She grabbed Niamh's hand.

"I hope we can open that thing again and get back through."

The shield closed around them.

"Guess it's time to find out what's been hidden in here."

The city's buildings appeared to be intact. Trees had long since claimed everything and covered the towering buildings with greenery.

Carts and carriages stood abandoned in the streets. It almost felt as though everyone had simply vanished.

"This place feels so eerie." Nyx shuddered. "It's so quiet."

No sounds of birds or even the wind passed through. Everything remained still, including the trees.

"I'm surprised anything could grow in here." Niamh glanced round, uneasy.

"The shield must let the elements through."

"What are you hoping to find?"

Nyx shrugged. "I don't know. Something. If we can find the place where the murders occurred, maybe we can find the other mind whisperer."

"I still want to know who they are."

"Just so we're clear, you're not going to kill them, are you?"

"What else would I do with them? They sent me to kill my sister. If that doesn't warrant death, I don't know what does."

"Niamh, your first instinct shouldn't be to kill."

Niamh narrowed her eyes. "What do you expect me to do, then? Get them to apologise and we forgive them?"

Nyx gave a harsh laugh. "Of course not."

"There's no justice in this world. It's kill, or be killed."

"Being a mind whisperer is about more than killing. People look to our kind for justice. Or at least they did. Don't you want to use your powers to help others?" She put her hands on her hips. "You can't go back to the Order of Blood, can you?"

Niamh sighed. "No, I don't know what I want to do now."

The crystal on Ambrose's staff glowed brighter.

"Why is it doing that?" Niamh furrowed her brow.

"I have no idea."

"Maybe you should use that to find the murder site. If Ambrose used magic, wouldn't it leave a trail?"

Nyx focused her mind on the staff and tapped it on the ground as Ambrose did. A glowing trail of energy appeared.

She and Niamh hurried down the street and past several buildings. Doors stood open, broken items littered the ground along with other debris.

"What happens when we find the other mind whisperer?" Niamh wanted to know. "Our powers won't work on them."

"We'll talk to them."

Her sister snorted. "Talk? What good will that do?"

"Fine, we'll wing it. You have weapons and so do I. But don't use them unless we have to." Nyx knew she would have to keep an eye on Niamh since she was always quick to go for her weapons. "We need to figure out who it is first. The queen could be possessing anyone."

"You have a weapon?"

Nyx pressed her bracelet and the sword blade popped out.

"Nice." Niamh grinned. "Where did you get that?"

"Darius made it for me. As a servant I can't go around with visible weapons."

The trail grew brighter. Up ahead loomed an enormous palace with spiralling towers and turrets. Its white stone had turned grey with age, but that didn't take away from the sheer magnitude of the place.

"No wonder the Archdruid wanted this place. It is twice the size of the Crystal Palace." Nyx held up the staff and the crystal pulsed with energy.

She scanned the building with her mind. The whole place hummed with energy.

"There are still wards here. How can that be? Wards require energy and maintenance."

"I should share minds with you. Your druid knowledge could come in handy." Niamh ran a hand through her long, blonde hair. "Do you think someone could be living here?"

"I would say no, but I don't know what to believe anymore."

They headed up the steps to the palace doors. Nyx turned the handle, but it wouldn't open.

"Why would a door in an abandoned city be locked?" She furrowed her brow. "It makes no sense."

"Maybe someone sealed it to prevent it from being looted."

"The Archdruid was forced out the moment the queen died. I doubt anyone would have had time to do that."

"Let's see if we can find another way in."

They moved around the side of the palace.

"Odd. There's no bodies here either."

"They'd be dust after a century." Niamh shrugged.

"Wouldn't there be bones or some remnants of them if they weren't burnt?"

"I don't know; I don't deal with bodies after death."

They pushed through some trees until the area opened into a massive courtyard.

Nyx winced. A heaviness hung over the place. "I have—I've seen this before."

"When?"

"In people's memories and in the vision I got from the Great Guardian. This is where the Archdruid slaughtered all the mind whisperers and the queen."

Niamh shuddered. "But we know at least one escaped. Maybe two. The killer and whoever is related to us."

The burnt-out pyre stood as a blackened mass of charred wood. Nyx shivered as she approached it.

"What are you doing?"

Nyx ignored her and reached out to touch the pyre.

"Nyx, don't touch that."

Ambrose's staff flared brighter. "It might show me what happened that day." She tapped the staff on the ground. Light glowed from the crystal and swept around them like a tidal wave.

"Nyx, what are you doing?" Niamh repeated and rushed over as the light expanded. Dozens of people appeared around them. "What's happening?" Niamh grabbed her arm.

"I think it's showing us the past. This is the day of the queen's execution."

Fergus stepped out in front of the crowd. Around him, dozens of scorch marks littered the ground.

"Finally, the scourge of mind whisperers is gone forever. Except for one." He grinned as two Dragon Guards dragged a bruised and bloody woman over to the pyre.

"No, please, don't," someone called out from the crowd.

They turned around and Nyx gasped. "Gods, that's Ambrose."

Ambrose looked younger and had no beard, but it was still him.

"You can't do this!" Ambrose yelled, as the guards held him back.

Fergus laughed. "Indeed, I can. Your wife's reign has come to an end."

"You may kill my body, but you'll never win, Archdruid." The queen spat blood at him. "You will never own my soul. I will come back and get my revenge on you. You'll never own me or my powers like you do the others."

"Your queen's reign ends now." Fergus threw a ball of fire at the queen.

The flames enveloped her body. White light exploded from the queen's burning corpse. The force shook the air around them.

Fergus stumbled back, then raised his hand to shield his eyes. The light from the queen's body expanded, then blinded everyone.

The sisters covered their eyes from the glare.

Through the whiteness, Nyx spotted something as she lowered her hand. Orbs of gold lights hovered near the queen's body and shot straight into the screaming crowd. Lyra stood there and flinched as the light flowed into her. Then a grin spread across her face.

In the chaos and the screaming, Ambrose's staff winked out. It left an eerie silence around them.

Nyx let out a breath she hadn't known she'd been holding. "I think we just found out where the other mind whisperer is. The queen never left."

A wave of energy reverberated through the air, knocking both sisters off their feet.

"Very good, Nyx. I wondered when you would figure it out." Lyra stepped out from behind a tree. She held out her hand, and Ambrose's staff flew into her grasp. "But it's good you are here. It saves me having to come and take you myself."

"Take us where?" Niamh growled.

"Oh, not you, Niamh dear, you're not the one I need. Nyx is."

"Need for what?" Nyx scrambled up. "Why are you doing all this?"

"You'll find out soon enough." Lyra laughed.

"You are not doing anything to my sister." Niamh threw one of her knives at the priestess.

Lyra waved the blade away as if it were an annoying insect. She tapped the staff on the ground. Niamh vanished in a bright flash of light.

"What did you do to her?" Nyx cried.

"I got rid of her."

Nyx raised her hand. "Stay back."

Lyra laughed again. "You know your powers won't work on me."

Yes, she did know that. She might not be able to use her touch against Lyra, but maybe the force of her magic would be enough to keep her away. Or she could move something and use it as a weapon.

Staff! Nyx willed it to come to her. If she could get hold of it, she could go back through the shield.

Green orbs sparkled around the staff, but it didn't move as Lyra gripped it tighter.

"Stupid girl, you really think your power can match mine?" She raised the staff.

A blast of energy sent Nyx crashing into the remains of the burned-out pyre.

Nyx winced from the force of the blow. "I won't help you."

"You won't have much choice." Lyra raised her free hand. An invisible pulse of energy dragged Nyx into the air. "I'm the first mind whisperer. I have lived for thousands of years. My power allows me to control my own kind."

An invisible noose tightened around her throat.

Nyx reached for her magic and let go of all the control she had over it. It crashed around her, shaking the air like thunder. But it did nothing to free her from Lyra's grasp.

Lyra came over to her. "I could end you with a single thought, little girl."

Tears sprang from her eyes as she choked for breath.

"I need a mind whisperer's blood to help restore me to my former self. You're going to help me return to my true body and bring about the rising."

CHAPTER 31

Darius sat in the garden with his grandmother for a while as she continued pruning flowers. She ignored him for the most part.

He went over the list of names. How were they connected? It made no sense. The deaths were so random.

"What have you got there, boy?" His grandmother's voice made him jump.

"Oh, nothing."

Rhian came over and glanced over his shoulder. "Are you going to punish all those people?"

"Why would I punish them?" He furrowed his brow. Darius knew he shouldn't mention who he was again, or he'd confuse her.

"All of those names are servants, courtiers. People who lived at the palace before the queen was killed. I remember helping them after they were forced out of their city. They are probably the ones who helped Ambrose spirit his wife's body away."

"Why would Ambrose kill them?" Darius flinched when he realised he'd asked the question aloud.

"Ambrose? I doubt he wants her back. She would want revenge on everyone, including him, for letting you kill her."

"Revenge on Fergus? I mean me?" He hated referring to himself as his father but didn't want to create any further confusion.

"Yes, because you enslaved the fae and the rest of the ancients." The rest of the ancients?

"What do you mean?" He furrowed his brow.

"Why, the Twelve, of course. The Twelve they call gods." She scoffed. "They are the oldest of Magickind. I warned you never to go up against them."

"The Twelve gods that the sorcerers worship? Did my father— Fergus do something to them?"

"Of course. How can you not remember? You spent the last millennia tracking them all down."

Realisation dawned on him. If the queen was still alive and, in their realm, he had a pretty good idea whose body she might be in. After all, who else wanted the Twelve back more than Lyra?

"What did I do to the Twelve?"

Rhian shook her head. "I don't know. Nor do I wish to know. You can't hold on to power forever, boy. The idea of using those boys of yours when your latest body wears out worries me. Haven't you slaughtered enough of your children?"

"What?" His mouth fell open. "What do you mean?"

"I mean, you using your children as vessels to host your spirit. Druids weren't meant to be immortal, even if we can live a lot longer than most Magickind."

"Wait, are you saying my father—I mean I—have used my powers to transfer my spirit into the body of one of my sons?" Darius's heart pounded so hard he thought it would jump out of his chest.

"Why do you keep acting like you don't know this, boy? I am one of the few people who knows what you've been doing to stay in power so long. It's not right. Your children have souls of their own. Killing them is unforgivable."

Light flashed as Niamh appeared. "Good, this power still works."

"Niamh, what are you doing here? How are you here?"

"I'm a projection—it's part of my gift. You have to come back. Right now." Niamh brushed her hair off her face. "Lyra has Nyx."

"What? How? Why—?"

"We went into the old city and found her there. She's the queen. The queen spirit is inside her body and has been since the queen died."

"Where'd she take Nyx?"

"I don't know. But I can't get back through the shield without Ambrose's staff." Her fists clenched. "You have to help me save my sister."

"I can't leave my grandmother alone."

Niamh's jaw tightened. "She's not in danger. Lyra just wanted you out of the way," she cried. "Are you going to stand back and let my sister die? I thought you loved her."

Darius sighed. "I do, damn it." He glanced at his grandmother.

"Go, boy." His gran put her hand on his shoulder. "I can take care of myself."

Darius waved his hand. Smoke billowed as Zephyr formed.

Niamh yelped. "That's a dark spirit."

"Zephyr, stay and watch over my gran. Kill anyone who tries to harm her."

Darius and Sirin used a portal to get to Andovia as fast as they could.

"Tell me everything that happened." Darius leapt from his dragon's back before Sirin even landed.

Niamh stood outside the shield, close to the guard tower.

"We used Ambrose's staff to get through and track Lyra. Nyx used it and conjured some sort of remnant of the past that showed us the execution."

"Ambrose was married to the queen."

"I know that. She somehow threw me out of the city. She said she needed Nyx for something."

"Yes, I think I know what. My gran told me the queen wants to find others like her. The gods most races worship aren't gods. They are immortal beings—some of the first Magickind. My father did something to them. If she wants to find them, she'll need her true body back. If she has been possessing Lyra for the last century, her body will be wearing down by now. She's probably running out of time."

"How could a spirit possess a body for so long?"

He shook his head. "I don't know. Most possessions only last a few months because two souls can't occupy the same body. They will burn it out. She must have found a way to stay inside Lyra all this time."

"But what does that have to do with Nyx? Is she going to possess my sister?"

"I can't be sure. Maybe she needs Nyx to somehow restore her to full strength. Perhaps the blood of another mind whisperer would help her do that. She wouldn't have access to her full power inside a body that's not her own."

"Why not?"

"Because Lyra's body probably wouldn't be strong enough to handle the kind of power the queen possesses."

"Just help me get through. So I can crucify that bitch." Niamh hit the shield with her fists and yelped from a jolt of static.

"I don't know if I'll be able to get through this time." Darius drew magic between his fingers.

"You did before."

"Yeah, but Nyx was there. The combination of our powers opened the shield." Darius called up power from the earth itself and Niamh used her touch. Energy shook the shield and blasted them off their feet.

He winced in pain. "I don't think forcing the shield will work this time. Lyra has probably reinforced it somehow."

He reached out to Nyx with his mind but couldn't feel her. Damn it, at least if he could talk to her, he might know what they were up against.

"Sirin, use your fire against the shield."

"Dragon fire? Will that work?" Niamh frowned. "Won't you make the Varden angry?"

"I'll deal with it later. Now, Sirin!"

Sirin roared and sent a column of fire at the shield. Flames thrashed around the glowing wall of light, then faded away.

"This will take forever." Niamh groaned. "Why can't you call on your father's power?"

"Because that wouldn't be enough to get us through. My father couldn't get through after he was forced out."

Niamh ran her hand through her hair. "What about the temple? Maybe there's something there." She shook her head. "No, that would take too long. Don't you have a bond with Nyx?"

"A link, not a soul bond. It is not the same thing."

"If we can't get into the city, maybe someone else can get us in."

Darius transported himself and Niamh to the temple.

He stormed into Isabella's chambers.

His stepmother jumped in alarm when she saw him. "What are you doing here?"

Niamh grabbed Isabella by the throat. Her eyes turned black, and her power shook the air. "Tell us how to get into the old city."

Isabella laughed and slapped Niamh's hand away. "Your power won't work on me, girl. I serve someone far greater."

"Lyra must have control of her. Damn it!" Darius clenched his fists. "What did she plan for you to do?"

"Once the queen is back in her body, she will find the other ancients and your father will finally get what he deserves." Isabella laughed again. "I thought you would be glad of that."

"I could get answers out of you." Niamh pulled out one of her knives. "And I don't need magic to do that."

"Fools, the ancients will return and there's nothing you can do to stop it."

Isabella raised her hand. A blast of energy sent Darius and Niamh flying across the room.

Power flared between Isabella's fingers as she prepared to strike them again.

Niamh threw her knife. The blade cut through the air. Isabella gurgled with blood as the blade embedded itself in her throat.

"No!" Darius shot to his feet as Isabella slumped to the floor. "Why did you do that?"

"She was going to kill us. I heard her thoughts."

"I would have stopped her! I could've protected us."

"From this?" Niamh got up and yanked a crystal from Isabella's fingers. "I sensed she was about to do something. I've seen these before. They are powerful and release a pulse of magic. You wouldn't have stood a chance."

He sighed. "I don't know another way to get through the shield."

"I saw another crystal in her mind." Niamh rummaged through Isabella's pockets and pulled out a different crystal. "This looks like the crystal on Ambrose's staff."

"Maybe we have found another way in."

CHAPTER 32

Lyra dragged Nyx into a spell circle where she had placed a stone coffin. She had put a cuff on Nyx's wrist that rendered her powerless. "What's that?" Nyx frowned at the coffin.

Gods, was that meant for her?

"My original body lies in there. It took me years to finally find it. That's why I had Ambrose kill those people since they were the ones who helped him dispose of my corpse." She laughed. "It took longer to break him than I expected, but he will be dead soon enough. Once I'm back to full power, I'll finally get my revenge on the Archdruid."

"What do you need me for?" Her heart pounded in her ears. She wasn't sure she wanted to know the answer. Heck, she half expected Lyra to possess her body.

"The Archdruid destroyed my body. I need the blood of another mind whisperer to restore me."

Lyra took her hand. "Finally, after a century of being stuck in this weak vessel, I will be free. I'll be my true self again."

Nyx pulled back, but Lyra gripped her tighter.

Lyra began chanting in an odd language. The words sounded familiar, yet she didn't know what they meant. Nyx screamed as pain jolted through her.

Lyra cried out as something burned through her skin. "I should have known that no-good husband of mine would cast a protection spell on you."

Nyx yanked at the cuff, but it wouldn't come off.

Instead, she grabbed Ambrose's staff, that Lyra had placed on the ground beside them. "Stay away from me." She aimed the glowing staff at her.

The queen laughed. "You can't use that against me. I control this city." She raised her hand. An invisible noose wrapped around Nyx's throat. "Pity. I did enjoy the time we spent together. You're the first mind whisperer I've been around since my demise. But your time has come to an end now."

Nyx gripped the staff so hard the top part cut into her fingers and drew blood. *Come on, work. Help me!*

She aimed the staff at Lyra. A blast of energy shot out and pinned Lyra in place. The queen screamed. The staff stood erect, and flew from Nyx's grasp. The crystal grew brighter as a projection of Ambrose appeared.

He smiled at Lyra. "Hello, wife. If you're seeing this, I've no doubt you've done something to dispose of me. Did you really think I wouldn't recognise you in Lyra's body?"

Pure hatred covered Lyra's face. "You couldn't see anything that's right in front of you, you fool."

"Don't think you've won. I know you want your true body back, but that will never happen. Not whilst I'm still alive."

The light grew brighter, and Lyra screamed in agony.

Nyx, listen to me. I can't maintain this form for long. Ambrose spoke in her mind. *I can't force the queen out of Lyra's body. The only way to stop her is to contain her.*

How? I am powerless. Nyx tugged at the cuff.

You can fly. Use your wings. Lead her somewhere you can trap her.

Where? I don't know this place.

There's an old well nearby. I don't think it was covered up. It should be enough to contain her. Whatever happens, don't let her touch you. She needs your blood to restore her true body. She will kill you if she gets near you. Hurry!

Nyx flapped her wings.

Oh, you need to fatally wound her, Ambrose added. *It won't kill her, but her spirit won't be able to leave if she is injured and trapped somewhere solid.*

How am I supposed to get close enough? Nyx flapped her wings harder and slowly rose off the ground. Her body felt like dead weight.

She couldn't take the staff with her, it still held Lyra in place.

She flew higher and looked around for the well. Trees spread out before her, she didn't even have her senses to help her detect it. Her eyes would have to do.

Nyx circled around the trees. Ambrose's staff wouldn't hold Lyra back forever.

Come on, where is that well? Why didn't he tell me where it was?

A blast of energy zipped through the trees. Wonderful, Lyra was free again.

Nyx flapped her wings harder and dodged the blasts to keep out of the way.

She dove lower and screamed as a blast struck her back. She lost momentum and fell.

Sharp teeth grabbed hold of her tunic and swung her around into a pair of strong arms.

"Sirin," she gasped. "Druid." She threw her arms around Darius when he caught hold of her.

"Are you hurt?"

"That doesn't matter. Get this thing off me." She motioned to her wrist.

Darius yanked the cuff off and tossed it away.

"Time for that bitch to die." Niamh perched in a tree beside them.

"We need to trap her somewhere. She won't die because her soul is immortal. Ambrose said there's an old well nearby. We need to get her in there then block it up somehow."

"Ambrose? How did he tell you that?" Darius gaped at her.

"There's no time to explain. Ambrose said the only way to keep her from leaving Lyra's body is to somehow fatally wound her but keep the weapon inside her."

"I can do that." Niamh grinned.

"It won't be so easy. Her powers are incredible, and she has Ambrose's staff."

Blasts of light bombarded the tree. Darius conjured a shield around them. "That won't hold for long."

"How did your father overpower her?" Nyx winced as more blasts battered the shield.

"He said something about using her true name. Like I do with spirits."

"What is her true name?"

"I don't know. He never told me that, but I think the quickest way to weaken her is to force her to use her power as much as possible. The more power she uses, the more Lyra's body will weaken."

"But what is to stop her from jumping into another body?" Nyx furrowed her brow.

"Try and use your power to repel her spirit. Since you can move things, you might be able to push her away. Better yet." Darius waved his hand so that a metal band formed on her wrist and Niamh's wrist as well as his own. "These are made of cold iron. It repels spirits."

"It also burns." Nyx winced as her skin prickled with a painful burning sensation.

"Cold iron repels fae too. But I'll take her down." Niamh leapt from the tree and threw one of her knives. It missed Lyra by inches.

We need to find that well. Darius let go of Nyx as she scrambled onto the branch. *Can you fly?*

I think so.

Good. Be careful. Darius pulled her in for a quick kiss.

Her eyes widened in shock. He and Sirin flew away.

Nyx took off. *I'll keep her focused her on me. Be ready.*

Sirin rose higher and sent a plume of dragon fire at Lyra. Lyra deflected it away from her with Ambrose's staff.

Nyx flew further away as Darius and Niamh continued their assault on the queen. Hitting her with both weapons and blasts of lightning.

She had to find that well. She pushed through trees and waved her hand to make them move.

A large, black uncovered hole stood up ahead. That had to be the well.

Nyx waved her hand, so branches and leaves covered it.

Lyra pushed her way through the trees. "You think you could outrun me?" She gasped for breath and blood trickled down her face.

"It's over, Lyra." Darius jumped from the dragon's back. "Your body is burning out. Look, it's falling apart."

Lyra glared at him and raised a hand.

Seeing the queen's distraction, Nyx called out with her mind. Green light sparkled as the staff appeared in her hands.

Darius struck low to the ground with a lightning bolt.

"The more you use, the faster your body burns out. You should know that." Darius gave the former queen a pitiful look. "Lyra's body was never built to handle your powers."

"You are right, but I have a way to get into my own body."

Nyx blasted the queen with the staff.

"You can't kill me," Lyra smiled.

"Maybe not, but we can make sure you don't hurt anyone else." Darius moved to Nyx's side.

The former queen snorted. "I'm part of the prophecy. I'm immortal. You can't stop me," Lyra spat. "I will bring the other ancients back."

"There's no coming back for you." Niamh threw one of her daggers and it embedded itself in the queen's throat.

Nyx waved her hand and Lyra fell straight into the well.

"Now, Sirin!" Darius told his dragon.

Sirin covered the well with fire that Darius forced to stay in place.

"There. With the flames in place, she'll never get out." Darius took Nyx's hand.

"I hope it's enough to keep her down there." Nyx grazed his hand.

"That's too bad, I lost one of my favourite knives." Niamh sighed. "I'm glad you're safe." She turned to Nyx and hugged her.

Nyx returned her embrace. "What happens now? Will you stay?"

Niamh shrugged. "I don't know."

"Let's go home. We need to check on Ambrose."

Ambrose's condition hadn't changed—much to Nyx's disappointment. Killer or not, they would never have defeated Lyra without his help.

Isabella's death hadn't gone down well with Gideon. Lyra was blamed and now presumed missing.

Nyx sat perched on the branch where Ambrose's treehouse stood.

News of Niamh's betrayal of the Order of Blood would soon spread and that meant she couldn't stay.

Nyx knew she'd have to face a choice, too. Whether to stay in this realm or to leave with her sister.

Darius came to sit beside her. They hadn't really talked since they defeated the queen. Not about their relationship, at least. They were quiet for a while as he watched her.

"You should go with your sister. It's not safe here."

She didn't know what she had expected him to say. Not that, though.

"That's not true. The old city is the second safest place I know."

"Where is first?"

"With you." She gripped his hand. "I'm not leaving you." She pulled him in for a kiss. "I know it's not been easy and we'll both have tough choices to make, but we owe it to ourselves to make this work. To find out if we can be more than friends."

Darius pulled her in for another kiss. "What about Niamh?"

"I will talk to her."

Nyx raced down to the dock where *The Vanity* stood waiting.

"Niamh?" She spotted her sister hidden by a long black cloak.

Niamh peeked out from under the hood.

"You're not coming with me, are you?"

"No, I'm not. For now, my place is here. You could stay too. The city is—"

"Even that wouldn't stop the Order from getting to me. I have to keep moving."

"We can still see each other. We can talk mind to mind whenever we want to." Nyx threw her arms around her sister and blinked back tears. "Be safe, sister. I know you want me to be safe, too." Niamh returned her hug.

Nyx smiled. "You be safe too. Where are you headed?"

"I need to keep moving, but Yasmine says there is a resistance stronghold not too far away. I need to figure out who and what I am now. So maybe that's a good place to start. Helping others instead of hurting them. If we do have another sister out there, we'll find her."

Nyx hugged her again. "I'll miss you."

"I'll miss you too, sister." Niamh jumped onto the ship. "Oh, and that druid isn't so bad. For a Valeran, at least."

Nyx chuckled and waved as she watched the ship disappear into the distance.

"She'll be back." Darius appeared beside her.

"I hope so." Nyx nodded. "But something tells me Lyra—the queen—won't stay gone forever. We need to be ready for whatever comes next."

Nyx and Darius headed back into the old city after saying goodbye to Niamh. Ambrose's staff still allowed them to get through the shield. She hadn't set foot back in the city since they had trapped the queen, but she knew Darius had been back a few times to make sure she was secure.

The city still remained as eerie and quiet as ever. Not even the wind blew through the empty streets. The old palace remained locked up and inaccessible, but they knew Lyra must have been working somewhere within the city.

She didn't know what Darius hoped to find there. When they had searched the temple, they hadn't found much of anything. But they hoped to find something that would help them save Ambrose. Killer or not, he had helped Nyx defeat the queen.

"Maybe there's nothing here to find," Nyx remarked.

Darius furrowed his brow. "She must have been holding the victims somewhere. What if there are more people trapped here in the city? We have to keep searching until we know for certain. Maybe you should use your senses and see if you can hear anyone."

She lowered her mental shield and let her power run through the city. The constant hum from the shield echoed through her ears. And something turned to her senses.

Help me! someone called out.

"Druid, there's someone here." Nyx ran off in the opposite direction towards a smaller stone building close to the palace. When she reached for the door handle, it wouldn't move.

She stepped back and raised her hand. A burst of light shot from her hand and exploded the door in a shower of sparks.

Someone coughed as they stepped out from the shadows. A girl covered in dirt. Her long, curly, green hair fell over her face.

"Are you hurt?" Nyx asked.

Wide blue eyes met hers and the girl threw her arms around Nyx. "Nyx, I'm so happy to see you. I knew you would come save me."

She furrowed her brow. "Do we know each other?"

"Of course we do. I'm your sister Novia."

If you enjoyed this book please leave a review on Amazon or book site of your choice.

***

For updates on more books and news releases sign up for my newsletter on tiffanyshand.com/newsletter

EXCERPT FROM BOUND BY BLOOD

Ann Valeran crouched low in the bushes as she stared at the small stone building. It was round in shape and made of crumbling grey stone. A remnant from before the dark times, before all the world of Erthea had changed.

Branches snagged at her long cloak. Its black colour helped her blend in with her surroundings, and she pulled its long length over her knees.

You sure this is the right place? she asked in thought, then turned to stare at Edward Rohn, her best friend.

He knelt beside her, unmoving. *This is where the message said the witness wanted to meet us.*

How do we even know this so-called witness is legitimate? Her eyes narrowed at him. *It's been five years. It seems strange someone would come forward after all this time.*

Isn't it worth finding out? Ed's dark brown eyes seemed almost black in the darkness.

Ann sighed, pushing her long, wavy blonde hair off her face to tuck it underneath her hood. This was it. The chance she'd been waiting over five years for. A chance to prove to all five lands that she hadn't murdered her family.

How did the witness even know where to find us? she asked, sitting back on the cold, hard earth.

Above, the night sky hung like a heavy blanket of darkness, without a cloud or glittering star in sight. It made it much easier for Ann and Ed to stay concealed without using magic. Magic would make it easier for Gliss or any other potential enemies to find them.

Ann could see easily in the near blackness. As a druid, she used her fire element to make everything seem lighter and enhance her vision.

She knew as one of the Black Guard, Ed saw clearly too. It was strange how the magic of her father's old guard had survived after all this time.

Ed touched her shoulder. *Don't you want the chance to prove your innocence?* In the low light, she made out his short brown hair, golden brown eyes, and chiselled face.

His touch felt comforting, but Ann bit her lip. She hated being hunted by Orla's forces, not to mention all the others who sought to profit from the price on her head. She didn't know how high the price had grown but had heard it was almost ten thousand coins now. Enough to make someone comfortable for the rest of their life.

Yes, Ann said. *But it won't bring my family back or restore my father's lands to me.*

Darius Valeran had been the archdruid of Caselhelm on the night of the revolution. He had not just controlled Caselhelm, but parts of the other territories as well. Under his rule, the lands had been at peace for the first time in ten thousand years. The Realm War began that night at the hands of the Fomorian demon Orla, when Ann's parents, Darius and Deanna, had been murdered. After the latest realm war, peace was a distant memory. Orla had won control over most of Caselhelm and placed a bounty on Ann's head.

A witness had reached out to one of Ann's contacts in the resistance, claiming to be one of Orla's associates. She said she would approach the council—a small governing body who oversaw the rule of the five lands—to tell them the truth about what happened to Ann's parents.

Ed gave her hand a comforting squeeze as she rose.

Ann took a deep breath. *Let's get this over with. I want to get back to the warehouse before Xander wakes up.* She was glad she hadn't brought her brother along with them. At least then he'd be safe if this turned out to be a trap.

Ann stayed alert as she scanned the area. She searched for potential threats but sensed no other presences nearby.

She and Ed moved over to the building, which only had one outer door. That made Ann more uneasy; she liked having more than one escape route when she went somewhere unknown. *Do you sense anyone inside?* she asked.

He shook his head. *No one.*

Let's make this quick. The familiar weight of her knives at her back felt comforting.

Ed pulled the wooden door open. It gave a groan of protest as he did so. Ann half expected it to fall off its hinges given the age of the building.

Ann paused, scanning the building with her mind. She used the earth lines, feeling the hum of power, but nothing suggested the presence of another living being nearby. Earth lines were veins of natural power that run through Earth itself. Some called them the world's lifeblood.

"Maybe the witness isn't here yet," Ed whispered, touching the hilt of the sword at his back.

"I don't like this," Ann remarked. "We should have picked a neutral location, somewhere in the other lands, not Caselhelm."

She glanced around the empty passageway, then touched the stone, which groaned and mumbled. Stone magic was rare among the druids, but her power could tap into almost all of the elements.

Ann closed her eyes, listening. This place had been a bunker. She heard people screaming and the sound of running footsteps as the stones showed her what had happened here.

Nice place to meet someone who claims they can prove I'm not a murderer.

Ann let go of the stone, and the murmurs faded. "What do we know about the witness? You haven't told me anything about them."

"Sage didn't tell me much." Ed shrugged and moved ahead of her, keeping a close eye out for potential threats.

"When does she ever?" She hated talking to the other druid at the best of times. Ann had been suspicious when Sage contacted Ed in thought with the news about the witness.

"She seemed to trust this person."

"This person who wouldn't even give us their name." Ann grimaced as she walked face-first into some spider-webs. She brushed them off with the back of her hand. "I like to know the details. Next time, *I'll* talk to Sage."

Ed chuckled. "Careful, there might still be spiders around here."

She scowled at him. "Don't mention spiders around me. They are almost as bad as Sage."

"You hate talking to her, even though she's your aunt."

"She is *not* my aunt. She's my aunt's lover, there's a difference." Ann rounded a corner, following a passageway that led into a larger room. Ancient debris and dirt littered the stone floor. Withered black leaves crunched under her feet as she walked in. No one here, and there was no other entrance, so they'd have had to come in the same way she and Ed did.

"Are you sure Sage didn't tell you anything else?" Ann prompted.

Ed pulled out his sword, the blade catching the light as Ann lit a crystal torch on the wall that filled the room with an orange glow. Shadows danced across the stone floor.

"Stop being so worried. That's my job." Ed grinned.

"Not anymore. You haven't been my bodyguard in over five years. You're my partner."

"I've always been your partner. Always and forever, remember?"

Ann smiled at the promise they'd made to each other as kids. Always and forever best friends.

She sighed, using the lines to tell the time. Just past midnight, when their witness had said she'd be there.

"Try to keep an open mind," Ed said. "What if this person truly wants to help?"

Ann didn't trust anyone, not after everything she'd been through. The only two people she did trust with her life were Ed and Xander. A lack of faith in others had kept her alive. She didn't dare hope this person would help.

"Let's be ready to make a quick exit. Stay close to me so I can transport us out as quickly as possible."

"Let's see what they have to say first."

Ann frowned. "You keep defending them. What aren't you telling me?" She put her hands on her hips. "Edward Rohn, you've never been able to lie to me. Tell me what you're hiding."

"Nothing." Ed shook his head. "I'm not…" He gritted his teeth. "I just want you to talk to her."

"*Her?*" Ann's eyes narrowed to slits. "You do know who's coming." She pulled out one of her knives as the once smooth earth lines became jagged beneath her feet, warning her of another presence. *Someone's here.*

Orla? No, Edward wouldn't set up a meeting with the demon bitch who'd helped murder her parents and had killed or enslaved thousands of Magickind in her tyrannical rule.

"Who's coming?" she hissed.

He said nothing and shook his head again.

A woman with long raven hair past her shoulders walked in. Her skin was pale, her eyes so dark they looked almost like obsidian. She wore a red version of the leather bodysuit all Gliss wore. It covered her from neck to toe.

It took Ann a second to place the woman's face as that of Ceara Mason, once a close friend, now a traitor who'd helped destroy her family.

Ed, you can't be serious, Ann growled.

Ann, please just listen to what she has to say, Ed replied.

Heat flared between her fingers as her fire magic burned to life.

Ceara studied them and smiled her perfect smile. Ceara had always been a dark beauty, which had drawn Ann's brothers to her.

Ann, with her own pale skin, long blonde hair, and pale blue eyes, looked slight compared to Ceara's darkness. Ed and Ceara were both taller than her.

"Rhiannon, it's been a long time." Ceara smirked. "I hear they're calling you the rogue archdruid now."

"What do you want, Ceara?" Ann folded her arms. Any hope of this witness being genuine had long faded. Oh, Ceara had been there. Only she'd been on the enemy's side. She knew this was a setup. Still, she couldn't believe Edward had agreed to go along with it.

"I expected a warmer welcome. I mean, we haven't seen—"

"Why are you here?" Ann snapped. "Don't give me some crap about wanting to turn against Orla. We both know where your loyalties lie."

Ceara's smile faded. "That *is* why I'm here. Spirits, I thought you'd be tired of life as a fugitive."

"What makes you think I'd ever accept your help?" The fire between her fingers blazed harsh and hot. Her magic wanted out, wanted to kill this traitorous bitch.

"Say what you want to say, Ceara." Ed took Ann's hand. The flames licked his skin but snuffed out as he squeezed her hand. Her fire wouldn't harm him; he'd always been immune to it.

"Wolfy, it's been a long time. I—"

Ed gave Ceara a hard look. "You stopped being my foster sister a long time ago. You don't get to call me that."

Ceara sighed. "I'm here because I made a mistake the night I helped Orla and Urien. I didn't kill either of your parents, Ann. If you don't believe anything else I say, believe that. Listen, I'm one of the few people who can prove you didn't kill your parents," Ceara snapped.

"You really expect me to believe you want to help?" Ann scoffed. "Why would you do that?"

"Because I'm tired of living under Orla's rule. She's…it's not important," Ceara replied. "Don't you want to come out of hiding, Rhiannon?"

Ann winced at Ceara's continued use of her full name. Rhiannon Valeran had died along with her parents. Along with her life as the archdruid's daughter. It wasn't who or what she was any more.

"I'd rather hide than be ruled by Orla."

"That's why I'm here. Since she took over, magic is outlawed in Caselhelm, and those who have it are kept under strict control. Even among the Gliss," Ceara said. "Orla has to be stopped, and you're the only one who can do it. I'll come with you and tell the council what really happened."

Ann shook her head, knowing Ceara wouldn't help her. This was ridiculous. Even as a child, selflessness had never been her strong suit. There had to be some other motivation. Anyway, on the slim chance she did want to help, there was no guarantee the council would believe her.

"If we buy this, what do you get out of it?" Ed prompted.

"Why can't you believe I just want to help?" Ceara demanded.

"Because you're a Gliss who helped Orla destroy everything my father worked for," Ann snapped.

"I've made mistakes, but aren't you willing to take the risk to stop Orla?"

Ann laughed. "You expect us to believe you want to turn on her. Do you take us for idiots?"

"Aren't you and your resistance friends trying to do just that?" Ceara arched an eyebrow. "I've heard the rumours. I know how you help them flee Orla's clutches."

Ann gritted her teeth. They weren't here to discuss the resistance. The last thing she needed was Ceara finding out anything about them. She only hoped Sage hadn't divulged any details about them to Ceara.

"If you truly want us to trust you, you're going to have to prove it," Ed challenged.

"I came here, didn't I?" Ceara threw up her hands in surrender. "You have no idea what Orla would do if she found out I came to see you."

Ed, let's just get out of here, Ann said. *I can't do this. We're wasting our time. Let's get back to Xander. She'll never help us. She's just leading us into a trap.*

Ceara reached into a pocket of her bodice. "I did bring something to help prove I'm telling the truth." She held up a small round crystal etched with glowing runes. "A list of all Orla's allies."

Ed tightened his grip on her hand. *You're right we should go. I don't like this.*

I'm glad you finally agree with me. Ann traced runes in the air, muttering words of power to transport them out of the building. Light flashed around them, enveloping their bodies.

As it did, Ceara threw the crystal toward them. Thunder roared as an explosion ripped through the air.

Ann screamed as the transference spell wrenched her body away and she felt Ed's hand let go of hers.

She landed hard outside the bunker, the air leaving her lungs in a *whoosh.*

Ann scrambled up, ignoring the wave of dizziness as she ran back inside. But when she reached the meeting room, Ed and Ceara were gone.

ALSO BY TIFFANY SHAND

ANDOVIA CHRONICLES

Dark Deeds Prequel

The Calling

ROGUES OF MAGIC SERIES

Bound By Blood

Archdruid

Bound By Fire

Old Magic

Dark Deception

Sins Of The Past

Reign Of Darkness

Rogues Of Magic Complete Box Set Books 1-7

ROGUES OF MAGIC NOVELLAS

Wyvern's Curse

Forsaken

On Dangerous Tides

EVERLIGHT ACADEMY TRILOGY

Everlight Academy, Book 1: Faeling

Everlight Academy, Book 2: Fae Born

Hunted Guardian – An Everlight Academy Story

EXCALIBAR INVESTIGATIONS SERIES

Denai Touch

Denai Bound

Denai Storm

Excalibar Investigations Complete Box Set

SHADOW WALKER SERIES

Shadow Walker

Shadow Spy

Shadow Sworn

Shadow Walker Complete Box Set

THE AMARANTHINE CHRONICLES BOOK 1

Betrayed By Blood

Dark Revenge

The Final Battle

SHIFTER CLANS SERIES

The Alpha's Daughter

Alpha Ascending

The Alpha's Curse

The Shifter Clans Complete Box Set

TALES OF THE ITHEREAL

Fey Spy

Outcast Fey

Rogue Fey

Hunted Fey

Tales of the Ithereal Complete Box Set

THE FEY GUARDIAN SERIES

Memories Lost

Memories Awakened

Memories Found

The Fey Guardian Complete Series

THE ARKADIA SAGA

Chosen Avatar

Captive Avatar

Fallen Avatar

The Arkadia Saga Complete Series

ABOUT THE AUTHOR

Tiffany Shand is a writing mentor, professionally trained copy editor and copy writer who has been writing stories for as long as she can remember. Born in East Anglia, Tiffany still lives in the area, constantly guarding her workspace from the two cats which she shares her home with.

She began using her pets as a writing inspiration when she was a child, before moving on to write her first novel after successful completion of a creative writing course. Nowadays, Tiffany writes urban fantasy and paranormal romance, as well as nonfiction books for other writers, all available through eBook stores and on her own website.

Tiffany's favourite quote is *'writing is an exploration. You start from nothing and learn as you go'* and it is armed with this that she hopes to be able to help, inspire and mentor many more aspiring authors.

When she has time to unwind, Tiffany enjoys photography, reading, and watching endless box sets. She also loves to get out and visit the vast number of castles and historic houses that England has to offer.

You can contact Tiffany Shand, or just see what she is writing about at:

Author website: tiffanyshand.com
Business site: Write Now Creative
Twitter: @tiffanyshand
Facebook page: Tiffany Shand Author Page

Printed in Poland
by Amazon Fulfillment
Poland Sp. z o.o., Wrocław
28 February 2022

f92fcd31-0dfd-4da3-813b-831aad3676b7R01